THE
NATIONS

THE AUTHORS

KEN FARMER – After proudly serving his country as a US Marine (call sign 'Tarzan'), Ken attended Stephen F. Austin State University on a full football scholarship, receiving his Bachelors Degree in Business and Speech & Drama. Ken discovered his love for acting when he starred as a cowboy in a Dairy Queen commercial. Ken has over 39 years as a professional actor, with memorable roles *Silverado, Friday Night Lights* and *The Newton Boys*. He was the OC and VO spokesman for Wolf Brand Chili for eight years. Ken now lives near Gainesville, TX, where he continues to write and direct quality award winning films like *Rockabilly Baby* and write novels like *The Nations* sequel, *Haunted Falls*.

BUCK STIENKE – Captain – Fighter Pilot - United States Air Force, has an extensive background in military aviation and weaponry. A graduate of the Air Force Academy, Buck (call sign 'Shoehorn') was a member of the undefeated Rugby team and was on the Dean's List. After leaving the Air Force, Buck was a pilot for Delta Airlines for over twenty-five years. He has vast knowledge of weapons, tactics and survival techniques. Buck is the owner of Lone Star Shooting Supply, Gainesville, TX. As a successful actor, writer and businessman, Buck lives in Gainesville with his wife, Carolyn. Buck was Executive Producer for the award winning film, *Rockabilly Baby*.

Buck and Ken have completed four novels to date. The first was *BLACK EAGLE FORCE: Eye of the Storm, BLACK EAGLE FORCE: Sacred Mountain* is the second *Return of the Starfighter*, the third. A historical fiction western, *The Nations*, the fourth and we are over 90,000 words into our fifth novel, this time back to the Black Eagle Force series: *Black Eagle Force: Blood Ivory*.

THE

NATIONS

BY

KEN FARMER
&
BUCK STIENKE

BASED ON AN ORIGINAL SCREENPLAY

THE TUMBLEWEED WAGON

BY

RUSS M~~A~~

ISBN-13: 978-0-9848820-5-2 Paper
ISBN-13: 978-0-9848820-6-9 E

Timber Creek Press
Imprint of Timber Creek Productions, LLC
312 N. Commerce St.
Gainesville, Texas
214-533-4964

DEDICATION

THE NATIONS is dedicated to the United States Marshals Service. They have served for over 200 years as instruments of civil authority by all three branches of the U.S. Government. We also dedicate it to all law enforcement personel through out the U.S. and their selfless dedication to duty.

ACKNOWLEDGMENT

The authors gratefully acknowledge the help from Kelly "Gunny" Jackson, Jodie Moore and Doran Ingrham for their invaluable help in proofing and editing this novel.

Contact Us:
Published by: Timber Creek Press
timbercreekproductions@yahoo.com
www.blackeagleforce.com
Twitter: @pagact
Facebook Book Fan Page:
http://www.facebook.com/TheNationsNovel

Cover Design by: Steve Daniels
Back Cover by: Warren Martin

TIMBER CREEK PRESS

BASS REEVES AND BOOT

ENDORSEMENTS

famously did so without serious injury, and while earning the respect of all who knew him. The Nations gives us a look into hunting outlaws in those days, and is a thoroughly entertaining novel.

****

5.0 out of 5 stars The Western Novel is Alive and Well!

By Gary Hancock - I own every western novel written by Zane Grey, Louis L'Amour, and Elmer Kelton and I had no interest in adding to my collection by two new upstart authors. However, being a lifelong student of Oklahoma history I decided to read "The Nations" and I have just added this novel to my best of the best section of westerns. Ken Farmer and Buck Stienke have captured the feel of the old west with action that hits you right in the gut and keeps you awake late at night as you read on, excited to find out what happens next. This novel begs to become a movie and Bass Reeves, the black US Deputy Marshall, will be a coveted role. I look forward to the next western from Ken and Buck, hurry!

****

5.0 out of 5 stars A True Western-Not Just for the Western Fan,

By Warren Martin - Authors Ken Farmer and Buck Stienke continue to exceed expectations in their latest novel. The Nations, is a story that takes place in the late 1800's about the real life US Deputy Marshall Bass Reeves who worked the Indian Territories for the infamous Hanging Judge--Judge Isaac C. Parker.

The Nations and the accounting of Marshall Reeves' encounters with the lawless, his thirty-two year career, and the fact that Bass Reeves was also a Black Man, is brilliantly told through the authors unique and excellent writing style of telling a story through the characters themselves. The reader is drawn into the story with the sense of participation through dialogue and details of the era that gives a true sense of being there. The Nations is more than a Western; it has characters, sub-story lines and subject matter that are identifiable with the problems and issues of people even today.

The Nations is a true western with a real hero and authentic characters and details. As with all of Farmer-Stienke novels, the Nations is packed full of action, adventure, twist and turns, and saying any more would ruin the story for future readers.

For the Western buffs, this is a winner, and for those who've never liked Westerns, the Nations will change your mind and give you a new admiration for the way of the West.

Forgotten Soldiers What Happened to Jacob Walden

****

5.0 out of 5 stars Buck & Ken have Written Another 5 star story.

By Wilma "Jay" - If you like a good Wild West story let Buck & Ken take you back to a place in the year 1885 , known as Robber's Roost and No Man's Land.

You'll feel like you are riding horseback with the good guys as they go after The Larson Gang.

You'll get a look into what life was like in the "latter part of the 19th century as the bloodiest and most dangerous place in the world."

The language can be a little rough at times but so were the men and the way they lived.I agree that it would make a good movie.

****

5.0 out of 5 stars So good that it should be made into a movie,
By Israel Drazin (TOP 1000 REVIEWER)

This book is so good that many readers will feel as I do that it should be made into a movie and hope that the authors tell future tales like it about the Wild West. The hero of the story is a real person, Deputy Marshall Bass Reeves, the first black US Deputy Marshal west of the Mississippi who died in 1910. He served as a marshal for 32 years and had over 3,000 felony arrests and fourteen men killed in the line of duty, twice as many as "Wild Bill" Hickok. He was never wounded. He had a wife and ten children, five boys and five girls. Many regard him as the best lawman in western history, regardless of color. He worked for Judge Isaac C. Parker who presided over the Indian Territory and who was known as the hanging judge; 79 men danced on his gallows.

This novel tells how he went after the notorious Larson Gang in 1885 with his partner Jack McGann, two other deputies, and two Indian lawmen, known as Lighthorse. Ben Larson was a vicious killer, a true sociopath, a man who killed simply because he delighted in doing so. Bass had a difficult time searching for Wes Larson and the rest of the gang and holding onto Ben Larson.

We read about Bass' encounters with other outlaws, including how the famous Belle Star got word that it was Bass Reeves carrying a warrant for her, that she rushed to give herself up to another marshal, Bud Ledbetter; such was the respect for Bass Reeves. We read how sensitive Bass Reeves was; how he cried when in self defense he had to kill a boyhood friend and what he did for a young girl and boy who were mistreated by their father who was an outlaw and who forced them to ride with him and his gang, and who sexually violated his daughter.

****

TIMBER CREEK PRESS

CHAPTER ONE

THE INDIAN NATIONS - 1885
WEWOKA
SEMINOLE NATION

Wewoka—a Seminole word that meant *barking waters*—earned its name for the small rapids found in the creek that ran on the north side of the town. Wewoka was a farming, ranching community as were most of the towns in the Nations.

A lone rider walked his tired red-roan gelding down the main street of the capital of the Seminole Nation. He was a handsome young man of twenty, wearing a spiffy black morning coat with a tall starched collar and a burgundy cravat. A dark gray uncreased low crown Stetson with a flat three inch pencil-rolled brim, sat atop his head, cocked at a jaunty angle—neatly trimmed dark hair showed out from underneath the back. Unlike many of the men of his time, the young man wore no facial hair.

It was midmorning and the main street had begun to fill up from the townspeople and farmers coming in for supplies or setting up to sell their wares. One wagon with several wooden crates of chickens and two pigs tied in the back was pulled up to the front of Haney's Butcher Shop, next door to Franklin's General Store and Mercantile.

The young man drew rein and pulled his roan up to a water trough between two hitching rails in front of Franklin's and allowed the grateful horse to dip his nose to the water. After a few moments, he eased up the reins and side-passed the gelding to the hitching rail on the right side of the trough, dismounted and tied up. He dusted his clothes down, straightened his vest, grabbed his saddlebags and stepped up on the eight foot wide boardwalk. All of five feet-seven—a tight one hundred fifty pounds—he moved with a somewhat confident, if not arrogant air.

He turned the knob and pushed the door open to Franklin's, ringing a three inch brass bell attached to the doorjamb overhead. There was only one other customer in the store—a man on the far right side looking at garden tools. A balding middle-aged store-keep in a white shirt with black garter half-sleeves and a white apron stood behind the counter. He looked up when he heard the bell. "Come in, Pilgrim. If we ain't got it, you don't need it. That's our motto. Whatcha lookin' for?"

"Oh, just need some supplies," he said as he walked over and flipped his saddlebags on the counter. "You can start by fillin' up those saddlebags with some Bull Durham smokin' tobacca, canned peaches 'n some stick candy."

The clerk took the bags, turned around and grabbed a couple of cans of peaches and the Bull Durham and put them in one side of the leather bags. He turned back around, laid the saddlebags on the counter and reached for the large round glass jar packed full of cinnamon, butterscotch and root beer stick candy.

"Oh…yeah, and all the money in yer cash register there."

"Wh…what?" said the stunned store-keep as he looked up.

The young man pulled a pearl-handled Colt, cocked it and shot the store clerk between the eyes. "Damn. I hate it when people act like they did not hear what I said."

He reached over, opened the cash register, cleaned out all the paper money, grabbed most of the hard stick candy from the jar then stuffed the booty in his saddlebags. Just as he turned around, he met the business end of a swipe from a hickory ax handle across his forehead. His hat went flying backward as his eyes rolled up and he dropped straight down to the floor.

The store owner, Millard Franklin, rushed out from the back store room when he heard the pistol shot with a ten-gauge long barreled shot gun to his shoulder. "What the Sam Hill…"

"I'm sorry Millard. He shot Barkley 'fore I could get to him. Most cold-blooded thang I ever saw. Just shot him dead, right there, on account of him askin' what the man said," said resident Deputy United States Marshal Stan Oakley.

"Who is he, Marshal?"

"Damn if I know," Oakley said as he slipped the toe of his boot under the unconscious man's shoulder and rolled him over on his back. "My God in Heaven!...This is Ben Larson, the youngest of the Larson gang. Got a new dodger jest yesterday on 'em. They's a two thousand dollar re-ward on Ben here and his older brother, Wes. Most bloodthirsty bunch since Quantrill's Raiders...Jesus Christ o'mighty!" Oakley stood there for a moment just shaking his head, and then he looked at the ax handle, quickly dropped it and drew his Colt Peacemaker. "Git some rope, Millard, a lot of it, and let's git him tied up good 'n proper...gotta send a telegram to Fort Smith. Hope they's a Tumbleweed Wagon in the area."

It was Indian Territory, 1885—comprised of most of the eastern half of what is now the state of Oklahoma given primarily to the five Native American civilized tribes or nations—the Cherokee, Choctaw, Chickasaw, Seminole and Creek—by the Indian Removal Act of 1830. The forced removal of the five tribes from their ancestral homeland in the southeastern part of the United States to the Oklahoma territory beginning in 1831, became known as *The Trail of Tears*. The Cherokees called it *Nunna daul Tsuny* or *The Trail Where They Cried*. Over four thousand of the fifteen thousand relocated Cherokees alone, died en-route.

The land of the Red Man became the stamping ground for outlaws from all over North America. The Territory—also called Robber's Roost or simply, the Nations—was under the jurisdiction of the Federal Court for Western Arkansas at Fort

Smith, presided over by Judge Isaac C. Parker—known far and wide as the *Hanging Judge*. This area of nearly 74,000 square miles was policed by a small, but courageous force of 200 white, black and Native American Deputy United States Marshals along with local Indian Police called *Lighthorse*.

Deputy Marshals often traveled in wagons in which they served warrants and collected their prisoners, many of them hardened criminals, and transported them to Fort Smith to await trial. They received 10 cents per mile for expenses and board plus $2.00 for each fugitive arrested. These marshals served nearly 9,000 writs or warrants during Parker's 21 years on the bench from 1875 to 1896. A prison wagon like this drifted back and forth across the territory like an uprooted, windblown weed and it is from that analogy it got its name—the *Tumbleweed Wagon*, the Great Wagon of the law.

ADA
CHICKASAW NATION

The green covered wagon creaked slowly toward town, as the team of four black-nose Tennessee mules plodded on, indifferent to the cold north wind at their backs. The wooden axle-grease pail swung to and fro from its hook just in front of the rear tailgate. A weathered gaunt man in his fifties sporting a full mustache, Deputy Marshal Hank McGann held the four reins and kept a sharp eye out for any sign of trouble. Beside him sat Deputy Marshal Joshua Nelson, a stocky black man in his early forties. Both men wore dark sackcloth suits and had their collars turned up to ward off the chill of the late winter cold front that was passing through. Hank had wrapped a charcoal colored woolen scarf around his neck and ears.

Nelson was singing softly to himself an old Negro spiritual he had learned from his grandfather who had been a slave in Mississippi before the war. The song had a direct reference to the Underground Railroad used for runaway slaves.

"Coming for to carry me home...Swing low, sweet chariot..."

"Hope that there chariot rides easier than this old prairie barge, Josh. My butt is about wore to a nub."

"Yessir, this seat is as hard as a widow maker's heart...Could stand me fresh cup 'o Arbuckle, too."

"Think I see the steeple of the First Baptist Church yonder. See there? Just to the left of the road where it crosses the rise."

"Cain't make it out. My eyes never was as sharp as yern's."

"Should be rollin' in just before noontime. How's eating somebody else's cooking sound to you fer a change?"

"Is that a complaint? Thought you liked my cookin'?"

"No complaint. Jest thought you might like to sit down inside and get out of the wind, not to mention have some vittles without the work."

"Never was afraid of work, but some fried chicken, mashed taters'n sweet-milk saw-mill gravy would stick to my ribs jest fine, I'm thinkin'," Nelson said as he grinned.

"Whoa there, boys. Hold on up, now," Hank coaxed the team to a halt outside the town livery. He set the foot brake and looped the reins around it. Joshua stood up and stretched his back

6

before he picked up his rifle and climbed down off the wagon. Hank followed suit and both men eased up beside the lead mules and began the process of unhitching the team from their traces. A young hostler in faded blue bib overalls and brogans exited the livery office door and approached McGann.

"Good day, Marshal. Y'all stayin' over?"

"Nope, just stoppin' fer a bite. Water 'em, check their hooves, give 'em a bait of grain and some hay," McGann replied. "Any place you speak highly of?"

The stable boy pointed down the street. "Lots of folks 'er partial to The Fried Pie."

"We were kinda thinking more about lunch than dessert."

"No, Marshall…That's the name of the cafe, The Fried Pie."

Joshua looked quizzically over at the boy. "Ain't never heard of frying a pie."

"It's somethin' Gussie May, just come up with, I guess. They sure are good, 'specially when you pour some fresh cream on top 'er some melted butter."

"Well, I'm game to try new things. How 'bout you, Hank?" asked Joshua.

"Same here. If we didn't try new things, we'd all still be nursing…way I figure."

The boy blushed. Joshua let loose a deep laugh. He glanced at Hank and grinned. "That would be a sight to see."

Joshua licked the crumbs off the four tined fork and set it reluctantly on the plate. "That fried apple pie makes me want to slap my momma, it was so good."

"Well, that just gives me an idea of a new trail dessert, if you have the fixin's," said Hank.

"Got everything, but ground cinnamon and vanilla. Think I'm gonna make me a stop by the mercantile a'fore we get outta town."

"Pick up some canned peaches while you're at it. That's what they used in this peach pie. It's worth a trip to Ada, all by its lonesome. Boy was right 'bout the fresh cream."

"We just might have to tip him a nickel for his suggestion."

"Uh huh, jest..."

"Howdy there, gentlemen. Willy over to the livery told me could find y'all here."

The two looked up to see a lean man of fifty in a brown three-piece suit with a badge pinned to his vest. They started to get up.

"Keep yer seats, boys, finish yer coffee," town marshal Burton Raines said as he pulled out a chair. "My lunch break, too."

Gussie May Davis, a portly woman in her fifties with her gray hair up neatly in a bun, approached the table. "The usual, Burt?"

"You know me too well, Gussie May, but I'm kinda extra hungry today, double up on the dumplins 'n bring me a glass of buttermilk."

"Comin' right up. You marshals need anythin' else?"

"No, ma'am...fuller'n a tick. That was mighty good," answered Joshua.

"I'll bring your ticket when I bring his lunch," she said as she walked away.

"How's everything in Ada, Burt?"

"Fine as frog's hair, Hank. Good to see you and Joshua. Guess you boys are working warrants out this way. Don't have any customers for ya, myself."

"Didn't figure you would. You keep most of the riff raff on the scout outta Ada. We been strikin' out so far on this trip."

"That's what the folks pay me for...Oh, hell! So busy flappin' my gums I forget to give you this here telegram from Fort Smith," he said as he pulled back his lapel and drug out a folded piece of yellow paper. "You're gonna love this one!"

Hank and Joshua exchanged glances. Hank took the paper and read it aloud to Joshua, who could cook like nobody's business, but reading was not his long suit. "To Deputy US Marshals McGann and Nelson. Stop. Proceed to Wewoka, Seminole Nation. Stop. Pick up prisoner Benjamin Larson. Stop. Additional personnel will meet you for transport assistance. Stop. Confirm this message upon receipt. End. Signed United States Marshal Fagan."

"Benjamin Larson? Ben Larson? They caught Ben Larson in Wewoka?" Joshua asked incredulously.

Burton Raines leaned back in his chair and smiled broadly. "Even a blind hog finds an acorn sometimes!"

SAND SPRINGS
CHEROKEE NATION
MORNING

A tall trim man, in his late fifties, with an unruly shock of salt and pepper hair sticking out from under his hat, carried a fifty pound burlap sack of oats out of Dennard's Feed and plopped it in the back of a faded blue buckboard on top of four other bags. His red and white border collie, Boot, trailed him from the door to the wagon, just as he had for the four previous trips. As he straightened up and twisted to limber his back, a town marshal badge pinned to his gray vest peeked out from the lapel of his black morning coat. He had a full mustache with the ends just beginning to curl upward—it matched his thick white eyebrows.

"Why don't you let Timothy's hired hand, Enos, to do that," said an attractive blonde woman in her late forties as she wheeled herself out the door onto the boardwalk. She was confined to a wheel chair with a tall wicker back.

"Plague take it, Molly darlin', I am quite capable of carryin' a sack of feed," said Marshal Tobe Bassett.

"I know you are, Tobe, but it is what the boy gets paid for. You should let him earn his money."

"I suppose, 'ceptin' that he was still loadin' Frank's wagon."

"How about we go over to Lucinda's cafe and you buy me breakfast. By the time we finish and have a cup of coffee, Enos will have loaded Frank's feed and mine too."

"You could have mentioned that 'fore I toted five sacks of oats out."

"Would have, but I was busy settlin' up with Miz Dennard and didn't see you start loadin'...Now you gonna buy me breakfast or just stand there with your mouth workin' 'till lunch time?"

"Remind me why I put up with this abuse?"

"'Cause you're a man and I'm a woman," she said with more than a hint of a smile.

"Noticed that some time ago, I did," he said in a mock grumble. "Well, come on Miz Allgood, don't want to stand here all day waitin' on Tim's boys. I have a reputation to consider."

He walked around behind her chair, and Molly placed her hands in her lap. Tobe smiled as he pushed her chair down the raised wooden boardwalk.

"Come on Boot," Tobe said, then added to Molly, "I wanted to tell you...you look particular pretty in the morning sunlight."

"Then what's holding you back, Marshall? I don't mean to be crass, but neither of us is getting any younger. If you have something to say, today is a good day as any."

"Tarnation, woman! I try to get up the nerve to tell you something nice and you cut me to the quick. There's no dealing with women folk, I would wager!"

"So, gonna give up on me just like that? No fight left in you?"

"Fight? I'm not tryin' to fight you, Molly. I wanted to say how pretty you are and you want to fight?"

She squeezed his hand on the top of her chair and then patted it gently. The two came to the entrance of Lucinda's. The smell of the strong coffee wafted out the open door as Tobe held it while she rolled herself in. "Stay outside, Boot. I'll bring you a biscuit."

Boot woofed and lay down beside the door and rested his head on his front paws.

Molly's eyes crinkled as she smiled at the welcome familiar scents. Homemade buttermilk biscuits, fresh churned butter, flapjacks and hickory smoked bacon complemented the eggs brought in fresh every morning for the eatery. Tobe could feel his mouth begin to water, and he almost forgot all about the attempted compliment. Molly saw the proprietor and spoke, "Miss Lucy, smells like a breakfast heaven in here."

"Why thank you, Miz Allgood. Pleasure seein' you as usual."

"I see someone knows how to take a compliment," Tobe said dryly.

"Pay no attention to him, Lucy. Marshal has his feathers ruffled."

"Do not."

"Do too."

Maybe he'll feel better when he's had his breakfast. You know how some men folk are before coffee," Lucy added.

Tobe stopped in his tracks. "Two against one?"

"I think you hit the nail on the head, Lucy. Better get us two blacks before he has a conniption."

Tobe settled in for a second cup of the stout black brew and was spreading some watermelon rind preserves on his fourth biscuit when Molly asked him a question that set him off again.

"When you gonna give up that badge and quit playin' lawman?"

"Woman, what do mean *playin'*?" he said as his head snapped up.

"Don't go gettin' all huffy on me, Tobias Bassett. It was a perfectly reasonable question."

"I'll decide what is reasonable when you are talking about my livelihood."

"Being a marshal is no job for a man of your age. There are plenty of young men willing to take the job, I am certain of that."

"While you may be all fired up to consign me to a rocking chair, I'm not inclined to join you."

The hurt in her eyes was immediate. She had been a most active horse trainer and excellent rider before her unfortunate accident in a buggy left her paralyzed from the waist down. He reached across the table and placed his hand on top of hers.

"Molly, that didn't come out right. I'm so sorry. What I meant was…I'm good at this job…John L. is still too wet behind the ears to take over full time. Besides, you have all the help you need at your ranch. Sky and them other boys do a good job for you, don't they?"

She nodded, but Tobe could tell she was still thinking about what he had just said. "I was just trying to figure out a way to make things easier on you, is all."

"Cain't say as it's easy. Molly darlin', I've asked you to marry me a dozen times and you have turned me down flat ev'ry time. Not inclined to live out on your place as a hired hand training horses...So here we are, neither of us givin' an inch."

"Like two bulldogs, I would say," she said with a slight smile.

"Took the words right outta my mouth...Why is so hard for us to talk about the future?"

"I wish I knew the answer to that. Perhaps I'll know what it is when I see it."

Tobe gazed into the golden brown eyes that had captivated him years before. His frustration tempered slightly. Each of them loved the other deeply, but something was holding her back. There was real love between them, but Molly would not give in to it. Overcoming obstacles was Tobe's stock-in-trade, but this was his future he was wrestling with and, like Jacob and that Angel, he was determined to prevail. He reached into his vest pocket, placed a half-dollar on the checkered tablecloth to cover the cost of the meal and grabbed the last biscuit from the platter for Boot. "I'll bring your wagon down. Enos should have you loaded out by now."

He rose walked around the table and kissed Molly on the cheek.

"Thank you, Tobe," she said as he patted her hand.

Lucy watched him walk toward the door. He tipped his hat to her and exited without a word. She glanced back at the table where Molly was finishing her coffee alone. *I'll never understand some women.*

THE NATIONS

CAMP
NORTH CANADIAN RIVER
PRE-DAWN HOUR

The scent of coffee boiling, beans and fatback frying in a cast iron skillet wafted across the campsite set atop the ridge overlooking the North Canadian River flood plain. Hank McGann rolled over in his bedroll to see Deputy Willis Scopes seated on a three-legged camp stool with a well-worn Winchester 1873 rifle across his lap. Scopes had a hand-woven Indian wool blanket pulled tightly around him to ward off the night chill.

"Any activity, Willis?" McGann inquired as he sat up and rubbed his nose across the back of his gloved hand.

"Nary a thing, 'ceptin' a couple packs of coyotes tunin' up. Purty quiet tonight," Scopes replied before he sniffed at his running nose. He leaned to the side and pressed one finger firmly against his rather large nose, closing one nostril off completely. He then proceeded to clear one, then the other nasal passage. Willis glanced round the small circle of light emanating from the cook fire and saw Deputy Nelson. Because he was the best at it, Joshua did the cooking for this group of lawmen. He could just make him out flipping thick-cut slabs of bacon with a two-tined fork. Other groups usually split the cooking chores up equally, but old Josh had a flair for turning out better trail rations than some of the small eating establishments could muster in towns. He liked to cook, but didn't like to scour pots, so a bargain had been struck that suited all five of the lawmen just fine. He'd do the cooking and the others took turns cleaning up.

Nelson grabbed the long cast-iron rod with a small shepherd's hook made on one end and fished around the coals and ashes atop the Dutch oven until he made solid contact with the arched bow cast into the rimmed lid. Satisfied the lid was securely hooked, the big man gently lifted it off, using care so as to not drop too many ashes into his prized biscuits. He set the lid downwind of the cast-iron convenience and lifted a small flaming stick from the fire to light up the interior. Inside, a baker's dozen of his signature buttermilk biscuits sat in their golden brown perfection.

"Come an' git it 'fo I tho's it to the hogs! The sorghum is warmed up too," Josh hollered, as was his usual jovial greeting to start the day, even though there were no hogs.

Momentarily, two heads appeared as they crawled to the back of the covered wagon. Once the tail gate was lowered, Deputy Marshals J.B. Donner and Bradford Tyler tugged on their tall cavalry style black leather boots, purposely built for riding and coming up almost to their knees, and slipped off the tailgate into the short buffalo grass. Donner snagged his leather galluses with his thumbs and pulled them over his shoulders as he walked towards the fire. Tyler, who had the six-to-midnight guard duty the previous night, walked out some thirty yards from the fire unbuttoned his brown canvas pants and relieved himself of the previous night's coffee. Deputy Marshals Donner, Tyler and Scopes were the additional personnel nearest to Wewoka. They had been sent by James F. Fagan, Chief

THE NATIONS

Marshal, Fort Smith, Arkansas, to assist Deputies McGann and Nelson in the transport of one, Benjamin Larson.

A sullen young man with blue eyes and the discoloration of a bruise on his forehead jealously watched the five deputies eat their fill and pour sorghum syrup or honey on top of the still streaming biscuits. Ben Larson wore heavy iron manacles on both his ankles and wrists and had a heavy logging chain wrapped around him twice and secured to the right front wagon wheel with a bulky iron keyed lock. "Hey! What about me? Don't I get to eat?"

"Shut up, boy! You don't eat 'til we're finished," McGann snapped at the prisoner.

"Who you callin' *boy*?" The prisoner spat back. "Ain't none of you Johnny Laws man enough to take me on! You'll never make it to Fort Smith with me, I wager you that!"

Donner looked over his shoulder at the young thug and shook his head. "Fer someone with a date with the hangman, the little piss-aint shore is full of hisself."

The other men laughed and finished off their breakfasts as the eastern sky began to turn lavender, and then shaded into apricot as the sun crept closer to the horizon. Flocks of passenger pigeons coursed through the sky low to the ground. The wind whistled across their wings as they flew past, creating a musical note.

NORTH CANADIAN RIVER
OSAGE COUNTY

Early morning sun crested over the tall cottonwood and black gum trees that populated the North Canadian River flood plain. The first rays glistened off the morning dew covered grass like thousands of scintillating diamonds. Ground-hugging winter fog which would be burned off by the sun later in the day still obscured the low-lying areas between the rolling hills. The faded green converted army wagon with its off-white canvas bonnet rolled up to the top of the yellow pine bows rattled down a dirt road that sloped toward the river. The melting snow in the New Mexico highlands and the late winter rains had swollen the river to almost flood stage.

Deputy US Marshal Bradford Tyler, with Deputy Nelson beside him, was driving the wagon, pulled by the four-up hitch of black-nosed Tennessee mules. Deputy Donner, on horseback, had been riding alongside with McGann and Scopes sitting in the back of the wagon on each side of the shackled twenty-year old outlaw, Ben Larson.

Tyler rode the brake lever with his foot to assist the mules as they eased down the bank toward a flat-bottomed ferry tied to the shore next to a six-foot diameter windlass. It was connected to a half-inch steel cable stretched across the one hundred yard wide river.

Tyler pulled up the team of mules just as they reached the ferry ramp and a middle-aged man in faded blue bib overalls and a battered old fedora standing next to the windlass and a sign that read:

HORSE & RIDER - 4 BITS, WAGON & TEAM - 6 BITS,
COACHES AND HEAVY WAGONS $1
MAX C. BURNS - PROPRIETOR

"Whoa up there, boys," Brad said as he eased back on the four sets of reins and locked the brake. "Mornin', you'd be Burns, I take it…River is up a mite."

"I be him, Marshal," Max said after he spit a stream of tobacco juice into the reddish brown water. "They's a lot of snow up north this winter…" he held on the end of the ferry. "Go ahead and pull your team on, Marshal. I got it."

Brad released the foot break and clucked to the mules as they gently stepped from the ramp onto the ferry—something they had done many times. "Come up there, Ted."

"Who's yer prisoner?" Burns asked as the wagon passed him and rolled onto the ferry.

The dark haired, chiseled featured Ben stood up in the wagon and took a theatrical bow toward Max. "Benjamin Larson is the name. Owl-hootin' and long ridin' is my game."

Deputy McGann reached over and roughly pulled him back down on the thirteen-inch wide seat. "Hesh up and seddown."

"Ben Larson? The Ben Larson?" the startled ferry-master said.

"I hope to hell there ain't more'n one," Tyler replied as he flipped Burns a silver dollar for the crossing fee.

"They broke the mold when the big man made me!" Ben said before he broke into a laugh.

Tyler remained seated in the wagon, while the other deputies all got out. Donner dismounted from his sorrel gelding and rolled a smoke as Burns stood on the bank and cranked the graduated gear assembly, turning the big windlass that started to move the heavily laden ferry out into the river. The current pushed the ferry downstream about ten yards, but the big double windlass was well anchored on both banks for the annual high water. Max cranked with a practiced motion as the ferry reached the middle of the river and proceeded until it was almost to the opposite bank.

Ben abruptly threw himself down to the floorboards of the wagon. McGann and Scopes looked over at him, puzzled.

"What the Sa...?" McGann started to say.

His words were cut off by a storm of gunfire from the bushes on the east bank. He and Scopes both turned forward quickly, looking around trying to see where the gunfire was coming from as they hastily drew their side arms. Multiple puffs of gray gun smoke rose from the low-lying willows lining the riverbank. Nelson, standing at the front holding the team steady, was blasted by the first volley. A well-aimed round struck Tyler in the left eye, blowing bits of brain and bone over Larson lying in the bed of the wagon. He toppled over the back of the seat without ever firing a shot. Nelson struggled back to his feet only to take two more rounds—one to the leg, another in the shoulder—and went down in a heap under the frightened mules.

At the rear of the wagon, Donner threw his partially smoked cigarette into the river and grabbed for his 1876 Winchester rifle chambered in 45-75 WCF riding in the saddle boot. He was shot twice in the back; .44 caliber bullets tearing into his spine and ribs. His wrist hung up between the rifle and saddle as the frightened animal plunged into the river, dragging Donner's lifeless body along.

Scopes fired twice before taking a rifle bullet in the throat. He grabbed where the blood was spurting with every rapid beat of his heart, and then staggered backward and toppled over the sideboards into the swirling muddy water on the upriver side of the ferry. The current pulled him immediately under—he never resurfaced.

McGann fired three shots at the smoke boiling out of the willows then took a solid hit and fell down beside the wagon.

There was a sudden eerie silence as the shooting stopped and the ambushers rose from their cover as the gun smoke hung like a pall in the still morning air. It was the Larson Gang—Ben's older brother, Wes; the half-breed Comanche Bob; Johnny Hawkins; Kell Brophy and the immigrant, Irish Buck Strong.

Ben's blue eyes peeped up over the side of the wagon—there was a wide grin on his strangely handsome face as he got to his feet. He managed to shuffle to the front of the wagon until his shackled ankles reached the end of the chain—he waved his cuffed hands at his brother. Ben stretched out as far as he could and pulled Tyler's Colt from its holster. Once it was stuffed securely in his pants, he searched through Tyler's gray vest under his coat until he found the keys to the manacles. He first unlocked the ankle shackles, followed by his wrists, and then climbed over the driver's sideboard and down to the jockey box. Ben knocked the lock open with the butt of Tyler's gun. He opened it, pulled out his own pearl handled nickel plated Colt Single Action .45 nestled inside his gun belt and buckled it on. Ben turned and threw the two sets of heavy restraints far out into the river with a, "Yeehaw," as they splashed into the muddy water.

Ben saw McGann was still breathing and clutching at a serious wound through his shattered collarbone. He kicked the wounded man's Colt to the back of the ferry, and then straddled the deputy and bent over to gloat. "See there? I told y'all you wuz not men enough to git me to the hanging judge…Know what's funny? The bullet that's gonna kill you wuz paid fer by Judge Parker! How is that for a howdie-do?" The younger Larson laughed and pulled Tyler's pistol out of his belt. He gut shot McGann twice in rapid succession as he fanned the hammer back. Then he turned his attention to Burns, a hundred yards back across the river. The fear-frozen man's eyes were wide as the blood and gore splattered outlaw called to him, "Ferryman, get your bony ass in gear. You got paid to take me all the way across this here river. Get to it, or my boys will drop you where you stand!"

***

CHAPTER TWO

CHOCTAW NATION
LATIMER COUNTY

Choctaw Lighthorse, Tecumseh Moore and Lyman Jackson, rode down into a draw, dismounted and tied their mounts to some brush. Both men wore dark broadcloth three-piece suits, homespun three button shirts and cravats. Tecumseh was a slight, wiry built full-blood and wore a black seven-inch tall uncreased crown hat with a Red-tail Hawk feather stuck in a beaded band around the base. Lyman was three-quarter blood Choctaw and quarter freedman—his hat was tall, gray flat topped narrow brim with a stampede string hanging down his back. He was taller and thicker built than Tecumseh—both wore their hair short in the white man style.

They pulled Winchesters from their saddle scabbards and started walking up the deep, steep-sided gully. There was a four foot wide wet weather stream flowing at the bottom, so the two men kept to one side as they approached an area where cattle, horses and wild life had crossed over time, creating a path up and down both sides. Tecumseh, being the smaller, led the way as they crept up the near side to the top. He lay down under a cedar tree growing close to the edge, removed his hat and peered over the lip of the draw.

Two white men, Seth Chantry and Ebitt Kimble, were sitting around a rock lined camp fire next to a grove of trees barely ten yards from the gully. Seth was a large bearded potbellied man dressed in bib overalls and a dirty fedora. To say Ebitt was skinny would be kind. He too wore bib overalls that seemed to be the norm for teamsters of the day. They were sampling a bit of their cargo mixed with hot coffee.

Nearby was a green buckboard with a single unhitched mule hobbled and grazing on the winter grass. There were a number of wooden cases in the back of the buckboard.

"Lilly is gonna hug both our necks when we bring in that load of whiskey," said Seth.

"Hope she does more'n than just hug our necks," replied Ebitt. "She's been waitin' on that who-hit-John fer goin' on three weeks now."

"'Fraid she be waitin' longer than that, boys."

Both men spun their heads around at the same time to see Tecumseh and Lyman standing at the edge of the gully, Winchesters trained in their direction.

Tecumseh continued, "We are Choctaw Lighthorse, Tecumseh Moore and Lyman Jackson. We have warrants for your arrest on account of whiskey peddlin'."

"The hell you say," said Seth as he jumped up, drew a Colt Peacemaker out of the back pocket of his overalls and snapped a quick, ill-aimed shot at the two lawmen and then turned and ran toward the woods.

Lyman and Tecumseh both ducked as the shot went high. Tecumseh brought his well-used '73 Winchester to his shoulder and squeezed off a round at the laboring Seth as the fat man tried to run. The 200 grain 44-40 slug caught him dead center of his right butt cheek, exiting out below his hip joint, sending him tumbling ass-over-teakettle on his face in the grass.

"Ow, ow, ow! You shot me in the ass, you damn red-hide!" yelled Seth as he rolled over.

Lyman walked over and pulled him to his feet. "White man too fat. Run slow. Tecumseh coulda taken head off just as easy."

Tecumseh waved his Winchester at Ebitt as Lyman was walking Seth back toward the fire.

"I'll patch this ya-hoo up whilst you have this other'n dump out all but one bottle of that whiskey," said Lyman.

"Aw, we brung that all the way from Fort Worth. It taken us over two weeks just to git this far. You jest gonna dump it out?" whined Ebitt.

"That is the law. Savin' one bottle for the court," said Tecumseh, stoically.

"Make a grown man want to cry," Ebitt said as he started opening the bottles and pouring the low grade alcohol on the ground.

"Ow! Dammit, Injun, that burns!" yelled Seth as Lyman pushed a putty-like paste of wood ash mixed with coal oil into the wound. Seth had his overalls around his knees with the flap of his red union suit down—his white bare butt seemed to shine like a beacon in the morning sun.

"Better burn a bit than bleed to death," replied Lyman. "Whiskey peddlin' not hangin' offense...yet. White men be out of jail in few months."

Lyman finished his doctoring, walked over and started hooking up the mule to the buckboard.

A few hours later, the Lighthorse rode into the farming community of Red Oak following the buckboard with Ebit driving and Seth standing behind the seat. They drew rein in front of the High Sheriff's office.

Sheriff Bennett stepped out of his door before the smaller of the two Lighthorse could dismount. "Tecumseh, Lyman, good to see you. Got some ne'er-do-wells for me I see," the sheriff said.

"We do, Sheriff. Couple of white eyes we caught peddlin' whiskey...again. Third time for this pair."

"One needs a doctor...Tried to argue about us servin' the warrant, Tecumseh shot him in ass when he tried run away. Rode all way here standin' up in the wagon," added Lyman.

"Stupid is like ugly, goes all the way to the bone," said Bennett. "Bring 'em in, just happen to have a vacancy. I'll send a deputy to fetch the doc."

"Packed the holes so's he wouldn't bleed to death 'forc we got here," said Lyman as he and Tecumseh dismounted, tied their horses up and helped the prisoners down. "Have an execution, did you?" continued Lyman as he noticed a Choctaw body in a casket leaned up against the undertaker's wall across the street.

Nailed across the coffin was a hand-painted sign that read *ASSASSIN*. The body was shirtless and a flour circle had been drawn on his chest. There was a single bullet hole dead center of the circle.

"Silan Lewis," the sheriff said. "Shot Deputy Sheriff Joe Hoklatubbee of Gaines County, a staunch Progressive and a political rival, last fall. Lewis led a band of Standpatters that had targeted Hoklatubbee and shot him dead as he stepped out on his porch with his little girl. A special term of the Moshulatubbee Court was held in January. Lewis had fired the fatal shots and the jury found him guilty of murderin' his red brother. Had eight men with him that were convicted of complicity in the assassination, they were executed last week."

"Guess we were a shade late for the doin's, Lyman."

"'Peers as though," replied Tecumseh. "Who was Silan's best friend?"

"Lyman Pusley, Gaines County Deputy Sheriff. He and Lewis had known one another since they was kids, hunted together. Silan requested that Pusley be his executioner and gave Lyman his own Winchester to do it with," the sheriff said, then added, "Promptly at twelve o'clock, per the Moshulatubbee Court order, Silan Lewis rode into town, turned his rifle over to me, peeled his shirt off so's the execution committee could powder his chest...He said, 'Time up. Choctaw law say Silan Lewis must be shot. Want Lyman Pusley do it.'

So, we walked down to the courthouse. I blindfolded him with a big red bandana. He knelt down while Pusley stepped back a dozen paces, levered a round into the chamber and fired one shot from Lewis' rifle, dead center...Some of his friends had tried to get him to run off to Texas, but Silan had told 'em, 'Choctaw law say I die, it must be right'." The sheriff paused for a moment. "Would have been a war between the Progressives and the Standpatters if he had violated the court order...not to say anything of Choctaw tradition."

"Know Pusley. Good man. He did duty," said Tecumseh.

"So did Silan Lewis," added Lyman.

"Here is paper work on whiskey peddlers, Sheriff. We destroyed their stash, 'ceptin' for this one for evidence," Tecumseh said as he handed the surviving bottle to Bennett.

"Pity," mumbled the Sheriff. "But the law is the law,"

"It is," said Tecumseh.

"It is," agreed Lyman, then added, "If you don't need anything else, Sheriff, we head north toward the Canadian. You know how to reach us come time for the trial."

"Under control. You boys watch each other's backs, ya hear?"

Tecumseh and Lyman nodded, mounted up and rode north out of town.

OSAGE COUNTY
EARLY AFTERNOON

The two Lighthorse sat their horses on a knoll as they scanned a mule drawn wagon a little over a mile away through binoculars.

"Mules are wandering, Lyman," said Tecumseh.

"Maybe the driver sleeps."

Momentarily, the wagon disappeared behind a hill—they put the glasses away and reined their horses down the knoll in the same direction the wagon was heading.

In a few minutes, they caught up with the wagon. Lyman rode to the front, grabbed the reins of the lead mules and pulled the team to a stop. "Whoa up there."

"Hells bells, Lyman! These men are Deputy US Marshals and are both dead. They been propped up to look like they was alive!" Tecumseh said as he got close enough to the drivers for a look.

Stripped pine boughs had been shoved down the backs of the dead deputy's jackets and wedged between the wagon seat boards and the back slat.

Lyman rode to the back of the wagon, side-passed his pinto pony up against the tailgate and stepped directly from his saddle to inside the wagon. "Two more dead marshals, Tecumseh..." he said as he examined the first two—and then..."But one is still alive!"

SAND SPRINGS
LATE AFTERNOON

There was a professionally painted two-by-three foot sign hung over the wooden sidewalk in front of a solid six-paneled door that read:

ELWOOD W. THACKER, M.D.,
PRACTICE OF MEDICINE IN GENERAL

Inside the office, white haired Dr. Thacker cinched up the laces of a ladies black high-button shoe top on Molly Allgood's right wrist. The vamp part of the shoe had been cut away; just the top was being used as a brace. Molly was a rugged blond-haired beauty in her late forties who was confined to a wheelchair. A beautiful, but not delicate, raven haired young woman—in a white blouse buttoned up to the neck and a dark green ankle-length brushed twill skirt with a complementing Abigail vest that accentuated her tiny waist—stood beside Molly's wheelchair. She was eighteen year old Nellie Ruth Bassett.

"Ouch! Dammit! Elwood Thacker, this is enough! You have ruined a perfectly good pair of my shoes to make this contraption...Ouch! That is too damn tight!"

"Hold still...It is not too tight! This will keep your wrist in place, so it will heal quicker...That's a good girl."

"Don't you *That's a good girl, me!* You old sawbones!... Nellie Ruth, let's go shoppin'. I need a new pair of them St. Louis shoes...No thanks to Thacker here...How much do I owe you?"

"I'll let you know...Keep this brace in place and come on back here in three days. Nellie Ruth, bring Miz Allgood back here Thursday...please?"

"Yes, sir, I'll see to it."

"Now, git us out of this den of pain before he kills me... You'll have to push, since this quack has got me trussed up like a turkey!"

Nellie Ruth moved in behind Molly's wheelchair and wheeled her toward the door Thacker held open. Molly's tall wicker-backed wheelchair bumped over the narrow threshold onto the boardwalk and left a chuckling Doc Thacker behind as he closed the door.

Nellie Ruth wheeled Molly down the boardwalk. "Why don't you go ahead and marry Daddy? I know you think the world of him and he's crazy about you...It's been eight years since your husband passed away...'Sides..."

"Sides, what? Why don't you commit yourself in marriage to John L.?...Well? You're a lot younger and a hell of a lot more active than me, that's for damn sure...Come around here, in front of me."

They stopped and Nellie Ruth walked around to face Molly. She took Nellie Ruth's hand in her good one. "Does it hurt?" Nellie Ruth asked.

"Of course it hurts...Are you going to marry him?"

"Who?"

"Don't you play games with me, Nellie Ruth Bassett...John L. Patrick, that's who!"

"Oh, Molly. That's all he talks about...I don't want to marry, yet...I want to live. Experience things, meet people...Is that so awful wrong?"

"Sakes no!...We're in the same crack, you'n me...You with your John L. and me with your daddy."

Down the street almost a half block away, Marshal Tobe Bassett walked in a hurry toward the women. He was followed by Deputy John L. Patrick, a younger, leaner version of Tobe, endeavoring to keep up. They were both being tailed by Tobe's red and white Border collie, Boot.

"What the hell do you mean, she's broke her wrist?" Tobe demanded.

"Been tryin' to tell you...Molly got banged into the fence by one of her green colts!"

"I heard ya the first time!...Shit fire and save matches!"

Tobe and John L. hurried up behind Molly and Nellie Ruth as they slowly rolled down the boardwalk—they were almost even with the Marshal's office.

"Plague take it, Molly, darlin'! I have told you and told you to let Sky and the boys take the edge off those green colts before...Before you start puttin' a handle on'em...Before!... Damn it to Hell!...Where are you hurt and how bad?"

Molly stopped her chair and spun it around with her uninjured hand when she heard Tobe's rant behind them. "Tobias Reese Bassett, I'm the one person around here you *don't* tell what to do. After five years of courtin', I'd think you would accept that!"

"She's broken her wrist, and it's very painful, Daddy."

Boot kissed Molly's hand.

"Thank you, Boot...'Tis not! Hush up, Nellie Ruth!"

"Dammit to purgatory, Molly!"

"Now, I'll be expectin' you for supper as usual...and quit using those vulgarities."

"You...You...Ohhh, damn. You really got me by the short string, Molly Allgood," Tobe said as he bent over to kiss Molly on the cheek, but she spun the chair back around the direction she and Nellie Ruth had been going with her good hand before Tobe could complete the peck.

"I know...Come along Nellie Ruth, I need to add a sugar tit to our shoppin' list. That bossy father of yours won't be fit to be around for at least a week."

John L. put his arm around Nellie Ruth and gave her a squeeze. She slipped free and grabbed Molly's chair from the tall back. "See you men at supper."

"Nellie Ruth is helping me tonight. Don't you dare come late!" Molly said over her shoulder, as Nellie Ruth rolled her down the boardwalk toward the mercantile.

Boot waved good-bye with one paw.

"Marshal, why don't you go ahead and marry Miz Allgood? You been a widower now most ten years and..."

"Mind yer manners, Deputy Patrick. You're a fine one to be givin' ad-vice....Nellie Ruth ain't said *yes* to you yet...Has she?"

"Huh?"

"Has she?" Tobe said louder.

"No, sir…" he said then added sotto, "You know that."

"Boy, let me…"

Tobe was interrupted by a wagon thundering down the street.

"Damnation! It's Choctaw Lighthorse Tecumseh Moore and Lyman Jackson with a Tumbleweed Wagon!…What in tarnation?…" Tobe exclaimed as he and John L. stepped out into the dirt street.

Tecumseh reined the lathered mules to a stop right beside Tobe and John L.—he swung down as Lyman dismounted and both hurried to the rear of the wagon. "Marshal, we need some help here!"

"What is it, Lyman?"

"Wagon load of dead deputy marshals!"

"Good God!"

"This man is just barely alive," added Tecumseh as he unlatched the tailgate.

Molly and Nellie Ruth had stopped and turned around. Molly motioned to Nellie Ruth to roll her closer.

"Merciful Heaven!" "Oh, my God!" they both exclaimed at the same time as they saw Deputy McGann lying on a blanket in the back of the wagon..

"John L., fetch ol' Doc Thacker. Be quick about it!" Tobe shouted.

John L. spun on his heel toward the doctor's office as Tobe helped the two Lighthorse unload McGann.

"Hell, I know this feller...He's Hank McGann. Git him inside...Be partic'lar with him now. Molly, ya'll go ahead and supper without me."

"Supper will wait!" Molly retorted.

Carefully, Tobe and the two Lighthorse carried McGann inside the marshal's office and back to a dark open cell. They laid him on the bunk chained to the stone wall.

Tobe bent down over McGann. "Hank...Hank, this is Tobe Bassett."

"Yeah...I hear...you," Hank whispered.

"What happened?"

Hank painfully turned his head to look at Tobe. "Larson gang...ambush...Burns...Ferry," he managed to say before he passed out.

Boot crawled under the bunk and covered his eyes with both paws.

Thacker and John L. rushed into Tobe's office followed closely by Nellie Ruth pushing Molly into the room.

Doc moved immediately to McGann, took out his surgical scissors from his black bag and began to cut away his wool vest, shirt and union suit. He peeled back the thick blood clotted clothing from the wounds in his stomach made by the 44-40 caliber rounds. One look at the location of the entries told him all he needed to know. Thacker looked at Tobe and sadly shook his head.

McGann's eyes fluttered back open and he continued to try to tell what happened, "We picked up...Ben Larson...this... this...mornin' in Wewoka...from Marshal Oakley...was tryin'

35

to…" He paused to gather some measure of strength. "…git him…him to…to Fort Smith." Hank lost consciousness again.

John L. lit a one of the several coal oil lamps that were in the office.

Nellie Ruth lit another and handed it to Molly, who held it close to McGann so the doctor could see. Nellie Ruth got the water basin and several clean towels for Thacker as he fruitlessly tried to staunch the flow of blood.

Hank finally opened his eyes again and looked up into Thacker's face knowingly, and then turned to Tobe. "They kilt us, Tobe…kilt us all…" McGann managed to get out before his death rattle.

Doc Thacker reached over and gently closed the dead man's eyes. There was a moment of silence in the room, and then Tobe spoke softly, "I've knowed Hank McGann since we rangered together down in Texas with McNelly…Damn good man to ride the river with." He paused for a moment, and then continued, "I'm goin' over to the telegraph office. Judge Parker will need to know what happened to his deputies…and who done it."

"Don't much think I would wanta be in the room when he reads that telegram," John L. said.

Tobe took a last look at the corpse, shook his head in pity and frustration, turned toward the door and spoke to the Lighthorsemen, "Tecumseh, I would 'preciate it if you and Lyman would see to the other bodies."

"I'll have to look 'em over before you move 'em to the undertakers," added Doc Thacker. "They'll want a medical record and death certificate for the trial record."

Tecumseh and Lyman nodded their understanding to Thacker as Tobe walked out into the now dark street followed by Boot. He looked up at the full moon just rising on the eastern horizon as Boot scratched at the side of his leg and whined. Tobe reached down and rubbed Boot's ears. "I know, Boot. I know," he said as he tried to choke back the lump that had started to grow in his throat.

***

CHAPTER THREE

CHEROKEE NATION
BARTLESVILLE

It was not quite nine in the morning when Wes, Ben, Kell, Comanche Bob, Irish Buck and Johnny Hawkins approached the single lane wooden bridge over Caney Fork of the Verdigris River on the west side of the bustling farm settlement of Bartlesville. The dirt road—with spindly scrub oaks scattered on both sides—they traveled on that passed through the town would become the famous Route 66 in the next century. Bartlesville, which would be the center of the Oklahoma oil boom in less than twenty years, lay just forty-seven miles north of Tulsa.

The outlaws all wore suits or morning coats of various description, vests and cravats or bow ties and looked for all the world like common businessmen or drummers. Only their saddle guns were visible, handguns would have made them immediately suspect. They had camped overnight near a small branch of Caney Fork located some two miles north. They had all shaved after their meager breakfast—then Wes had brushed the trail dust from their clothing and hats with a boar-bristle brush he carried in his saddlebag. He had wet an old rag with water from his canteen, wiped his boots, pitched the rag to Ben for him and the rest to do the same. After all the footwear was clean, Buck slung the dirty rag into the brush.

Irish Buck was a typical Irishman with freckles, red hair and beard and bright blue eyes. He always wore his favorite hat—a dark green derby. Wes had passed around a small tin of pomade for everyone to comb into their hair and smooth it back. The group looked at least respectable.

They passed by a small neat white painted clapboard house surrounded by a short picket fence. A somewhat heavyset woman in her thirties in an ankle-length gray house dress, her hair pulled back tightly in a bun and three wooden clothespins held in her mouth, was hanging wet-wash on the braided cotton clothesline strung between two 'T' posts at the side of the house. A couple of children, a boy around six and a girl seven or eight, were playing with a yellow cur dog in the yard. The woman looked up as the riders passed. Wes and Johnny nodded and touched their hat brims. She nodded back as the children stopped their play momentarily and waved. Everyone in the group, save Ben, waved back.

The woman continued to watch the group of six riders as they clopped across the bridge, the shod horses hooves making a hollow thumping sound, and rode on toward the town. She turned, took one of the wooden pins from between her teeth, and resumed hanging her wash.

As they rode closer to the center of the business district, Wes turned to his cohorts, took out his gold pocket watch and opened it. "Ben, you are with me, Kell, Buck, follow in two minutes. Johnny, you two minutes later and Bob, a minute after Johnny. Take your positions where we talked about and don't do anythin' stupid...Got it?"

"Aw, Wes, we ain't kids. We..."

"Don't need none of your mouth, Bob. Just do what you're told."

"Didn't mean nothin', Wes, just..."

Wes's eyes flashed at Bob, effectively silencing him and then he and Ben nudged their horses into a fast walk. The others held back until it was their turn to ride in.

"Ease your horse back, Ben. Let's drop off to a slow walk. Don't need no attention from the natives."

"I know."

They worked their way down Bartlesville Road until they came to a wide newly bricked street and reined their horses to the right to head south on Washington Boulevard.

"Do what I do, Ben," Wes instructed his younger brother. He nodded and touched his hat brim to any lady that happened to look their way. Ben would do the same.

THE NATIONS

A matronly woman holding hands with two young children stepped out into the street to cross to the opposite side. Wes and Ben pulled their horses to a stop, acknowledged the woman as she and the children crossed in front of them.

"Thank you, sir," she said as she passed.

"Yes, ma'am, anytime," Wes answered and lifted his hat a few inches.

The early morning sky was beginning to cloud up. A dark bank of a late winter cold front lay off to the north.

"Looking like rain," the woman said.

"Yessum, surely does. Surely does at that," Wes politely replied as the woman and her children reached the other side and stepped up on the limestone curb.

Wes and Ben squeezed their horses back into a walk. They were both handsome men, blue-eyed, dark haired and clean featured. Wes sported a full mustache while Ben was clean shaven.

"'Peers as though they bricked the main street since the last time we was here," observed Ben.

"That's very observant, Benny, since we've been on it for almost a hunderd yards."

"Just makin' conversation, Wesley."

"Yeah, well…Huh! Now looky there. They done built a new two-story brick bank, too. The old one next door is a haberdashery now. Times must be good."

There were numerous wagons, buckboards and buggies moving in both directions on the main street in addition to a half-dozen citizens mounted horseback and one black man on a mule. The day was just getting started in Bartlesville, IT.

"Bet that new bank is chock full," agreed Ben.

"Fixin' to find out," Wes said as he eased his horse up to one of the hitching rings on iron posts set in the limestone curbs directly in front of the bank. Ben picked the next one on the right. The large sign on the front of the building above the front door read:

CATTLEMEN'S AND MERCHANT'S BANK

Wes dismounted, tied his horse to the ring with a lead rope, took out his pipe and filled it. "Roll yerself a smoke, kid, while Kell and the boys are gittin' in position. Wes struck his match on the ball atop the iron post as Ben took out a bag of Bull Durham, a rolling paper and built a cigarette. They enjoyed a leisurely smoke while they surreptitiously watched Kell, Buck, Bob and Johnny ride in and take their positions. Bob and Johnny tied up in front of the newspaper building next to the town marshal's office, walked over and took seats on the benches on both sides of the door. Kell and Buck took their places at each end of the block.

Everyone set; Wes knocked the ashes out of his pipe on the heel of his boot and put the pipe back in his vest pocket. He removed his hat, smoothed his light brown hair back with his fingers and replaced it—the signal. He nodded at Ben to get a set of saddlebags from his horse, turned and entered the door to the bank.

Inside, there were six teller windows with steel bars down to within six inches of the counter. At the far left side of the counter there was a two-way swinging half-door and the president's office off to the side. The four foot wide, five foot tall steel safe was inset into the wall next to the president's office. The massive door had not yet been unlocked. There were two men and one woman at the three open teller windows. Wes calmly took a place behind the man at the far left window and patiently waited for him to conclude his business.

"Thank you, Mr. Carlisle, you have a nice day," the teller — dressed in a morning coat, high collared white shirt and a bow tie —said as he handed the man a receipt.

"You too Charlie," Carlisle said as he turned, nodded a greeting to Wes as he passed, and left the bank.

Wes stepped up to the window. "We'd like to make a deposit...Charlie, is it?"

"Yes, sir. I don't believe you have an account here, do you, sir?"

"No, we're new in town."

"Of course, sir, and how much would you like to deposit?"

"Well, it's sizable. I'd like to meet the president, if you don't mind."

"Yes, sir, just a moment," the teller said as he turned and stepped over to the president's door and tapped on the upper glass portion with the word *PRESIDENT* in gold lettering in the center.

The rather portly balding man with mutton-chop whiskers inside looked up from his desk at Charlie and nodded. Charlie opened the door and said, "Got a new customer out here Mr. Wingate. Want to meet you."

Hiram Wingate looked past his teller at Wes and Ben in their business suits standing outside the two-way door. "Of course," he said as he got up from his high-backed burgundy leather executive chair and straightened his silk brocade vest.

Charlie moved back to his window after he opened the half-door for Wes and Ben. Wingate stepped forward with his hand out. "Hiram Wingate, at your service, sir. I am president of the bank."

"And a fine new bank it is, too, Mr. Wingate. Very impressive," Wes said as he shook the proffered pudgy hand.

"Thank you, sir. And you are?"

"Henry Daniels, that's my brother, Benjamin."

"Please to make your acquaintance, Mr. Daniels...Proud to say we have the most secure bank in the territory. The latest fire and explosive proof safe in the nation from Diebold Bahmann Company of Cincinnati, Ohio. Absolutely impregnable, sir, absolutely impregnable. Paper documents inside one like this survived the great Chicago fire back in '71," Wingate said as he puffed out his chest a little.

"Yes, impressive. May I see the safe, sir?" asked Wes. We have a sizable amount of business we'd like to take care of. We just sold a herd up to Abilene and are a little uncomfortable carrying around such a sum."

"Of course, I was just about to unlock it for the day."

"Benjamin, would you give Mr. Wingate the saddlebags after he opens the safe," Wes said to Ben.

"Of course, W...uh, Henry, my pleasure," Ben said as he stepped forward and stood behind Wingate while he rotated the two dials and then spun the large stainless steel spoked wheel to open the vault. As soon as he swung the massive door open, Ben drew his Colt from his shoulder holster and shot Hiram Wingate in the back of the head. Wingate dropped directly to the floor. The woman at the window screamed. Ben wheeled about and fanned off three shots at the tellers before they realized what was happening. The three dropped like dominoes.

Wes moved quickly to the lobby and drew his own weapon. "Please, Ma'am. Do not make any more noise. Just sit down on the floor, you'll not be hurt."

The other man, a rancher by his dress, started to draw his revolver. Wes shot him between the eyes.

The woman screamed again. "You killed him!"

"Yes, Ma'am, I surely did. Now I told you to not make any more noise...Hurry it up, Ben."

"Should have brought two sets of saddle bags."

"Git what you can, no gold, paper only."

"I know, I know."

Across the street, the marshal and a deputy rushed out of the marshal's office at the sound of the gunfire. The marshal was drawing his side arm as he stepped out on the boardwalk. The deputy right behind him was shoving shells in a sawed-off double-barrel shotgun. Bob shot the marshal in the back before his pistol even cleared his holster while Johnny put two rounds into the deputy—they both dropped to the boardwalk—their momentum carried them all the way to the street where they lay still.

Buck and Kell moved immediately to their horses, mounted up and started moving at a trot toward the bank from each end of the block. Wes and Ben exited out the front door. Ben carried the now full saddlebags and even his coat pockets were bulging. They quickly untied their horses, mounted up and started to head down the street. The storekeeper from the haberdashery next to the bank stepped out of his door with a double-barreled shotgun. He started to raise it to his shoulder, but Ben shot him in the chest. The gun discharged into the water trough between two hitching posts, blowing water fifteen feet into the air. The rest of the people in the street, on horseback, wagons and on the sidewalk began to scatter out of harm's way.

"Let's ride!" yelled Wes as he spurred his mount down the brick street with a clatter and a shower of sparks toward the edge of town opposite of the side they came in.

Just south of town, they cut off the main road to a lesser traveled one to the east leading to Nowata. The gang topped a rise outside of Bartlesville and stopped. Wes took out his brass binoculars and scanned the road all the way back to town.

"Anybody on our tail, Wes?" asked Kell.

"Hang on...Nope, don't see a soul. What with Bob and Johnny takin' the marshal and deputy down, ain't nobody got guts enough fer a chase. See, told you nabobs that would work... Let's scatter and meet up at..."

"Wes! Listen!" interrupted Johnny.

They all turned their heads toward the east and tried to identify the sounds.

"Let's get behind that grove of wild plums over yonder, somebody comin'," said Wes as he turned his horse to the thick stand of trees on the north side of the narrow road.

Behind the thicket, they sat their horses until the travelers on the road came into view.

"Drummers," whispered Buck.

A single mule was pulling a box wagon down the rutted road —the pots, pans, scrub boards and wash tubs hung on the sides of the tall box wagon made enough racket to raise the dead. A sign on the side read:

HARVEY BERNBAUR
HOUSEWARES, SUPPLIES &
MEDICINE SHOW

On the seat at the front of the wagon sat two loudly dressed traveling salesmen of the day. One was thin as a rail and the other was more than rotund with a round red-cheeked face. The heavy set one was handling the reins to the mule.

"Nowata was shore good to us, Willie, made over two hundert. 'Spect we'll double that in Bartlesville. How much of that Chief Potawatimi Cure-All we got left?"

"Got nearly a case, Harv. If we can stop at the next creek, got enough 'shine, asafetida powder and turpentine to make another two cases. 'Bout all the bottles we got left anyway," the thin drummer said.

"Can git some more bottles and corks when we git to Tulsa."

"Good enough...Pull up here, Harvey, gotta water a tree,"

47

Harvey pulled back on the reins with a, "Whoa up there Blackie...Don't take all day."

The big black mule gratefully stopped walking and looked over to see if the winter grass growing alongside the road was in reach. It wasn't. He lowered his head and waited to start walking again. Will climbed down, walked over to a bare scrub oak just off the road, unbuttoned his striped trousers and got rid of his morning coffee. "Damn, Harvey, this feels good...You know, if I had my choice on how to die, think I'd just like to melt and run out the end of my tallywhacker."

"Don't think you are goin' to have that choice, pilgrim," said Wes as he stepped out from behind a large cedar tree with his gun held on Willie.

Willie looked up at Wes and then at the other outlaws as they stepped around the cedar. Bob started laughing. "Looks like yore tool is kindly drawin' up there, drummer. Why don't you put that ugly thang away 'fore I shoot it off."

"Faith, but you'd not be that good a shot, Bob Miller," said Buck.

"Got a point there, Buck. It's a gittin' smaller all the time."

They all laughed again.

"Step down off that wagon. You'd be Harvey Bernbaur, I take it," said Wes as he waved his pistol at the big man.

"Yessir. Listen you kin have our money...all of it..."

"Now I kinda doubt that is even open to discussion, lard ass. We are gonna just take what ever in the hell we want," said Ben as he cocked his pistol and shot Harvey right between the eyes.

The fat man fell forward to the ground off the wagon seat with a sound like someone dropping a ripe watermelon off the porch. The mule jumped at the shot and started to lunge, but Kell caught his headstall before he could take a step.

"Please, sir. We..." Ben turned and shot Willie in the mouth, the bullet tearing through to the back of his neck spraying a cloud of red behind him as he dropped where he stood.

"I just hate it when people speak without bein' spoke to. Bad manners," said Ben.

"Yep, just plain rude," agreed Johnny.

"Ben, git their pocket money, Buck you and Bob, git what ever supplies we need outta the wagon, especially the whiskey, then burn it. Kell, shoot the mule," ordered Wes.

SAND SPRINGS
OSAGE AND TULSA COUNTIES

The biggest difference between the Tulsa County side of the small town of Sand Springs—population three thousand—and the Osage County side was the sale of alcoholic beverages and the presence of saloons on the Tulsa County side. That influence alone made for a slightly shadier type character found late at night along the wooden boardwalks.

Deputy John L. Patrick cradled a double-barreled shotgun under his right arm with a coal oil lantern in his left hand as he made the nightly rounds. He stood a full six feet tall, and was a well proportioned young man at 180 pounds. His sandy brown hair was cut short, his face clean shaven, like his father's had been when the now departed man was his age. John L. never knew his dad. Corporal Horace Patrick had died in a battle near Petersburg, Virginia, on March 25th, 1865, only four months after his baby boy came into the world. John. L lived with his widowed mother Annette, and treasured the sole tintype of his father in uniform.

Just past midnight, he finished his rounds on Main Street, located on the Osage County side. He turned west at the end and crossed the railroad tracks into Tulsa County. A mongrel dog barked at him twice, then disappeared into the darkness beyond the small circle of lantern light. Most of the wood frame houses were dark, as one would expect on a Thursday night. He passed the modest house occupied by his boss, town marshal Tobe Bassett and his eighteen year old daughter, Nellie Ruth. He thought about her in her comfortable feather bed as he transferred the lantern to his right hand and flipped up the collar of his gray woolen frock coat. The night had turned cold, but he drew a measure of comfort in the fact that his girlfriend was safe and warm inside. He continued a quarter-mile down Hickory Street until he reached the end and then turned left and worked his way over to Poplar Street and back east.

Along the more commercial Commerce Street, saloons and bawdy houses dominated the second block west of the tracks. Coal oil lamps illuminated the painted wooden signs enticing entrance to the smoke filled rooms. John L. perked up at the sound of heated conversation spilling out through the swinging doors of the Double Diamond Saloon. He looked inside the front glass window to see a pair of large unknown men squared off next to the bar. One man, dressed in overalls, had his arm around the waist of a red headed saloon girl.

The other man was pointing his finger and yelling, "You had yer chance, Burt! She is agoin' up with me!"

"Like hell!" the man in a dirty oilskin jacket yelled back.

John L. shook his head and stepped to the swinging doors. "Here we go," he said to no one at all as he strode into the bar and spoke out in a loud voice, "Nice night for a peaceable drink, ain't it, boys?"

Both men turned to see who was talking. The bartender reached under the bar for a two foot long billy club.

"Stay outta this mister, ain't yer concern," the drunk with his arm around the girl slurred.

John L. eyed the burly man and set his lantern on a nearby table. He swept the frock coat back exposing the Single Action Colt on his right hip, riding high in a brown leather belt with .45 cartridges stuck in sewn loops all the way around the back. "That's where you are wrong, friend. My job is to make sure you gentlemen keep everything peaceable in our little town."

The young deputy pulled back the lapel of his coat slightly to reveal a shiny five point star pinned to his vest. Light from the four coal oil lamps adorning the wagon wheel suspended from the ceiling by a heavy rope glinted briefly as he turned to face the bigger man.

"Looky here, Earl! We got us a wet nurse for a lawdog, tryin' to tell us what to do!"

"Nope, already told you," John L. commented

The other man with whom the burly man had been arguing chimed in. "Why hell, let's just wipe the floor with his young ass, and git back to seeing who gets to poke this red haired filly!" Earl said. He spit out a wad of tobacco that bounced off the sawdust covered floor once before it rolled up to stop. Earl grinned drunkenly, exposing two missing front teeth.

Oh crap. These two are friends, maybe even kin. What was it Tobe always says about drunks? The inexperienced young deputy never had chance to remember the sage advice—*Make haste slowly.* The larger of the two cousins, Burton Wilson, threw the red-haired barfly to the filthy floor like a rag doll. She slid almost to the bar and hit her head against the thirty foot long brass foot rail at the foot.

Other patrons grabbed their glasses, bottles cards and money off the tables and headed for the far wall. Burton lowered his head and charged John L. like a bull. Cousin Earl took a step in the deputy's direction when he sensed motion from the bartender. He lifted his left hand to block the billy club and countered with a right cross to the barkeep's jaw. The blow sent the man crashing back into the shelves behind the bar, where he quickly slid to the wood floor, unconscious.

John L. reacted instantly to the charge by raising the double-barrel shotgun up slightly and coming down on the back of the bigger man's head. The blow felled him like an ox, but his momentum knocked John L. backwards, sending him sprawling. He struggled to get the man's dead weight off his legs for a split second, tried to avoid a kick to the head from Earl—and almost succeeded. The drunken man's right boot

52

glanced off his jaw, stung his ear and sent his hat flying. The lawman sent a right fist hard to the man's exposed crotch.

"Aiiee!" Earl bellowed and crossed his eyes as he folded over.

John L. tagged him with a left hook that sent him spinning around, and then pushed the prone body of Burton clear. He jumped to his feet as Earl recovered enough to throw a roundhouse right. John L. leaned back and let it pass by harmlessly before he countered with a sharp left jab and right cross that didn't.

Earl staggered back and cursed the deputy, "Slippery damn cockroach! I'm gonna…"

He never got the rest of his sentence out, as the young deputy threw an uppercut to his belly, just beneath his sternum, that took his breath away and doubled him over momentarily. John L. grabbed the man by his hair and pulled his head down as he slammed his knee up into the man's face. The sound of the drunk's nose breaking resonated across the quiet bar. Earl flipped back on to his butt and then to his back where he laid still—blood gushing from his smashed nose. A smattering round of applause erupted from the ten remaining patrons.

John L. turned round to scan the bar, reached down to retrieve his hat and brushed the sawdust off. He rubbed the boot burn on his left ear, "Ow." With his hat back in place, he approached the red haired girl who had a slight bump on her forehead. "You okay miss?"

He helped her stand. She brushed herself off and gave him a kiss on the cheek. "At least there are some gentlemen left in town," she said as she looked at the other patrons, turned and huffed out the door.

The bartender staggered to his feet and rubbed his sore jaw as John L. approached him.

"Anythin' broken?"

"Don't think so." He looked over at the two prone patrons and pointed. "They owe me two dollars for the whiskey."

John L. dug through Earl's vest pockets and found a couple of silver dollars. He tossed them to the barkeep. "Wanna press charges?"

"Guess not, officer. Just get 'em the hell out."

"I'd be happy to oblige," John L. said as he slipped handcuffs on the first unconscious man. He stepped over and locked his last pair of cuffs on Earl, grabbed a mug of stale beer of a table and tossed it in the man's face.

The man shook his head and returned to consciousness. "You had enough now, Marshal?" Earl cried out when he saw John L. bent over him.

"Got it bassackwards, mister," he replied as he pulled the man up to a sitting position

Earl reached up and touched his battered nose. "Damn!" His bloody hands told him what a mirror would have confirmed. "You broke my nose."

John L. hauled the drunk to his feet and looked him in the eye. "Yes I did," he deadpanned. "Help me get yer runnin' buddy on his feet."

"Burton, wake up!" Earl yelled at his cousin as John L. dragged him over closer to the swinging doors.

Burton's eyes fluttered as he came to, trying to focus on his cousin's face just inches away. He finally brought the two fuzzy images together and winced at the sight of the misshapen nose. "Look like hell, Earl. Did we kick his ass?"

"Not exactly."

The door opened just after 5:30AM on the tiny jail with three cells in the back of the one story brick building. Marshal Bassett stepped in and greeted the night shift lawman seated behind the single mahogany veneer desk. "Mornin', John L., I see by the horses tied up outside, you had some activity last night."

"Yessir. Couple drunks, up at the Double Diamond. They are sleepin' it off now, but I got charges on both. Disturbin' the peace. Assaultin' an officer."

"That so?" Tobe said as he poured himself a cup of coffee. "Locals?"

"No, sir. From out of town, looking for work, what one said."

"Well let's have a look at you...Bein' assaulted an all."

"Not much to show, Tobe, just a scrape and bruise from one of the jackass' boot," John L. said as he stood and walked closer to the coal oil light on the jailhouse wall.

Tobe studied the minor injury to his jaw as John L. pointed to the red spot on the upper portion of his ear. "Now, this one kinda burned."

"Bet it did," the older lawman said as he stifled a smile. "What happened here?" he asked.

"What?" John L. replied as Tobe placed a finger on his right cheek.

Tobe grabbed the white cotton handkerchief from his deputy's vest. "Looks kinda bad. Better not let Nellie Ruth see this."

"What?" John L. exclaimed as Tobe wiped his face.

"Lip paint...One of them boys kiss you while they was assultin' you?"

"No! It weren't like that!" a flustered John L. retorted. "There was this girl..."

"It's always about a girl," Tobe cut in.

"Yeah, and anyway..."

By the time he finished his story it was almost 6:00AM. Tobe smiled at the story and saw himself two decades earlier. "Remember what I taught you about haste?"

John L. grinned sheepishly. "Yessir...'bout thirty seconds too late...But I'll remember it sooner next time, you can count on that."

"Imagin' you will. Listen, you better go home and get yourself some sleep. Get rested up for yer pick-nick with my little girl."

"I'm on my way," he said as she hurried to the door. Two seconds after the door closed, it opened again. John L. stuck his head in. "Thanks for understanding, Tobe."

Tobe put his feet up on the desk and grinned. "That's my job, boy."

THE NATIONS

"Wake up, son, it's 11:30," Annette Patrick said as she gently nudged his shoulder.

He raised one eyelid, looked around and then slowly allowed the second lid to raise. The middle-aged attractive, but worn woman, pulled open the dark curtains installed in his bedroom that normally allowed him to sleep soundly after working all night.

"Nice day for a picnic, John L.," she said as she looked at the weather outside.

Whoa. That's right. Today is Friday. He threw back the covers and began to get out of bed before he realized he was stark naked. "Dang it!" he said as he flipped the covers back across his torso.

Annette chuckled as she turned her head. "Ain't nothin there I ain't seen a thousand times. I'm still your mama and always will be."

As soon as she left the room, John L. leapt out of bed, dusted his armpits with talcum powder and pulled on his red union suit. He was so excited, he almost forgot to shave, but lathered up with the basin of cold water in the porcelain wash basin on the dresser—nicked himself once in the lamp light and cursed for hurrying. He donned his blue bib front shirt, tucked it into his pants, slipped his leather galluses over his shoulders and added a green neckerchief that Nellie Ruth had commented she preferred because it matched his eyes.

"Thanks, for washin' my shirt for today, Mama."

"You look nice, son. Pass my regards to Nellie Ruth."

He walked briskly to the barn and hitched the buggy to the family horse. Ten minutes later, he pulled up in front of the Bassett house and tied off the lead to the concrete post set at the edge of the front yard. He walked up to the house and knocked on the door. The petite dark haired beauty opened the door. Even through the screen door, her classic bone structure and wasp waist was easily recognizable. Her smile lit up a room with a natural, unselfconscious style. He opened the screen door and reached out to grasp the wicker basket from her hand.

"You look beautiful today, Nellie Ruth."

"You always say that."

"Only because it's true."

"My goodness! What happened to you? Did it hurt?" she said as she touched his bruise jaw.

"Couple drunks early this mornin'…Fightin' over a woman."

"That almost sounds romantic."

"Well, think what you want, but the big man threw the woman on the floor before he came at me," John L. said as he held the door open for her.

"I hope you arrested him."

"I did…after he come to."

DIRT ROAD
RODGERS COUNTY, NEAR CATOOSA,
FULL MOON
A MONTH LATER

A red and yellow Butterfield stagecoach, pulled by a six-horse hitch, clattered along the rutted road. There were two railroad type coal oil lanterns hung on each corner of the coach up by the boot, casting a pitiful yellow glow that barely reached the rumps of the lead horses. The coach splashed through a shallow stream and headed out across a level open meadow toward some distant wooded hills.

Inside the bouncing vehicle, were three male passengers and one woman. Topside, on the box, rode the driver and a shotgun messenger.

The coach, with its horses at a trot, rounded a bend in the road, when two masked outlaws charged out of the woods at a full gallop, firing their pistols. The flashes of their weapons created brief moments of brightness in the moonlit darkness.

"Damn! Road agents!" the driver said as he whipped the team into a run. "Heaahhh, up there, you slab sided cayuses! Heaahhh!"

The messenger leaned back over the top of the stage and fired one barrel of his 12 gauge Greener sawed-off coach shotgun at the outlaws, but they were too far back.

The outlaws continued the chase barely out of range for almost a quarter-mile until the coach approached a fork in the road, just visible in the moonlight. As the coach neared the fork, two more outlaws rode out of the brush from the left, also firing their pistols. The driver reined the team sharply to the right as the messenger tried another useless shot from the bouncing coach. This road was much rougher and less used than the main road. The horses lunged as they started to climb the increasingly steeper grade; much of the wheel ruts were enlarged by the winter rains causing the coach to bounce violently. The thick eight-inch wide, multiple-layered leather suspension straps under the box were virtually useless for dampening the roughness of the road.

The passengers were being bounced roughly around the inside, desperately trying to find something to hold on as they reacted fearfully to the gunfire and the chase. One man, a drummer, was dressed garishly in a loud yellow and green plaid suit and green bowler hat—another man was garbed like a rancher. The other two passengers were a young, attractive newlywed couple destined for their honeymoon in Tulsa.

Still wearing his finest gray pinstripe frock coat and matching pants, the young attorney-at-law had just married his redheaded high school sweetheart in their hometown of Claremore, in the Cherokee Nation.

"My God! What's happening?" the young bride fearfully asked.

"Road agents! Get down!" admonished the rancher as he drew his pistol.

The four outlaws pursued the careening coach up the steep hill. As the coach neared the hilltop, the surprised driver jerked the team to a sliding stop to avoid a tree that had been felled across the road and set ablaze just as the coach arrived. The kerosene soaked tree rapidly began to burn and created a spooky flickering red glow on the rutted road, as well as the winter naked trees alongside and the rearing horses.

Several shots rang out and the driver jerked from the impact of a bullet to his lower ribcage. The shotgun messenger got off a wild high shot, and then took a hit to his right shoulder. He dropped the weapon to the ground and raised his left hand in surrender.

Wes and Ben Larson stepped out from behind the burning tree and continued firing from the hip at the driver and messenger with their Winchesters as they walked forward. The driver was struck again in the chest as he tried to pull his hand gun. He grunted and toppled off the seat to the ground with a sickening thud and lay still.

The horses continued to lunge in their traces and scream in fright, but could not advance because of the burning tree that blocked their path.

The other four outlaws—Kell Brophy, Comanche Bob, Johnny Hawkins and Irish Buck Strong galloped up to the stage just in time to see the defenseless messenger take a head shot from Wes. He fell over the front of the boot onto the back of the horses and then slid between them to the ground. One leg remained hung over the tongue and double-tree.

"I'm gittin' outa here!" the terrified drummer yelled inside the coach.

"Don't be a fool!" the rancher warned.

The drummer emerged from the coach with panicky caution, glanced wildly around at Wes and Ben and then at the others just arriving, and started running as fast as he could back down the hill in the moonlight. The brothers ceased firing; Ben nudged Wes, pointed at the drummer sprinting for his life, took careful aim with his carbine and squeezed off a round.

The slug hit the drummer in the middle of his back and its impact sent him sprawling awkwardly. Ben laughed as he watched the drummer somersault three times and then roll to a stop against a wash tub sized rock at the side of the road. He and Wes started cautiously forward toward the coach.

"All right! You in the coach…Come out with yer hands up…or suffer yer death!" Wes yelled.

The rancher, his six-gun held ready, knelt down on the floorboards, and watched out of the corner of the window as the outlaws approached. The young married couple were crouched fearfully in a corner of the coach holding each other, the bride was sobbing.

"You hear me?…I said come out…Ain't in the habit of repeatin' myself!"

The rancher suddenly aimed over the edge of the window and squeezed off a quick shot, lifting Ben's hat off his head. He and the other outlaws all hit the dirt fast and recommenced firing at the coach, punching holes and knocking chinks out of the sideboards near the window.

The couple cowered in abject terror as they tried to get even lower. The rancher caught a bullet in his arm—his gun flew from his hand and clattered noisily to the floorboards.

"All right! All right! Hold yer shootin'!" he yelled out.

The outlaws continued firing.

"We give up! There's a woman in here!"

Wes waved to the others to hold their fire. Everyone stood up and moved forward warily, their guns at the ready. Ben stooped over, picked up his hat and grimaced unhappily at the bullet hole in the crown then followed behind the rest. As the outlaws approached the coach, the rancher and the couple emerged nervously. The rancher was holding his wounded arm.

"All right, which one of you got sassy with the shooter?... Well?" Wes asked.

"I...I guess it was me," the rancher replied with trepidation.

"Well, now that were not very bright," said Wes.

Ben caught up to Wes, still holding his hat. "Looky what he done to my brand new hat, Wes." Ben turned to the rancher and poked his finger up through the hole in the crown of the flat-topped, Plainsman hat. "Looky there. You see what you done? I give a double-eagle for this hat last month in Little Rock...and you done ruin't it."

"Aye, you know what they say, Ben Larson, turn abut's fair pley," suggested the big red-faced Irishman.

"That's right...Reckon I'll just have to put a hole in yer bonnet."

The fear in the rancher's eyes increased as Ben tossed his Winchester to Buck, and then slowly, deliberately pulled his pistol.

Comanche Bob started laughing and said, "But, Ben, his head is still in it."

"Say, that's right, Bob...Oh, well, he don't seem to be using his head much anyhow."

Ben suddenly cocked his pistol. The team of horses reared and lunged in fright as his shot rang out. The woman screamed.

There was a hole through the crown of the rancher's hat just above the sweat band and a thin rivulet of blood started to trickle out from under the brim down his forehead. His eyes rolled back and he slumped to the ground like a felled ox. The coach behind him jerked and shook from the lunging of the team.

Ben's cold, indifferent eyes followed the body of his victim to the ground. Then he swiveled his six-shooter toward the couple holding each other as the woman tried to choke back her tears. "You see that?"

The couple put their hands over their heads and began to beg.

"Please…Please, we done nothin' to you," the groom said.

"You can have everything we got," his bride added.

Ben ejected the spent cartridges from his gun and reloaded from the rounds in his belt.

"Here is my wallet," the groom said as he pulled his wallet from inside his coat.

"That's our startin' out money. Just please don't hurt us," begged the bride. "It's all we have."

The groom held the bulging leather wallet out to Ben who took it as he snapped the loading gate closed, cocked the hammer and fired in a single motion, hitting the groom in the middle of his chest. The bride screamed as she tried to keep her husband from falling to the ground and failing. She dropped to her knees, sobbing, to hold him. "No! Please! Oh, God, no!

Calab? Calab! Please dear God, no! Don't leave me. Please don't leave me!"

Ben pitched the wallet to Wes who caught it and slipped it in his coat. Ben turned back to the terrified bride who was cringing in terror. A large cameo broach hung from a gold chain around her neck and nestled just at the top of her ample cleavage that peeked out of her open bodice dark gray travel dress. Ben reached forward slowly and lifted the broach up from her bosom and studied it for a moment. He smiled at the bride, and then jerked the broach away, breaking the gold chain, his soulless eyes locked on hers as he put the necklace in his vest pocket.

The terrified bride looked to Wes. "Help me! For God's sake, help me! He's killin' us all!"

Ben placed the muzzle of his .45 between her breasts where the cameo had rested a moment before. The young woman looked up at Ben in a brief second of disbelief before he calmly pulled the trigger and she toppled over onto her dead husband.

"Damn you...You go too far!" Wes said as he stepped in and backhanded Ben across the face, knocking him to the ground.

Ben rolled over and jerked his pistol around toward Wes. Wes drew his gun, cocked the hammer and pointed it straight at Ben's forehead. "Not on your best day...If you weren't my brother..." Wes paused. "Git yer sorry ass up and git that drummer's valuables...Now!...Kell, you and Johnny, the strong box."

Ben got up, glared at Wes, holstered his pistol, reached over and grabbed the bride's purse, and then spun around and stomped off down hill toward the drummer's body.

Kell and Johnny moved to the front of the coach, climbed up and drug the money box from the boot and tossed it to the ground. Kell jumped down after it while Johnny grabbed the ax from the front of the boot, tossed it to him and jumped down. Kell raised the ax and chopped at the lock. On the second swing, the lock was broken. Kell and Johnny knelt over the box and began to lift out stacks of paper money.

Ben looked down at the drummer, who was still alive and bleeding profusely. He drew his pistol, deliberately fired four shots into the helpless man's head and reholstered his nickel plated Colt. Ben searched through the pockets of the drummer's three piece suit until he found his wallet, removed the folding money, stuffed it into the bride's small travel purse and walked back up the hill toward the others.

.

Comanche Bob and Irish Buck removed the valuables from the driver. The two proceeded to drag the shotgun messenger clear of the double-tree and then picked him clean as well. Buck grabbed up the messenger's Greener shotgun, extracted the empties, looked it over approvingly and draped it in the crook of his left arm. When finished, they headed toward Wes eagerly. Wes distributed equal shares of the loot to his henchmen. Ben arrived in time to get the last handout and gave Wes the purse.

"Same as usual. We split up and meet again in two weeks at the Reese out-shack along the Arkansas," he said as he divided up the money from the bride's purse.

Bob, Kell and Buck walked toward their horses, mounted up and rode away in different directions. The Larson brothers stood and watched the rest ride into the darkness. Wes turned to his younger brother, anger still in his eyes, "You comin' with me?"

"No! Goin' to Sand Springs to see Tillie, and cut loose the badger."

"You take a caution, hear? Don't go runnin' into none of Parker's marshals…again."

"Take care of myself," Ben mumbled as he turned away from his brother and walked to his horse. He stepped up into the oxbow stirrup, swung his right leg over, wheeled his horse and loped away toward the south west. A battered old Mexican guitar tied behind the cantle of Ben's saddle bounced in rhythm to the horse's rocking chair lope.

Wes gazed after him for a moment, shook his head hopelessly, and then walked back over to the stage. He found a blanket inside, covered the dead bride, paused for a moment as he looked down at the inanimate mound, and then turned and walked to his horse. Wes mounted, surveyed the gang's handiwork once more and rode away in the opposite direction from Ben into the moonlit darkness.

***

CHAPTER FOUR

MUSKOGEE, OKLAHOMA
DECEMBER, 1909

A seventy-one year old white-haired black man, wrapped in a thick shawl, sat in his rocking chair near the fireplace in his modest house on North Howard Street, Muskogee, Oklahoma. His face was slightly puffy from the edema caused by his failing kidneys—an affliction known in that day as Bright's disease—he held a cup of hot lemon and mulberry tea, but he spoke in a strong clear voice to the young reporter from The Oklahoma Daily News.

The twenty-eight year old man in a three-piece hound's tooth suit had his flip-over spiral notebook on his lap and brought his yellow number two stub of a pencil to his mouth and wet the lead with the tip of his tongue. His dark green Burberry cabbie cap was on the couch beside him. "So they killed how many, Mr. Reeves, sir?" the reporter asked.

"Bass will do fine, son."

"Yessir...Uh, Bass, sir."

"Now as to how many they killed...Best I can recollect, believe it was nineteen, meby twenty that we know about in that last spree, son. And that was just in the Nations. Word had it they ranged from the Nations, over in the Oklahoma territory, to Arkansas, Missouri, Texas and up into Kansas. No telling how many they was all told." Bass paused and took a sip of his tea, and then continued, "In my opinion, they made the James', Daltons, the Doolin gang and the Martins all look like choir boys. The others only killed when they felt they had too. The Larsons...they was just pure killers. Killed for the love of it."

The young reporter finished writing a sentence in his notebook then looked up at Bass. "How long had you been a Deputy US Marshal at that time?"

"Oh, I 'spect I'd been marshallin' fer the Judge 'most ten years by the time the Larsons hit their stride."

"How did you come to capture Ben Larson again?"

"Oh, hell, wadn't me the first time, boy. Didn't have nothin' to do with the catchin', just the transportin'. See, back 'bout the time they had hit that stage, Jack and me were down in the Choctaw Nation on the trail of a gang of horse thieves. We had gotten a telegram from Captain John H. Rogers of the Texas Rangers that they had chased Dirty Bill Trotter and his clan...wanted for horse stealin' and rustlin' in Texas...cross the

Red. Cap'n Rogers said they believed the Trotters was headed to the Kiamichi Mountains to hide out in the wilderness..."

KIAMICHI WILDERNESS
CHOCTAW NATION
1885

Bass Reeves was a big man for the time at six foot, three inches in his stocking feet and weighed over one-hundred-ninety pounds—lean and hard like spring steel. The forty-seven year old black man was in his tenth year as a Deputy US Marshal for Judge Parker. Bass' long time partner, Jack McGann, was a crusty, tobacoo chewing, fifty-year-old white man with twelve years of Marshal service under his belt. Not as tall as Reeves at five foot ten, Jack was built like a bull with the attitude to match.

Bass and Jack were deep in the Seven Devils in the Kiamichi Mountains. The Seven Devils were so named because they were seven identical shaped large hills that covered over four hundred and fifty square miles—completely forested over with heavy timber. Many a pilgrim traveler had gotten lost in the Seven Devils, never to be heard from again, but Jack had spent several years living with the Choctaw and knew the Kiamichi Wilderness like the back of his hand. To hear Jack tell it, there wasn't a creek he hadn't fished, a cave he hadn't spent the night in or a bear 'er panther he didn't know on a personal basis in the Kiamichi's. Of course, Jack had been known to stretch the truth on occasion.

"They gonna have to stay fair close to Gates Creek, Bass. Only good water in between Cane Creek and Little River."

"Makes sense. Any grass in the area for the horses? Cap'n Rogers telegram said they had more'n twenty head."

"There's a couple of small meadows along the south bank of the Gates. My bet is they'll be in one of them."

"We need to take 'em easy. We go in there shootin', them horses will scatter to hell and gone. Rangers won't be none too happy...Think I'll go in as George Shields, the colored outlaw from Texas..."

"Satan Shields?"

"Same. You stay hid out in the trees and watch my back. If'n everythin' goes right, I can get the drop on Trotter, the rest of 'em will fall in line,"Bass said as he removed his badge and slipped it in his inside coat pocket.

"And if'n everythin' don't go right?"

"Then come a shootin'."

"Damn, Bass, why don't you just crawl in with a nest of vipers?"

"Think I've done that already."

"Oh, yeah...Forgot," said Jack.

"My old grandma used to say, iff'n you go amongst the Philistines, go armed."

Bass rode down the narrow game trail that ran along Gates Creek. He made no attempt at stealth as he whistled a old slave tune. He had just rounded a sharp bend in the tree canopied trail when two unkempt youths, the oldest no more than eighteen stepped out in front of him. "Where the hell you think you be agoin', nigger?" the older one asked.

"Who'd be askin'?"

The older one looked over at his brother, somewhat confused. He didn't expect that kind of answer from a colored man. "We be the Trotters…"

"Bill Trotter. And I think my boy asked where you be agoin'…I'm askin' who you be," interrupted a big man with a full beard, pointing a single-shot ten-gauge shotgun at Bass as he stepped out of the brush into the trail next to the oldest boy.

"George Shields…Texas way," Bass replied, as he looked the big man straight in the eye.

"George Shields?…Satan Shields?" Trotter asked, as his eyes noticed a hickory ax handle stuck in a leather scabbard tied to the saddle.

"Some call me that…some call me other things."

Trotter turned to his boys. "Damn good thang you boys didn't piss this man off. He be Satan Shields…killed five men…"

"Six," interrupted Bass.

"…Uh, six men at one time in a saloon in Texas with that there ax handle." He turned back to Bass. "Dodgin' the laws, air ye?"

"Could say that. Y'all got a camp set up nearby?"

"Just through the woods a piece."

"Mind if'n I light fer a spell, boil up some Arbuckle?" asked Bass.

"You got coffee?" Trotter asked excitedly.

"Yep. If'n you got the water."

"Damnation! Ain't had no coffee since Bully was a pup. Foller us," Trotter said as he and his two boys struck out down a side trail.

Bass followed the Trotters for several hundred yards through the thick woods. *Easy to see how folks can get lost in here. All looks the same. Hope Jack is still behind me.* They broke out into a small meadow split by the creek. Half of the grassy area was roped off as a corral for twenty-four horses. The horses had grazed the winter grass—wild oats, vetch, rye and cheat—down about half way. *Looks like they been here for 'bout a week.* Bass rode over toward the campsite where they had built a brush arbor lean-to. By the fire was the forth member of the Trotter clan—his fifteen year old daughter.

"This here's my baby, Mary Alice. I calls her Mame. Those other two are Ellis, he's the oldest, and Hubert, he's the middle young-un."

Bass tipped his hat to Mary Alice. She just glanced at him and went back to stirring her pot.

"She's cookin' up some possum stew with wild onions 'n acorns. Just give her a handful of yer coffee beans so's she kin grind 'um up...How long 'fore that stew's ready, Mame?"

"Be ready in thirty, forty minutes, I 'spect, Papa. Gotta add some water, since you invited comp'ny."

Bass stepped down from his dun gelding and tied him to the rope corral. He undid his poke sack and took it to her. "Git what you need of the Arbuckle, Mame."

"Thankee," she said as she looked at him with some curiosity.

Bass then took out his corn-cob pipe, filled it from his pouch and lit up with a burning twig from the fire. "Just the four of you move all them horses, did ya?" he asked in between draws.

"Naw, they's another. My brother. He's out huntin'. Rekon he'll be along directly," said Bill. "He ain't one to miss supper."

"That's a nice lookin' hoss you got there Mr. Satan," observed Ellis. "Real nice."

"He'll do to ride the river with," responded Bass without looking up.

"Care to trade?"

"I guess not," Bass said as he sat down on a log near the fire.

"Sure?" Ellis asked again.

Bass looked up and eyed the young man for a moment. "You heard me the first time, boy…Don't ask again."

Ellis settled back, eyeing Bass cautiously. In a few minutes, the smell of coffee drifted across the camp. Bill inhaled deeply. "Damnation, that smells good! We gotta git ourselves into town more oftener!" he pronounced.

"Nuthin like the smell of fresh made coffee to git a man's mouth to waterin'," Bass agreed.

Mame took a sip of the possum broth with a hand-carved wooden spoon. The flat tasting liquid did not meet her expectations. She took a bit of fatback and rendered it in a cast iron skillet. Afterwards she added a handful of flour from a cloth sack kept inside a saddle bag and stirred the resulting roux until it turned a deep golden brown. As a final touch, she scraped a Green River style kitchen knife across the sharp corner of a chunk of pink rock salt and stirred the seasoned mixture to incorporate it and thicken the thin stock. She tasted the result and nodded to herself. "Supper's awaitin'," Mame called out.

All four men gathered around as she dished out the meager meal onto tin plates. Steaming mugs of coffee were poured out and the family sat down on logs rolled up by the lean-to.

Bass took a seat on the grass, sitting cross legged as he dug into the possum stew with gusto. "Right tasty, missy," he said without too much fanfare.

She smiled and she savored the black brew Bass had provided. "Yer coffee, too," she said as she took another sip.

"Too bad Uncle Chesley ain't here to enjoy it. Might have to have me another plate," Ellis added.

"Yer mama learned you good, little one," Bill said as he wolfed down the possum and lapped up the gravy from his plate like a dog.

"Shore do miss Mama," Mame said with a look of sadness.

Bass scanned the rest of the family quickly. The young boys were nodding in agreement.

"Lost the kid's mama, did you?"

"Yep. The consumption taken her last sprang," Bill said just before he belched loudly. "Teachin' her to take her mama's place," added with a lecherous grin. "Doin' right good if'n I say so myself. Right boys?"

The black lawman kept his poker face, but inside, his stomach churned. Incest was one mortal sin he could not tolerate in any fashion. The image of Trotter taking one of his own bullets to the head flashed into his mind. Bass' face showed just a hint of a smile and he kept on with his supper as if nothing had transpired. He had almost cleaned his plate when motion caught his eye.

Bass looked up to see Jack riding in, followed close behind by a big man with a full mustache on foot, holding a shotgun in his left hand like it was a toy. Bill rose as did his two sons, all three glaring at Jack.

"Whatcha got there, Chesley?" Trotter asked.

"Lawman. Badge say Deputy Marshall, United States, IT…Step down off'n that horse, lawdog."

Jack stepped down and stood beside his horse, Pepper, eyeing Bass. All of a sudden, the possum stew tasted flat and greasy. Bass set his plate on the grass.

"What you adoin' 'round here?" asked Bill Trotter.

Jack looked around and fixed his eyes on Bass. He pointed his gloved finger directly at the big black man. "I've been trailing that nigger there fer some time. Wanted for murder, robbery and arson back in Texas."

"That so?" Trotter laughed. "In case you don't know, this here place is better'n thirty miles north of the Red."

Jack didn't flinch one eyelash. "I know exactly where we stand. I'm a Federal officer, rivers don't mean much to me. That there buck nigger is goin' back with me to stand trial in Grayson County."

Bill shook his head. "Don't rekon so, mister. See, me and the boys don't cotton to the law. On account of our line of work, you understand."

The other Trotters laughed at the weak joke. Ellis' eyes narrowed. He looked over at his father. "Paw! Let me kill him? Won't nobody ever find him out here in the Kiamichis."

Bass stood up. He knew the situation was not good, not by a long shot. His horse was tied thirty yards away, with the ax handle still stuck in the scabbard. He spoke in a loud clear voice, "That law's been a doggin' me for nigh on three weeks. Anybody gonna kill him, it is gonna be me." He walked up to Jack and decked him with a hard right hook.

"Hold on there!" Trotter objected. "In my camp, I git last say on who kills who!"

Bass ignored him and walked over to his horse and pulled the hickory ax handle out in one fast motion. He slapped the head flat against the open palm of his huge hand. The resulting *smack* of wood on flesh sent shivers down the two young boy's spines.

Jack scrambled to his feet rubbing his bruised jaw.

"Hey, now! There is a five hundred dollar re-ward for this smoke bastard back in Sherman. I'll see that you folks get it!"

Chesley Trotter chuckled. "Hell, mister! We got more than a thousand Yankee dollars on the four of us over in Texas! Don't think we'd be a galavantin' down thar to pick up five hundred on some darky."

"Listen here, we can work sumphin' out!" Jack pleaded.

Bass believed him. Or at least he thought the Trotters did. He walked closer to Chesley, who now held the double-barreled scatter-gun chest high, aimed at Jack's face. Dirty Bill Trotter held the single barreled shotgun aimed at Jack's midsection. One wrong move and Jack was dead. Bass raised the wooden club high. Jack's heart beat wildly as he looked at Bass for a sign, any sign. Bass took in a deep breath. His eyes flicked toward Bill Trotter for a split second.

Bass started forward with the ax handle—Jack crossed his arms overhead in preparation to block the lethal blow. In a lightning move, Bass redirected the handle across Chesley's right wrist. The sound of bones breaking echoed across the campsite like a rifle shot. The shotgun flew out of his hands as the man screamed in agony.

Bill swung right to fire at Bass, but Jack was too fast. His panther-like leap snatched the smokepole from Trotter's hands and swung it hard against the horse thief's head like a boxer's left hook. The buttstock struck him just behind the ear—his head snapped over at an unnatural angle. Trotter's body never moved after it hit the ground.

Bass recovered from the downward blow on Chesley by coming back up with both hands on the smooth hickory handle. The resulting uppercut caught the bent-over Chesley Trotter across the mouth, sending yellow tobacco stained teeth flying across the leaf litter. Chesley landed on his back and cried out in pain. His hands went to his mouth and felt for the mangled lips and gaps in his gums.

Ellis went for a Colt .41 Thunderer on his hip. He almost cleared leather when the .45 six-shooter worn by Bass roared to life. Fired from only ten feet away, the heavy lead bullet lifted the skinny teenager off his feet. Blood sprayed up from the torn arteries in his chest wound as his sister screamed at the top of her lungs. Hubert wet himself and sank to his knees when Jack turned the single barreled shotgun at him.

"Don't shoot, mister! I give up! Please don't kill us!"

Mame turned and started running away, still screaming hysterically. Marshal Reeves reached down beside Chesley and retrieved the double-barrel.

"Go git her a'fore she hurts herself or gets lost," he yelled at Jack, who took off in pursuit.

He addressed young Hubert. "Keep your hands up there, boy. You got any guns or knives hid out?"

The boy nodded, tears streaming down his face. Bass kept staring at him. "Well, don't you keep me guessin'. Whatcha got there?"

"Mister Satan, I got me a foldin' knife in my front pocket and a .32 inside my coat."

"Real slow like, take off that coat and throw it over here. Chunk the knife on top of the coat...And the name is Reeves, Bass Reeves. You and your Uncle Chesley are under arrest."

The boy's mouth fell open at the mention of the name. Even Texas based rustlers and horse thieves had heard of Bass Reeves. His tears fell faster, and he shucked himself clear of the tattered coat in short order.

In a few minutes, Jack returned with Mame. By that time, Bass had manacles on the hands of both Hubert and Chesley as well as a green wood stick cut for a splint for the elder man's broken arm.

"How bad is it?" Jack asked as he motioned at Chesley's arm.

"Ain't through the skin. He'll be able to ride once we slap some creek mud and flour around the splint and sling it."

"Ya'll got any that supper left? I ain't had a chance to get me anythang since mornin'," Jack said as he looked at the empty plates.

"Got a little," Mame said as she sniffed up her tears. "Don't think Uncle Chesley is gonna be eating anythin' solid for a spell."

"Don't rekon so," Jack said, looking over at the pitiful outlaw.

As the night closed in on the camp, Bass pulled the two corpses out by the rope corral, rolled them up in blankets and wrapped rope around them. He came back to the fire and took a seat on one of the logs. Jack pulled out a plug of tobacco and cut off a hunk with his Bowie.

"Chaw?" he, said offering the plug to Bass.

"Pass...Got my pipe," Bass said as he appeared deep in thought.

After a couple minutes of silence, Hubert spoke up, "Marshal? Ain't you gonna bury 'em?"

"'Fraid not, boy. They's re-ward money posted on both of 'em, and yer uncle, too. We got to deliver all y'all over to Antlers for the Texas Rangers to make final disposition."

"Don't seem right, not burying a man and his son," Hubert grumbled.

"What's not right is what you all done over the past year and a half. Robbin', killin' and stealin' horses from folks," Bass replied. "Did y'all bury all the folks your family killed?"

The question froze Hubert for a moment. Jack studied the boy while the wheels turned.

"No, sir. Guess not...but Mame and me, we never killed nobody. Honest Injun."

Bass studied the boy's face and then looked hard at the girl, seated on the ground near the fire. "Haf'ta say it...I believe you," Bass said slowly.

Jack spat a stream into the fire, the brown spittle hissing on a burning log for a second. "The same cain't be said 'bout yer uncle. We got paper on him for two counts."

Chesley just glared back defiantly, nursing swollen lips over mangled gums.

Jack stared down Chesley, who found another place to fix his eyes. "Bass, how you see this playin' out? We got almost three days travel to Antlers with two dozen cayuses in the corral...Plus two stiffs and three prisoners."

"I been cogitating 'bout that, Jack. Figured we pack up camp of a mornin'. These folks, here, they travel light."

Jack nodded in agreement. "Yep. One horse for each Trotter, and one for camp gear...let's see...that still leaves us nine horses each to wrangle. And we got the Kiamichi River to cross."

"See your point, Jack," Bass said, looking over his shoulder at the small herd of horses grazing in the meadow.

"Uh, Marshal Reeves?" Mame asked.

"Yes, missy?" he said turning around.

"Daddy 'n them usually tied four or five horses, injun style, behind each rider. They's plenty of rope in the panniers over yonder. They all'ays picked the most gentle as lead horse."

"Why there is a right smart idea, young lady. I 'preciate you sharing it with us."

She nodded and began to rock herself slowly back and forth with both her arms wrapped around her knees. Bass looked at her carefully and noticed she was no longer crying.

"Miss Mame, mind if I ask you a question?"

She shook her head, and looked him in the eye.

"Why did you offer to help us marshals...particular after we killed your Pa 'n brother?"

She cast her eyes to the ground for a while. When she looked up, she had found a clarity that she had trouble articulating. "Well sir, see...it's like this...my daddy and the others done some stuff that I know is against the Bible teachin's. He oughtn't have done whut he done to me. That goes for my uncle and brothers, too." She looked at Hubert who could not stand to have her eyes on him. "So when you killed them, I figgered you wus gonna kill me, too...You bein' Satan Shields and all. That's how come I run off like I did. I wuz sceered for my life. But now, I knows you men is the law, and I am glad you killed them...fer what they done to me...and my Ma." Tears rimmed her eyes and Hubert began to cry also. "Does that make me a bad person, Marshal?"

Bass turned away for a second as tears filled his eyes, too. He felt the young girl's pain and tried to conceive of the shame she must feel for all those months. Images of his own childhood spent in slavery and memories of the women folk in his extended family during that awful time flooded back He shook his head and looked back to her. "No, child. That just makes you human. You be a lady some day and you hold your head up proud, you hear?"

"Yes, sir. I...I hear you," Mame replied softly and put her head back on top of her knees folded up against her chest.

Dawn broke slowly over the camp as a deck of low clouds had moved in. A murder of crows woke the camp with raucous chatter as they moved from tree to tree. Jack sat up from his soogan, rolled his shoulders and stretched his arms out wide before he yawned. Glancing toward the fire pit, he saw Bass was already blowing on a tiny bit of tinder to start the morning fire. Jack looked around behind him to see that Mame was awake and pulling together the fixings for breakfast. Chesley and Hubert were still chained together and shackled hand and foot. A pair of the birds dropped their residue of the last night's meal and the white semi-solid feces splattered across Chesley's chest .

"Damn you crows! Git out of here!" he yelled, then realized he should have been a lot more careful with his jaw movements.

The dried blood and scab cracked painfully in response to his mouth movement and another line of fresh blood ran from his lower lip, down his chin and mixed with his scraggly beard. He tasted the saltiness of his own blood and glared back at Bass for the fifty-fifth time. "Hey! Lawdog! You gotta git me to a sawbones 'afore I bleed out!"

Jack slowly moved to his feet and looked down at the injured man. "Now, ain't that a caution? Mo-ron here sets up camp, sixty miles from the nearest whistle stop, and says we got to git him to a doctor right quick. What should we do 'bout that, Mr. Reeves? I vote we put him in a cannon and shoot him clean to Antlers."

"Fresh out of cannons, Jack. Got a couple sticks of dynamite we can stick up his ass."

"That'll work for me...Suit you, Trotter?"

"Ain't funny. I could die here," Chesley groused.

"Always that possibility. Got 'nother blanket we kin roll you up in," Jack said as he smiled.

Hubert sat up against the tree to which he and his uncle were chained. His bladder sent signals that it was seriously full. "Marshall, I gots to go pee. How 'bout you unchain me?"

Jack tugged the key out of his vest pocket, tossed it to the boy, and then dropped his hand to his Colt and made the usual warning, "Try anything dumb and I'll kill you where you stand...That's the only real cure for stupid I know 'bout."

Hubert turned the key and opened the heavy lock attached to the welded rings on the chain. He turned and began walking away from the fire.

After ten feet, Jack called out to him. "Far enough."

Hubert struggled with the suspenders and buttons on his fly, but eventually managed to complete his necessary morning ritual.

"That's enough time for that," Jack called out.

"I'm movin' as fast as I kin," the boy pleaded.

"Hook yourself back up the way you were before. Lock it up and pitch me the key."

Hubert complied and sat back down.

Forty minutes later, the five had finished the bacon, beans and flatbread, and Mame had the cookware cleaned and stored in the pack horse panniers. The marshals ran the lead rope around the tail of the lead horse, back through the hair and tied it off with a half-hitch. Jack and Bass had the first ten of the stolen horses rigged up with the short four-foot lead ropes connected to halters. The first eight horses settled down and it appeared there was not going to be problem. However, the next eight proved to be more of a challenge.

"They are a bit green, ain't they?" Bass commented.

"May not have been rid in some time," Jack observed.

"Some don't have no sign of no saddle ever bein' on 'em 'afore."

"We can just do what we can. Turn aloose any we cain't round up."

Bass shook his head. "I'll saddle up. Meby they work better round horses."

'Wellsir, we can try, but I don't want to spend all day at it. Got a lot a riding ahead of us, and these two dead bodies are gonna be kinda ripe 'fore we get to Antlers. Just glad it's still fair cool."

Bass nodded and frowned a bit at the thought of two bloated corpses tied to the saddles. "We'll pour water on 'em and soak the blankets ever chance we git."

After camp was cleared and packed, Jack removed the leg irons from Chesley and Hubert. He stuffed the rusty shackles into his saddle bags as the two prisoners mounted their horses. Bass had tied a short string of the stolen horses to each of their saddles using a slip knot and stood back as the man and his nephew got settled in.

"Now, ain't gonna say this but once. Either of you try to make a run for it, my idea of a warning shot is one that'll take off the top of yer head. Won't do you no good a'tall, but it warns the other one not to try nuthin' dumb. That clear?"

Both men nodded their agreement.

"Jack, go on an' lead us off. Mame, yer next, then Hubert and Chesley. Be right behind you with my eye on you," Bass said.

Jack grabbed a lead rope to a string of horses daisy-chained together and started out of the meadow. He was soon out of sight in the woods, as were Mame on her grulla mare and the two pack horses. Hubert hesitated for a second.

"Boy, don't make me light a fire under you. Keep it tight with Mame. I am the last person on the face of this earth you want to piss off...Believe me."

Hubert could readily imagine a dozen bad things that could fall under the category of *light a fire*, as dug his heels into the sides of the bay mare. He had no stomach for pushing the big black man in any fashion.

"Come on, girl," he said to his horse as he looked back over his shoulder at Bass.

Jack was relieved when the group finally cleared the timber and had a stretch of buffalo, blue stem and gamma grass that fanned out for several miles ahead of them. Working through the thickets and heavy timber was slow going and Jack also didn't want to accidentally stumble across another band of lawbreakers hiding out in the Kiamichis. The sun came out shortly after noon and it was a welcome sight. A rumble in his stomach told him what time of day it was as much as the position of the sun. He dug a piece of venison jerky out of his poke sack and began to gnaw on the highly peppered leather-like meat. It was tough even though it had dew berries and bone marrow fat pounded into it with the edge of a tin plate before drying over a slow smoke fire. It was what the Indians called *pemmican*.

Mame looked up as he rode in silence. "'Scuse me there, Marshal. Have y'all got inny more of that?"

Jack looked over his shoulder and frowned. *Dammit. Hadn't planned on hauling in a couple kids, 'specially a split-tail.* He ground tied the string he led and circled back to the young girl—reached back into the poke sack and glommed on to a few more strips of the prairie staple. "Here you go, missy. Just hold up here a minute."

She took the two proffered pieces and nodded. "Thankee kindly, sir."

"You bet," Jack said as he eased his legs into his horse slightly.

He stopped at Hubert, who gladly accepted the trail lunch then moved on back to Chesley. The older man glared at him as he pointed at his mouth. Jack smiled. "Rekon it'd take you all day to gum this jerked deer to death. Here…Got a corn dodger you can wash down after it softens a bit."

Chesley took the corn pone and stuffed it in his shirt.

"Name yer poision, Bass. Got dodgers or jerky."

"Better stick with the jerky. Trotter is likely to need all our dog bread."

Jack handed the big man three large strips and gazed back west. "There is a good creek up ahead two, three miles. We can water the stock and take a short break. That all right with you?"

"If we keep it short. Like to camp over to Big Creek tonight."

Jack nodded his agreement and wheeled back to the head of the procession without another word. He leaned over to the quietly grazing lead horse and snagged the halter rope with his gloved hand, did a double dally around his saddle horn and eased off down the trail.

Arriving at the creek, the five dismounted and partook of the cool clear spring fed waters as the hobbled horses grazed the gamma grass growing unchecked just outside of the summer shade line of the towering pecan trees.

"Good lookin' country," McGann observed.

"That it is. Too bad it's so far from civilization," Bass replied, cracking a couple of the previous season's pecans against each other in his calloused hands. He picked out the sweet meat and tossed it in his mouth. "My wife could sure make us a good eatin' pie out these here nuts." The smile faded soon after the words left his mouth.

Jack watched Bass for a few minutes as they sat in silence. Bass cracked a few more pecans, tossing the moldy ones from two years previous into the creek. Finally, Jack spoke up, "Whatcha thinkin' 'bout? You got a case of the dismals?"

Bass glanced sideways at the husky marshal, then shook his head slowly. "Boy howdy! You be knowin' me like the back of yer own hand...Started thinkin' of the family. This job is good one, but shore do make a man miss his wife and kids."

"Guessin' it would."

"How come you to never git hitched up, Jack?"

Jack stared at the ground as he mulled the question over. "Never thought about marshalin' as a thing for married men. We are gone too damned much for most of the gals I ever courted. They wanted a man home ev'ry night to talk to and fawn all over 'em. Just not in the cards, I rekon. Don't know who'd have me, ornery as I am, anyhow."

"Yep, guess I lucked out with my Nellie Jennie. She's a wonder." Bass nodded then looked off in the distance with a thousand yard stare. After a couple minutes, he turned back to Jack. "When we git done with this rotation, I'm gonna ask Judge Parker for some time off. I needs me some home time. The trail gets wearisome after a bit."

Jack looked downstream at the three Trotters. "The quicker we git those reprobates to Antlers, the quicker you git home. What say we fork the saddles?"

Bass smiled. "If yer waitin' on me, yer a backin' up."

A hour before sunset, Jack led the group across a three-foot deep fording of the twenty mile long stretch of water known as Big Creek. Where the stream cut through sandy ground, deep gorges with exceptionally steep sides characterized the terrain. But here, the dense clay soil spread the water out with some deep pools that teamed with catfish, bream and black bass. Massive red oaks, mixed with stands of native pecans and walnuts in the bottoms, lined the flood plain on both sides. Jack lifted both his feet up to keep his boots dry when the water reached the bottom of the leather wrapped wooden stirrups. He reached the far side, climbed a short embankment and led the string of horses downstream where he allowed them to drink.

Once the whole hundred-yard long procession had crossed and been watered, Bass looked around for a suitable campsite. Mame began unpacking the cooking gear, but stopped and walked over to Bass who was busy making a lean-to out of a tarp.

"Marshal? I was wonderin' if'n you two menfolk would like some fish? I spied some over yonder in the creek when we wuz watering the horses."

"Sounds good to me, Mame. Whatcha got fer bait?"

"I'll cut me some pork rinds off'n that fatback."

"Catfish'l love it, I bet," Bass smiled at the young girl.

"Hope so!" Mame beamed at the smile she had caused to come to Bass' face. She whirled around and ran back to the leather covered panniers and quickly unwrapped the cloth bound salt encrusted slab bacon. Mame expertly sliced of some of the dark brown rind and cut it into narrow strips, roughly resembling worms. Finishing the bait, she dug into the pack for a small metal tin box where she kept the four fishhooks the family owned. Mame chose the two with sharpest hooks, rubbed the points on a piece of Arkansas soapstone to knock the rust off and then attached those to a twenty foot length of cotton twine. She walked across the pecan bottom and cut a couple sections of dogwood saplings as her poles. In short order, she was planted beside the slow moving pool, with tiny pieces of dead pecan limb in the line to act as corks. "Come on, little fishes. You know that bacon is sumpthin' special. Come on now," she whispered.

A few minutes passed before one of the pecan-wood corks disappeared beneath the surface. She watch the line cut a V shaped path through the water's surface and slid over to grab the dogwood pole. She expertly set the hook, let the fish tire himself out, watched the pole bend as she lifted it up and was rewarded when a three pound blue cat flopped beside her on the bank. Ten minutes passed and she added another slightly larger catfish and a black bass to the stringer she had made out of a willow branch.

"Looky here what Mame has got!" Bass called over to Jack as the proud girl walked back into camp.

"You are something else, Miss Mame," Jack said in a booming voice.

"Figured you fine gentlemens would like a change from beans and jerked meat."

"You sho' figured right, girl," Bass said licking his lips.

"I'll get to cleaning these and dustin' 'em with salt 'n cornmeal. Supper'l be ready in a two shakes of a lamb's tail."

Bass dug a shallow trench around the uphill side of the tarp and buried the edge of the tarp with the dirt. Jack looked up at the clear skies and then back at Bass.

"Think we got rain a'comin'?"

"'Fraid so. My elbow been painin' me some. Usually rains when that happens."

Jack sniffed the air for an scent of rain, but there was none on the slight west breeze. He shook his head, but didn't say a word to Bass. He glanced at the young Hubert Trotter who had just dropped a load of firewood near the pit dug three inches into the rich soil in the pecan bottom.   "Two more loads and you can call it a night, boy."

"Yessir," Hubert dutifully replied as he continued his assigned chore.

Chesley had a blank look on his face as he studied the manacles attached to his wrists and legs. It was as if he had never noticed them before.

Fifteen minutes later, Mame had rendered some fatback to fry up the mess of fish she had rolled in cornmeal, salt and fresh ground pepper. When the meal was done; the wind suddenly shifted to the east north east. The setting sun shone on clouds building in the east and moving west. Jack looked at Bass and motioned eastward with his thumb.

Bass smiled broadly. "Told ya. Elbow never lies...Mame, ya'll get these dishes cleaned up and get yourselves under the tarp. Fixin the have us a frog strangler."

"Yessir, Mr. Reeves," she replied, looking over her shoulder at the line of dark clouds. In the distance, the sound of thunder could be heard as it rumbled up the Red River valley.

Later that evening, the rain came down in sheets with lightning crashing overhead every few seconds. Mame looked at Bass, clearly frightened from the raging storm.

"Marshal, are we gonna git kilt by this lightnin' storm?"

"It ain't up to me, chile. The Lord decides when it's yer time to come home...If'n yer afright, come sit over by me. Ain't nobody gonna git any sleep for a while, anyhow."

She moved her blanket beside his as the rain pelted down and leaned her head against the big man. Bass wrapped his arm around her and rocked back and forth gently to calm the girl. By two in the morning, the rain had subsided and the front, with all its natural light show had moved west of Marietta. Jack got up to check the status of the swollen creek. It had risen a full four feet and was menacing in its dark raging power. He eased his way back to the lean-to.

"Rainin' like a cow peein' on a flat rock...Creek's up to the banks. We need to keep an eye on it, in case we need to move higher."

"I'll take the first watch. Go ahead and get some rest."

With that, Bass picked up his rifle and donned his yellow rain slicker to keep himself dry as he sat on the soaked ground overlooking the creek. The creek crested just before dawn and the others awoke to find Bass sitting a mere thirty feet from the waterlogged fire pit.

"Cuttin' 'er kinda close ain't you, Bass?" Jack asked as he looked at a line of sticks extending into the water, the farthest ones barely clearing the surface of the chocolate colored muddy water.

"Already moved the horses up and out of the bottom," he replied as he unbuttoned his slicker.

"No sense in trying for a hot breakfast. We musta got four inches last night. Good thang Mame fried up some more corn dodgers last night whilst she had the drippins'."

Jack nodded. "You heard the man. Clean up, pack up and saddle up."

The long string of people and horses made good time for a couple hours before they came upon a oak forest that stretched as far as the eye could see across the gently rolling hills. A fringe of head high scrub oak brush surrounded the much taller mature red and white oaks, and was, for all practical purposes, impenetrable. Bass pulled up and raised his right hand, signaling a stop. Jack ground tied the lead horse in his string and rode around the three Trotters to confer with Bass.

"Hell, Jack, thought you knew this country."

"Brush growed up some since I lived here twenty year ago…So, what do you think?"

"If'n it was just the two of us, bet we could weasel our way through. What with the prisoners and animals…don't see how as we can do it."

"Me, neither. 'Nuther twenty miles and we come across the Kiamichi. It's gonna be high and fast with the rain. I say we try south then work along the Kiamichi through these here woods. North ain't nuthin' but a week of miseries."

"That's a fact, Jack."

"Then it's settled. Take us south, Bass. Prob'ly have to stop at noon and give the horses a rest…this mud is tiresome on 'em."

Bass glanced back at the three detainees and the pair of bodies tied across the saddles. "Better wet down the stiffs again."

"Yep," Jack agreed.

Marshalin' was steady work, with emphasis on the word *work*. Bass turned left to parallel the oak brush and began to whistle softly to himself. The sun came out for the first time as Jack took a long drink from his canteen.

After a lunch of jerky and corn dodgers, the five began the slow task of working their way through flooded pecan bottoms on the east side of the Kiamichi. The slow moving water was dark, knee high to the mounts and care had to be taken to not injure the horses on submerged deadfalls.

"Keep yore eyes peeled for moccasins!" Bass yelled back at Mame.

The warning was unnecessary, as she was already on high alert—her wide set sky blue eyes darted left and right for any signs of the ill tempered vipers. Squirrels chattered their warnings to each other along the river as the five passed though acre after acre of submerged bottom land. Occasionally, the pecan trees disappeared as stands of cottonwoods or elms took their place. The trunks were straight and tall as the closely spaced trees competed for sunlight along the river flood plain. Had it been late spring or summer, the canopy above would have blocked the sun—one reason so little vegetation grew under the towering elms.

Bass was almost asleep in the saddle, dozing off from time to time. The night of stormy weather and guard duty had taken its toll. His eyelids fluttered shut and his head nodded one more time when the relative quiet of the flooded forest was shattered by a pistol shot. Bass snapped back to alertness and he dragged his Colt from its holster in a flash. He anxiously scanned the area in front of him for a couple seconds, and then looked over his shoulder to see Jack limbering up his lariat.

"What in hell?" he muttered as he stuffed the pistol back in its bucket.

He watched as Jack built a loop and threw at something in the water. Jack gingerly tugged at the rope until it pulled tight on its unidentified target. McGann hauled on the rope until he had dragged the heavy object beside his horse. He leaned over and lifted the shape up until Bass could plainly see it. Only the head and shoulders cleared the murky water, but it was obviously a pig—in the ninety to one hundred pound range. Jack dropped it in back into the water, cupped his hands around his mouth and hollered up to Bass, "Supper!"

The water had begun receding before the marshals made the decision to camp for the night. It was easy to tell where the high water mark was, as branches and leaf debris had collected on willow clumps along the main channel as well as up on the bark of some trees. A grassy meadow ten feet above the flood stage turned out to be an ideal spot. The sandy soil had drained well from the previous night's deluge, although finding dry kindling proved to be a task. But soon, Hubert had a camp cook fire going and had broken off dead limbs from nearby beaver killed trees to feed it.

"Bass, any more rain tonight? What's the elbow saying?" Jack teased.

"Plant yourself under the stars, Marshal McGann. I'll be sleeping like a baby tonight."

"Not before I get some of those pork chops."

"Speakin' of that pig, was its ears notched?"

"Didn't notice. Why?"

"Just trying to figure if somebody owned it, 'er was wild. Thinkin' mebbe we'd be close to Antlers."

"Possible. I was thinking it'd be another twenty miles upstream."

"Flood could have floated the pig that far."

"Could have. But I'm voting for act of God on this one. Sure ain't seen no signs of habitation hereabouts."

Just then, Mame walked back into camp with a bucket of water to wash off the pig she had butchered.

"Marshal, they's some fish stranded down in the shallows. I could make a spear and get us a mess of 'em for supper."

Bass though about the offer for a moment, then shook his head.

"Little one, the Lord done blessed us with a fine pig already. Makes no sense to ask for more than we can eat tonight. We'll be in Antlers tomorrow."

She nodded and tried to understand a man who didn't take every thing he could when it was available.

After a dinner of pork chops, the last of the Trotter's potatoes and some wild onions, the sun sat over diamond clear skies. Bass packed his pipe while Jack rolled a cigarette. They both lit their smokes with a single match.

"Mighty fine meal, girl," Jack said as he exhaled a cloud of blue-gray smoke.

"Thankee kindly for roping us that pig," she said as she ladled the leftover potatoes into a shallow wooden bowl.

Bass caught Jack's attention and motioned with his head for Jack to follow him. The pair walked forty yards away, out of earshot of the Trotters.

"Jack, I've been thinkin' 'bout what to do with these Trotter kids."

"The law is kinda gray about dealing with kids this young. We ain't got warrants on 'em in partic'lar, but they was consortin' with known criminals...and that's a fact."

"I know what the facts are. Being with one's kin is not the same as consortin'. We turn them over to the laws in Texas and we both know what will happen to 'em. If Hubert ain't no criminal now, he damn shore will be when gets out of Huntsville. Plus, I heard tell of what them animals do to young boys inside..."

"Hell, Bass, we turn that sweet young girl to the court and they'll make her a damned indentured servant to the court until she is of age. No better'n makin' her a slave."

"I cain't do it, Jack...Jest cain't," Bass said as tears filled his eyes. "Been a slave...Won't make an innocent child one."

Jack looked on at him for a moment, and then glanced back to the youngsters sitting near the fire. When he turned back to Bass, tears were streaked down his weathered face, too. He took a long drag off the smoke, dropped it to the ground and crushed it with his heel. "What in hell we gonna do?"

Bass looked him in the eye. "Got me an idea."

"I'm all ears."

"Would you go ask the young 'uns to come here?"

"What you gonna do?"

"Just do as I asked, please."

Jack looked at him curiously. *Please* was a word Bass didn't use very often. It wasn't his nature. He brought the two over, Hubert still wearing the manacles, hand and foot. Both looked at the big black man and could see he had been crying, even in the fading light.

"Somethin' wrong, Mr. Reeves?" Hubert asked.

"Nuthin' like that. I am gonna lay it out for you chil'ren. Don't know any other way around it. We'll be coming into Antlers by noon tomorrow," Bass said. The faces fell on both youngsters. "Usually, we turn young folks like you over to the state to handle."

"What's gonna happen to us, marshal?" Mame said softly, a tinge of dread in her voice.

Bass stood up straight. "I got me a farm up outside of Van Buren, Arkansas. My wife, Nellie Jennie and me, we got us ten fine kids. Five boys and five girls..." He paused for a moment. "Don't see how one more of each would make much diff'rence."

Jack looked at Bass, then turned away. The hint of a smile could be seen under his mustache as his eyes teared up again. Hubert looked at Mame with uncertainty. She was just as confused as he. They both looked up at Bass.

"Does that mean we would live with you?"

"I would love to adopt you two, if you would have me. I know we ain't the same color, but..."

"I don't see no difference a'tall, Marshal," said Mame softly.

She and Hubert exchanged quick glances and nodded frantically. They both lunged at Bass and wrapped their arms around him, almost knocking him off his feet. Bass responded by reaching around the teens with a huge bear hug, lifting them both off them ground. Jack chuckled and shook his head.

"Marshall McGann, would you please take those irons off my son?"

"Glad to, Bass...Glad to," Jack said with a twinkle in his eyes.

Crossing the Kiamichi was a swim, but the sun and a south breeze made it bearable. The horses had become used to the daisy-chain configuration and had not panicked at the hundred yard wide stretch of water.

Five miles outside of Antlers, Bass pulled up. He motioned for Jack to come up front. "We'll rest the horses here. Go on ahead and wire the Texas Rangers that we are coming in with three wanted men. Advise them that Bill and Ellis are deceased, but we will accept the re-ward. The four of us will wait for you back here. We will set up a temporary camp."

Jack dropped the lead rope attached to his string of ponies and touched the brim of his hat. A minute later, he was out of sight beyond the grass covered rolling hill—his bright red sorrell at an easy lope. Bass dismounted and motioned for the others to take a break. Chesley sat back some sixty yards, preferring to not look at his captor any more than he had to. Hubert and Mame sat by Bass.

"Either of you two read or write?" he asked.

"I do a little, I learned myself by readin' the Bible," Mame allowed.

"That's good. It is a good thing to know. You picked a good book to start with...Now, what I'm gonna do is draw out a map of how to get to my place. Mr. Jack is gonna write the names and directions on it and write a letter to my wife when he gets back from town. That way she'll know who you are. Understand?"

The kids nodded. Mame's face reflected a dozen questions.

"What is it, child?"

"Do we call you Daddy or Mr. Reeves?"

"Whatever suits ya." Bass chuckled.

"I like Daddy. We never had a pa who cared fer us like you do."

Hubert nodded.

Bass smiled. "I know you chil'ren have good in your hearts. I can tell. I want to be proud of you and make you proud of your selves."

Mame asked, "How we gonna get to Van Buren? It's a powerful long ways, I 'spect."

"You are a smart girl, Mame. Always thinkin'. That's good. What I plan to do is buy tickets for the both of you on the train to Fort Smith with Jack and me. Then I am gonna give you two horses to ride and money fer the ferry to cross the Arkansas river to Van Buren."

"We never had our own horses afore!" Hubert blurted.

"Time you two learned some responsibility."

"Marshal...uh, Daddy, we ain't got no go-to-meetin' clothes. Meby they won't let us on the train lookin' like we do," said Mame as she pointed to her ragged, patched clothes.

"Got a point. Tell you what...we'll go by the mercantile when we get into Antlers 'n buy y'all some travelin' duds. And then we'll have a burnin' fer those rags yer a wearin'," said Bass.

"Ain't never had nothin' but hand-me-downs 'fore," offered Hubert.

"Well, that is gonna change. 'Fraid you still might get *some* hand-me-downs...waste not, want not...but all my chil'ren get their own go-to-meetin' outfits."

"What's gonna happen to Uncle Chesley?" Hubert asked as he looked back east.

"He'll have a fair trial down in Texas and the judge will sentence him accordin' to the law."

"Does that mean they'll hang him?" Mame asked.

"Most likely, I'm sure. He broke the law, killed and robbed, and got hisself caught. He'll have to pay the piper."

"He was just mean inside, like Pa," Hubert said.

"Don't know what makes a man do like that. But I ain't a judge. Just a Marshal. My job is to bring 'em in," Bass said as he looked back at the pitiful Chesley.

Later, when the Rangers arrived in Antlers on the 4:10 from Paris, Jack removed the manacles from Chesley and the Texans placed their own cuffs on him. The affidavits were signed concerning recovery of the stolen horses—less two that Bass paid for—and the Rangers went through the gruesome process of confirming the identifications of the two dead outlaws. Burial arrangements were made for internment in the local cemetery—pauper's section—as there was no longer any need to transport the bodies any farther. The whole process didn't take more than forty minutes, but the north bound train couldn't wait that long. Bass and Jack decided to take hotel rooms for the night and head north to Fort Smith on the 10:15 in the morning. They and the kids were looking forward to a hot bath at the hotel/bathhouse and a restaurant meal.

Bass tapped on the six paneled door across the hall from his, Jack's and Hubert's room. A still wet Mame, with a towel wrapped around her, opened it and Bass handed her a bundle wrapped in brown paper and tied with cotton string. "Somethin' for you to wear to supper, Mame. Managed to persuade the store keep at the mercantile to let me grab a couple of things 'fore they closed. Don't make no sense to put those dirty rags back on after you have cleaned up. We'll do a real live shoppin' spree in the mornin' 'fore the train leaves."

"I never imagined a hot bath would feel so good," Mame announced as she took the bundle from his hands.

"When you git them new duds on, you and brother gonna shine like new pennies!"

"Thank you, Daddy…Why you cryin'?" she asked as she caught sight of the tears rimming his eyes. "Did I do sumpthin' wrong?"

"No, baby," Bass said as he hugged her. "These are happy tears. Makes a man proud to do right by his chil'ren. Now comb and brush yer hair, like I told ya. Dry yerself off when you be through and slip into this here day dress. Gonna check on Hubert to see how the boy cleans up."

Across the hall in the men's bath room, Bass walked in to find Jack scrubbing on Hubert's back with a hog bristle brush.

"Ow! Ow!" Hubert protested.

"Hold still. You little turd rustler! We got some ground in dirt to git you shed of!"

"But yer a taking off my hide!"

Bass laughed as he laid down another small bundle of clothes for Hubert to put on after his bath and then started peeling off his own layers. Jack handed him the brush. "You start on the feet," Jack said as he took a course cloth, rubbed the bar of lye soap with rose oil on it and began scrubbing the boy's ears.

"Yer killing me!" Hubert complained.

"There's enough dirt in there to plant corn...Here, boy, yer old enough to finish up yer own self."

Jack stripped off and slid into the third cast iron tub and sank into the warm water until his face was just visible.

"Man, oh man. This feels good."

"Uh huh," Bass agreed from the second tub.

Hubert watched the older men and mimicked their every move, almost. In a couple seconds, he was screaming.

"It burns! It burns!" Hubert cried out as he tried to wipe the soap from his eyes.

Bass reached behind himself and pulled a white cotton towel off the wooden rack. He leaned over and grabbed Hubert's hand, pulling it off his the boy's face and wiped his eyes clean.

"Son, you gotta keep the soap outta yer eyes!"

Hubert blinked a few times and looked at his new adoptive father with red rimmed eyes. "Now, you tell me!"

Bass and Jack both burst out laughing. Jack shook his head. "Bass, you have taken on a major project, I would say."

"Right you are. Daddyin' can be a full time proposition. But, me and my Nellie Jennie have had some experience at it."

With a new chambray work shirt and denim bib overalls, Hubert looked like a different boy, as did Mame in her lavender calico print. Both kids entered the hall and knocked on the adult's door when they were ready. Bass opened the door wide and the two stepped inside.

"Looky here, Jack. Miss Mame looks prettier than a flax tailed pony."

She blushed at her first compliment—ever.

"And Hubert, he cleans up fine. Almost didn't recognize 'em," added Jack.

"We'll go to the mercantile agin of the mornin' and git the rest of yer new stuff. Didn't git any new shoes fer y'all…didn't know the sizes. Just eyeballed ya for the clothes. Feets 'er a whole 'nother matter."

Jack and Bass had donned new shirts Bass got when he picked up the kids clothes. They had dropped off their trail clothes at the Chinese laundry just down the street—to be ready in the morning.

The youngsters accompanied the men next door to the Blue Bird Cafe. The locals all stared at the four strangers as they walked in. A couple of men recognized Bass from newspaper photographs and spoke out as the four made their way to a table for four.

"Evenin', Marshal."

"Howdy, gents. How is the beef here?"

"Real good! They fry 'em up right here in Antlers."

"Nice to know that. "Preciate it. Ya'll have a pleasant evenin', hear?"

Mame watched the interaction, and once they were seated, pulled on Bass' sleeve. "Daddy! How did you know those men?" she whispered.

"Sweetie, don't really know them. Guess they read about me somewheres."

"Are you famous?" she asked incredulously.

Jack laughed. "Lots of folks know yer Daddy by his reputation...I call that famous."

Bass shot him a look, but ended up smiling anyway.

"A man gets knowed by his deeds, be they good or bad, chil'ren. Now who is hungry?"

After the steaks, with mashed potatoes, gravy, yeast rolls with butter, a side order of pickled beets and four glasses of buttermilk were delivered, Bass could see that the two children had absolutely no concept of table manners. Both held their forks and knives like grubbing hoes.

Jack had intervened a couple time with admonitions to keep their elbows off the table, take smaller bites and chew with their mouths closed. Bass looked on with a slight scowl. "Allrighty, you two. I see we have a lot a learnin' to do if I'm gonna take you out to eat in public. When you git up to home, Nellie Jenny, yore Ma, will peel yer head like an onion if'n you eat like that at her table. She's just as liable to send you out to eat from the trough with the hogs."

The crestfallen kids stared at their plates.

"I want you to watch Uncle Jack and do like he does. Yer in way too much of a hurry to shovel it all in."

Jack looked at Bass and grinned. "That's right. You want your Daddy and Uncle to be proud of you, don'tcha?"

Both kids nodded. Jack held up his knife and fork. "We're gonna start at the beginnin'. Hold yer utensils like this here."

The rest of the meal proceeded slowly, but the children were intent on pleasing the men. After coffee, Hubert glanced over to McGann.

"Mr. Jack, are you really our uncle now?"

He nodded as Bass beamed. "Seein' as how yer Daddy and I are like brothers, reckon that makes me yer uncle...yer Dutch uncle. And wipe that buttermilk 'stach off'n yer lip."

"Dutch uncle?" Hubert said as he started to wipe his mouth on his sleeve.

"Uh uh...not the sleeve."

Hubert quickly put his arm down, grabbed his napkin and wiped his mouth.

"That means I can light into you if need be, just like yer Daddy will," Jack continued.

"So keep doin right, or one of us will be on ya like white on rice," Bass added

Mame giggled.

"And just what is so funny, young lady?"

"The thought of a man black as you being like white on rice."

Bass roared in laughter. "You got me there, little bit!...How's this?...I will be on you like a duck on a June bug!"

"I bet you would, Daddy...I bet you would."

***

CHAPTER FIVE

FORT SMITH, ARKANSAS
TRAIN DEPOT

The whistle atop the vermilion red trimmed black 4-4-2 diamond-stack steam locomotive blew sharply twice. The massive engine with its number 409 shining in chromed relief at the front, centered above the imposing black cow-catcher, was one of many belonging to the St. Louis and San Francisco Railway. The short train, consisting of a single engine, a tender, two passenger cars, a dining car, a Pullman sleeper, a livestock car and ending with a caboose was stopped at the platform in Fort Smith, Arkansas. Bass Reeves and Jack McGann, stepped off the first coach car behind the coal tender followed immediately by Mame and Hubert. Bass took one last look up at the shiny behemoth—with its flashy red painted five-foot tall drive wheels and white outer rims—then looked up at the engineer's cab. The group was immediately engulfed in a seventy-foot steam cloud released from the train's boilers to relieve the pressure. Mame screamed. Bass and Jack held on to their hats with one hand—each grabbed one of the kids with the other—and walked quickly away from the hissing relief valve. They continued back along the train to a single livestock car where four saddled horses were being unloaded down a livestock ramp by a railroad yardmaster and his helper.

Both men were dressed in their normal field attire—Bass in a black three piece suit, Jack in dark gray. Each had dark olive cotton cravats, dark gray hats and calf high trail boots with the pant legs tucked in. They wore their custom made crescent and star Deputy Marshal badges with IT above UNITED STATES in the center of the star and the number 4 on Bass' and number 5 on Jack's at the bottom. The badges were pinned on their vests just above the left pocket. Mame was wearing a smart forest green riding dress, her now shiny corn-silk blonde hair tied low behind her head in a pony tail. Hubert wore tan canvas pants with suspenders, a calico shirt, short canvas jacket and a low crown, narrow brim hat. Each carried a small carpet bag containing the rest of their new clothes Bass had purchased that morning along with their new shoes.

Passengers were exiting and boarding the train as Bass and Jack were tightening the cinches on the kid's horses' girths. They each hugged the children and then helped them into their saddles.

"Now, you are sure you kin find the ferry 'n then the home place?" Bass asked Mame.

"Yessir. Cain't be but four, five miles to the river, then 'bout six miles to our new home. You drawed a good map...Daddy," Mame said and leaned down kissed Bass on the cheek.

"You mind yer sister now," Jack admonished Hubert.

"Yessir, Uncle Jack."

"Tell yer maw, that Jack'n I will be there just as soon as we finish up our next assignment. The telegram we got from the judge said we was to take the Tumbleweed Wagon out and serve a batch of warrants...Y'all be careful now, hear?"

"Yessir, we will," Mame said.

"Now skedaddle."

Mame and Hubert reined their horses toward the end of the train, crossed the tracks behind the caboose and disappeared from sight.

Bass stared wistfully at the departing children then he and Jack turned, cinched up their own girths and mounted up just as the train whistle blew again. The rodeo was on. Their horses had been cooped up in the livestock car for over eight hours since Bass and Jack had boarded at Antlers. To say the horses were *fresh* would be an understatement. After a few minutes of crow-hopping and bucking, they managed to get their mounts settled down by turning them in tight circles, then Bass and Jack headed up the dusty street toward the old Army barracks that had been converted into the Federal Court House with the jail in the basement for Judge Parker's court.

"Think that damned engineer did that apurpose, if you ask me. Damn near swallered my 'bacca," said Jack as he spit an amber stream of tobacco juice to the ground and wiped his mouth with the back of his sleeve.

"Wouldn't be surprised. Noticed he was watchin' as we was cinchin' up the boys."

They held the still high-stepping agitated horses on a tight rein as they walked past parked buggies and wagons.

"Reckon those kids gonna be all right?" Jack asked.

"'Spect so. Mame has a good head on her shoulders…she's purty resourceful. 'Course cain't say as much for Hubert…"

"Don't think his bread's quite done," Jack interrupted.

"Could be, but Mame looks out for him. She'll git 'em to the farm 'fore dark."

Closer to the court house, the massive gallows loomed into sight. Constructed of local rough cut loblolly pine, the broad structure was built overly strong to impress all that saw it. Thirteen steps led up the right side of the gallows, the same unlucky number as the wraps used in each noose. A heavy wooden roof sheltered the platform from inclement weather. The judge was adamant that the executions take place at the precise time assigned to the task. A shallow peaked archway across the front of the structure supported the roof and gave it a Greek revival architectural element.

Five condemned men were lined up side by side on the gallows platform that Parker had built to handle up to twelve at a time—their hands cuffed behind them and ankles shackled. All were mean-looking hardcases except for one frightened young man who wasn't out of his teens. Three men wore short dark colored sackcloth coats—shapeless, inexpensive ones made for those who could not afford the services of a tailor. Two wore cloth vests with brogans sticking out of their trousers. Well-worn boots and dirty cravats completed the outfits worn by the three convicted men with coats. A photographer entreated the men to stand still for his capture of the event on glass plate. They begrudgingly obliged at the stern direction from the hangman.

"Hold still, damn you, so this man can make his cursed immortal record!" Maledon commanded.

"Do they have to take my picture? My mama don't know I kilt somebody," pleaded the boy.

"It don't make no never mind, kid. She's sure to find out sooner or later," said the pock-faced man at the end of the line.

The photographer, who had made the ten hour train trip from Little Rock just to record the multiple hanging, placed his head under the black silk hood at the back of his Daguerreotype camera, reached around, removed the cap from the lens and called out, "Now!"

His assistant touched off the silver powder in the flash bar sending a cloud of foul smelling smoke up with an audible *whoosh* and a brief flash of white light. A chorus of *oohs* and *ahhs,* gasped from the startled assemblage, many of who had never seen flash photography. The photographer counted to three and replaced the lens cap. He lifted the tripod attached to the bulky wooden box and moved it closer to the unpainted platform to prepare to record the image after the trap doors were sprung. Six deputy marshals carrying double-barreled scatterguns provided security to the affair and stood between the crowd and the base of the platform. One of them caught sight of the sun glinting off the badge worn by Bass as his unbuttoned coat flared open with the breeze. He recognized the big man on the dun horse and his partner.

"Make a hole! Make a hole! Marshals coming through!"

The crowd looked around in confusion until someone whispered—but you could have heard it all the way to the court house.

"That's Bass Reeves!"

George Maledon—tabbed the *Prince of Hangmen* by the press— was a small, wispy, deceptively frail looking man in his sixties with a large white goatee. He wore twin .45 caliber Colt bird's-head revolvers in reverse holsters around his waist over his coat—Maledon always dressed in black. He had placed a black cloth hood over the head of the first man. The hangman followed the hood with the lightly oiled hemp rope noose. Next, he laid the thirteen wraps on the left side of the man's neck and pulled the slack to loop the rope at the top of his head. Maledon then moved on to the next man. The boy prisoner shivered as he watched in horror as the hood was placed over the second man's head.

Bass and Jack rode their horses past the gallows and up to the wagon yard and corral beside the court house, stepped off and handed their reins to the hostler. They looked back over toward the gallows at Maledon with his five customers and hesitated momentarily.

"Must be nigh on four hundred people here. Nuthin' like a good hanging to draw a crowd," Bass noted.

"Shoot, I reckon we could charge two-bits admission and make more money than serving warrants!"

"You gonna suggest that to the Judge, are ye?"

Jack paused for a second, then shook his head and grinned. "Not likely."

They slowly walked across the street past the gallows to the side of the courthouse, paused at a door with a gold lettered plaque that read:

JUDGE ISAAC C. PARKER

U. S. JUDICIAL DISTRICT OF WESTERN ARKANSAS

Bass and Jack entered the building and closed the door behind them.

Maledon started to slip the hood on the boy, who began to go to pieces, crying and begging. "Please, dear God! I don't wanna die! I don't wanna die!"

The condemned man, a middle-aged hardcase next to the boy, nudged him hard. "Hush up, boy! Stand straight like a man. Show 'em you got sand."

The boy, recovered a little, bit his lower lip and nodded his head.

The man continued, "There is a better place than this old world…And in a little bit, you and me are gonna git to see it…You hear me?"

"Y-yessir...I he-hear," the boy said as he lifted his chin ever so slightly.

The man nodded to George and the hangman placed the hood over the boy's head. The muffled sound of his choked backed sobs could only be heard by the men on either side of him.

JUDGE PARKER'S COURT ROOM

Judge Parker was a large barrel-chested man in his early fifties, with dark hair and full beard beginning to show some gray. He had just started to pronounce judgment on a convicted murderer, a large bullnecked black man. "The man you murdered was your friend. In an unsuspecting hour, when he no doubt was treating you as a trusted companion, you set upon him unperceived and with the fateful knife, you brutally murdered your victim. The sword of human justice trembles over you and is about to fall upon your guilty head..." He paused as the man in front of him dropped his head, then continued. "In a few weeks it will be springtime, the snow of winter will flee away, the ice will vanish, the air will become soft and balmy, the grass will be green, the flowers will be in bloom and all will be right with the world, but you shall not see it, sir, for you shall be hung by the neck until you are dead, dead, dead."

As Judge Parker slammed his gavel, the convicted murderer twisted away from the bailiff with a shout, sprinted toward the table in front of Judge Parker's cherry paneled five-foot-high desk, sprang from the top in an effort to fling himself over the bench and leap through the large window behind the Judge to freedom. As he cleared the desk, Judge Parker shot out his arm and hooked it around the man's thick neck. The force of the jump carried both men to the floor where Parker held him until the marshals and bailiffs shackled him hand and foot.

Without a word, Parker got up, straightened his robe and made his way toward his chambers. He took only a few steps when the defense attorney started toward the Judge in an apparent attempt to object to the harsh sentence. Judge Parker stopped and pointed his finger directly at the attorney, so startling him, that he fell to the floor, almost in a state of apoplexy. The attorney laid where he had fallen until Parker exited the court room.

Judge Parker entered his chambers and immediately began addressing a half-dozen Deputy US Marshals while he removed his black robe and hung it on a hall tree just inside the door.

"Gentlemen, I trust you have all read the telegram from Marshal Bassett in Sand Springs." He continued as he moved with long strides toward his large walnut desk. "The Nations have become a sanctuary for criminals of every stripe. I do not have to remind you that the killing of McGann and the others makes eight of our men lost in the last two months..."

The door opened and Parker turned, a little annoyed, to see Bass and Jack enter. He then moved over to shake hands.

"Mornin' Judge. Mornin' your Honor," Jack and Bass said at the same time as they removed their hats.

"Bass...Jack...Sorry about your brother, Jack...Be with you in a minute."

Bass and Jack nodded and then exchanged eye contact and nods with each of the other marshals being given their marching orders as Parker resumed his talk. "The Larson's could have robbed that stage coach, without murdering six innocent people, but those cutthroats kill for the love of it. For five years they have been on the scout, murdering and looting all over the Nations and laughed in our faces...And I damn well do not intend letting them get away with it any longer!"

Suddenly, there was the sound of five traps being simultaneously sprung from outside—Parker paused and everyone glanced toward the window. The Judge had the gallows built where he could witness the executions from his chambers. They all could see five bodies with five pairs of shackled ankles dangling lifelessly through the openings in the gallows platform.

Preacher Morse, a paunchy, round faced man with a large mustache, a stiff white collar and black suit began to pray from below the gallows, "Dear Father in Heaven, forgive them of their sins and accept them unto thy compassionate and understanding bosom...Amen."

Parker's gaze was still out the window, when he continued, "Gentlemen, it is not the severity of the punishment that is the deterrent...But the certainty of it..." He paused, and then turned to face the deputies again. "Now, as I was saying, I will tolerate no longer the Larsons and their gang of killers. If they will not respect the law...then by God, we will make them fear it! I want these murderers brought in alive...or dead! Anytime you need help, deputize whoever is available...God speed and watch your backs."

Bass and Jack stood waiting while Parker bid his other deputies good-bye. The two exchanged meaningful glances. Parker shook hands with the last deputy, then turned to Bass and Jack. "Boys, I'm sorry to keep you waiting. The commissioner and the marshal are both gone today, but they left a batch of warrants for you."

The Judge opened a desk drawer and began to sort out some official-looking papers.

"We'll be leavin' for the Nations in a few minutes...Sir."

"Fine."

"Unless..." Jack started.

"Yes?...Unless what?" the judge said as he looked up.

"Uh...Unless...well, Judge...uh, Your Honor...Sir...I have been wondering...that is, we have been wondering...uh..."

"Yes, yes?...Wondering what?"

"Uh...Well, Sir...I, uh...that is...we..."

Parker boomed out, "Well, confound it, Jack! Out with it man!"

Bass and Jack both flinched at the Judge's sudden outburst.

"We been wondering...Sir, if maybe somebody else could handle our duties with the Tumbleweed Wagon...We feel..." Bass offered.

"What?" Parker boomed again.

"Uh...We would like to join the others in runnin' down the Larsons."

Parker didn't hesitate. "Nonsense. I have enough men assigned to that job. Somebody has to go after these other hardcases. Besides, it's your turn in the barrel with the wagon, is that not true?"

"Yessir..." they said in unison.

"I...we just thought meby...since they killed my brother, Hank..."

"Well, you just quit thinking. You know I do not sanction revenge hunts, Jack. I understand your anger, but you boys have your own duties to attend to." He handed over the stack of papers he had put together from his desk. "Here are the fugitive warrants, and a few John Doe's for good measure."

Jack took the warrants—Bass had never learned to read or write efficiently—removed a pair of gold-rimmed reading glasses from his vest, and began to scan the paperwork. Bass and Parker both looked at him. They had never seen Jack with glasses before. Jack was nonplused.

"Any of them familiar to you?" asked Parker.

Jack read off the names from the warrants, nodding or shaking his head as he read. "Neely McLaren...Nope." He grinned. "Preacher Horatio T. Budlow...That highlacious old scalawag..."

"What's he done now?" Bass asked.

"Same as always...Whiskey peddlin'...Myra Maybell Shirley, huh! Finally got somethin' we can arrest Belle Starr on."

"What's she charged with?" asked Bass.

"Larceny of two horses."

121

"Better'n nothin."

"I reckon." Jack paused as he shuffled to the next warrant. "Boone Finley...Don't know him."

Judge Parker inserted a carved bone letter opener into an envelope and slit it open. "Either of you know the one he's running with?...Burkhalter?" he asked without looking up.

Jack read the next name, a look of regret came into Bass's eyes. "Otho Burkhalter..."

"Yessir,...I grew up with the Burkhalter boys back in Texas. Otho is the only one still alive," Bass said.

The Judge gave Bass a stern look. Bass looked him straight in the eye. "I know, your Honor. The law is the law."

OSAGE COUNTY

Ben Larson stumbled along on foot as he followed a game trail through the trees. He carried only his guitar and had his saddle bags slung over his left shoulder. His attention was caught by smoke swirling skyward two hundred yards on the other side of a grassy meadow in a small grove of trees. *A campfire.*

A lone cowboy squatted by a campfire in the grove next to a small flowing branch, cooking his noon meal. His Appaloosa gelding was tethered nearby. He looked up as Ben approached and greeted him good-naturedly, "Howdy, neighbor." Ben didn't reply. "Whatcha doin' shanks mare?"

Ben glanced around the small camp. "Horse broke a leg."

"Too bad."

"Yeah," Ben said suspiciously. "You travelin' alone, too?"

"Just me and my lonesome."

Ben unloaded his gear onto the ground beneath a tree, careful not to let the cowboy get a good look at his saddlebags.

"Name is Blue." Again, Ben didn't respond. "You're welcome to some vittles. Got some beans, bacon and branch water…run out of Arbuckle couple of days ago."

He handed Ben a tin plate and a fork. Ben, without even so much as a *thank you*, began to help himself. He wolfed down the food like he hadn't had a bite in days, which was the case.

PRAIRIE
SEVERAL MILES AWAY

A well-built black man, Jed Neal, loped his sixteen-hand mule through a grassy area with scattered post oak and cedar trees. He was well over six feet and pushed two-hundred pounds, wore a black broadcloth coat over a homespun four-button shirt, gray wool trousers with leather galluses and a wide-brimmed black hat. He was softly singing a Stephen Foster tune, *Oh! Susanna*, to himself. Over his shoulder was a well-kept Henry rifle with a leather sling. Abruptly he stopped when he noticed movement. "Whoa, Jacob," he said softly.

He quickly unslung the rifle and raised it to shoot a cottontail rabbit. Then he saw that it was a doe with several kitts. He fired into the air and grinned as the doe and her babies scurried back into their den.

OSAGE COUNTY
CAMPSITE

Ben finished up the last few scraps of food on his plate and took a drink of branch water from his tin cup then asked, "You a drover?"

"Yep. We just taken a trail herd up to Kansas. I'm on my way back home."

"Yer friends didn't wanta go back with you?"

"Nah. They's a mind to stay in Kansas a few days longer and chase the rooster."

"But not you?"

"And leave all my hard-earned money in them Abilene deadfalls? Nosireebob...got me a little redheaded gal back in Texas and we aim to get hitched."

Ben glanced over at Blue's horse. "Purty good lookin' paloose you got there."

"That's ol' Hank. Me and him rode a lot of rivers together," he said with a bit of apprehension.

"I reckon, then, it's about time ya'll parted company."

"Just a dang minute, here!"

Ben pulled his Colt and cocked the hammer. "Figure I done enough walkin' today...Now go put my bags on ol' Hank...You hear?" Ben reached over and lifted Blue's pistol and tossed it away into the brush.

"I thought there was somethin' fishy 'bout you...when you never told me who you was," Blue said with regret.

"I will tell you who I am, cowpuncher. I am the man that's fixin' to blow yer brains out you don't do what I say...Now, git movin'."

Reluctantly, Blue got up, walked over to the tree, picked up Ben's guitar and saddlebags and started strapping them on Hank.

NORTH OSAGE COUNTY

Marshal Tobe Bassett and Deputy John L. Patrick trotted their horses along a tree-canopied road. Tobe studied the ground.

"Any sign, Marshal?" John L. asked.

"Nothin'. Like they clean disappeared in thin air."

"Coulda headed up or down stream of that branch we crossed back a bit."

"Most likely. Just ain't no way of tellin' which...Damn horse thieves."

OSAGE COUNTY
CAMPSITE

Blue finished putting Ben's gear on Hank by tying his guitar behind the six-inch cantle of the trail-drover Visalia style saddle with the attached three foot leather strings—then walked several steps back toward Ben.

"Now then, peel off that money belt you got under yer shirt."

Blue stopped. "Aw, look, feller, not my money too! It taken me nearly four months to earn it. You got my horse...Ain't that enough?"

"Peel it off, I said! I declare, I never seen anyone in my life liked to argue more'n you."

Blue glared at Ben, pulled his shirt out of his pants, unbuckled the canvas money belt and tossed it to him. Ben moved past him over to Hank and stuffed the money belt into his saddlebags, buckled the flap back, stepped into the stirrup and mounted up.

"This here's a mighty ornery way to treat a feller human bein'…Stranded way out here with nothin' to ride."

"You don't like walkin' either, huh?" Ben retorted.

"Well, heck no!"

"Then I reckon we had better do somethin' 'bout that," he said as he brought his pistol around and blasted Blue.

PRAIRIE
SEVERAL MILES AWAY

Jed reined up, searching the distance with his eyes. "That sounded like shootin', Jacob." He paused. "Come from somewhere over yonder." He nudged Jacob toward a grove of trees in the distance.

NORTH OSAGE COUNTY

Tobe and John L. heard the same shot and both drew rein.

"Gunfire," exclaimed John L.

"Damn, son, you may make a lawman yet," Tobe said as he spurred his mare into a gallop in the direction of the shot, followed by John L. trying to catch up.

OSAGE COUNTY
CAMPSITE

Jed rode into the campsite, quickly dismounted from Jacob, ran over to Blue, lying on his back moaning, and knelt beside him.

"Mister?...What happened here?"

"Shot...me...stole my money."

"Who, mister?...Who done it?"

Blue shook his head, in real pain. "Oh, God! What's Lorena gonna say?"

"Lorena?"

"Bought her...a diamond ring...in Abilene..." Blue reached up and grabbed Jed's coat lapel and pulled him down closer. "Would you see...see that she...gits it?"

"I give you my word, mister. Wherebouts is it?"

"Shirt...shirt pocket."

Jed pulled Blue's vest aside, reached in and got the ring out of his shirt pocket. It was in a small leather draw-string pouch. "What's Lorena's last name, mister? Where does she live?"

"Lorena...Matthews...Gainesville...Gainesville,...Texas."

Blue suddenly took a sharp breath and then exhaled in a soft sigh as he died, his head rolled slightly to one side, his eyes stared sightlessly at Jed.

The big black man bowed his head and murmured a prayer, his lips moved silently.

Tobe and John L. galloped into the campsite—sliding their horses to a stop. Tobe immediately sized up what he thought was a very suspicious situation. They dismounted with their guns trained on the man as they approached.

Jed immediately realized his position and started to rise.

"Stay right where you are, and keep still...John L., take his rifle," ordered Tobe.

John L. walked over to Jed cautiously, took the Henry from his hand and smelled of the muzzle. "Been fired, Marshal...Recently."

"What's that he's holding?"

John L. reached over and took the small tan leather pouch from Jed's hand"

"Pouch," said John L.

"Well open it...Damn, boy, I take back what I said earlier about you makin' a lawman yet."

John L. slipped Jed's Henry rifle in the crook of his left arm, glanced embarrassingly at Tobe and pulled on each side of the draw-string pouch. He turned it upside down and shook out the small gold banded diamond ring into his palm. "Great balls of fire, Tobe! Looky here."

"I'd say we can add robbery on top of murder."

"Hold on there, Marshal! I didn't take the man's ring! He gave it to me to deliver it to his girl friend in..."

"No, you hold on, mister," Tobe cut him off short. "It ain't me you have to convince. Save it for the judge and jury."

SAND SPRINGS
NIGHT

A slow, steady rain pelted the dark dirt streets of Sand Springs, interspersed with an occasional flash of lightning and the accompanying crash of thunder common to Oklahoma's late winter weather. The streets were all but deserted at eleven o'clock. The only sound that could be heard between the peals of rolling thunder was a boisterous ballad being sung drunkenly to the accompaniment of a guitar.

Ben Larson was the inebriated singer. The enthusiastic noise masquerading as music was coming from the second floor of Maud's Parlor House on the corner of Main and Teneha streets. It was the local hotel/bordello and watering hole. Open saloons and the sale of whiskey were outlawed in the Nations and thereby gave rise to bring-your-own sporting-houses or parlor houses. Most bordellos had a large room in the center with a piano and numerous soiled doves or fallen angels available. Sometimes the main room was upstairs with the rooms or cribs on each side and other times, such as was the case with Maud's, it was downstairs with a walk-around balcony and the rooms upstairs.

Ben sat on the edge of the bed in Tillie's small room, holding his guitar—clad only in his pants. Tillie, a pretty nineteen year old girl-of-the-line with her long blond hair done in ringlets, was sitting up in bed—leaning against the brass headboard, clad in a not-too-new merry-widow and pantaloons. She looked very demure with a large cameo broach on a gold chain around her shapely neck.

On a table beside the bed stood several bottles of liquor along with Ben's holster gun and a smaller .32 Colt Rainmaker bird's-head double-action pocket gun.

Ben finished singing the ballad and he and Tillie both laughed loudly. He picked up a bottle and took a stiff slug.

"Benny, you're so grand and I love my new broach," she said as she looked down at the cameo nestled between her breasts.

"Sure, I'm the grandest. 'Cause I bring plenty of money and presents with me. Ain't that a fact, buttercup?"

"Benny, you know that's not what I mean. I'm really crazy about you, Sugar."

"That's right. You're crazy about my sugar. And the more of it I bring with me, the sweeter it makes things."

"Stop teasin'! Now come on, sing Tillie another song," she said as she moved closer and wrapped her arms around his neck and gave him a long, deep, lingering kiss. He dropped the guitar to the floor where it clanged and resonated as his hands reached up and caressed her ample breasts. She pushed herself away, picked up the guitar and handed it back to him. "Later, my blue-eyed angel. Sing me another sweet one."

He rambled through his version of a Irish drinking song, with an indecipherable attempt at an Gaelic accent.

Outside, Tobe, John L. and Jed Neal, each wearing yellow oiled slickers, rode down Main Street at a walk in the steady cold rain. The body of Blue, wrapped in a blanket, was draped across Jed's mule. They reined to a stop and dismounted in front of the Marshal's office.

A small group of citizens was standing in the shadows of the boardwalk outside the office. One of them, Maud, a handsome woman—although a bit heavy—in her late thirties, wearing a long dress and a hooded cape over her shoulders, approached Tobe. John L. escorted Jed into the Marshal's office. Several men lifted Blue's body off the mule and carried it towards Doc Thacker's office.

"Marshal, sure am glad you're back."

"Where's that drunken singin' comin' from?" asked Tobe, a bit preoccupied as he wrapped his lead rope around the hitching rail.

"My place...he's been up there with Tillie half the night, gittin' drunker and louder all the time."

Tobe turned to Maud. "What are you talkin' about, Maud? Who's up there?"

"Ben Larson!"

"Ben Larson?" Tobe asked as if he didn't understand her.

"In the flesh. Rode in 'bout sundown, bigger'n life 'n twice as sassy, bought him a mess of forty-rod and came straight on over to my place to see Tillie.'

"Was he alone?"

"Far as I could tell...Didn't see n'body else."

"Well, if that don't kill the corn ankle high! Every law in the Nations huntin' the Larsons and one of 'em walks right into my front yard."

Farmer,Stienke

Maud pointed toward her parlor house. "He's in that corner room, yonder."

"All right. Everybody git off the street and keep it quiet." Tobe said sotto, but with a degree of excitement.

"Marshal, I got a whole bunch of folks downstairs in the parlor watching that actor fella from England..."

John L. came back out of the marshal's office after locking Jed inside and noticed everyone scurrying for cover. Boot followed along behind the deputy, wagging his tail and, in fact, his whole body in excitement of his master's return. Tobe reached down and patted his faithful dog on the head. "Hey, Boot...Miss me?"

"What is it, Tobe?" John L. asked as he looked around.

"Shush...keep it down. Ben Larson's up there," Tobe said as he looked toward Maud's place and John L. followed his gaze.

"Larson? You sure?"

"Maud knows him by sight."

John L. stared eagerly up at the window. "Lemme take him, Tobe! Just give me a chance to put a bullet through that lowlife little..."

Tobe put a hand on John L's shoulder. "We'll do it together, boy...and we'll do it cautious. Ben Larson is dangerous as dynamite in a skillet." He paused. "Git yer scattergun."

John L. turned and took a shotgun from the scabbard on his horse and eagerly said, "Ready, Marshal."

"Now, John L., I don't want no killin' here if we can help it. I want him alive. Is that plain?...Maud says she has a mess of

132

folks downstairs in the parlor, so we take him easy...if we can...Now, you take the balcony."

John L. nodded and followed Tobe as he moved toward Maud's.

Ben strummed his guitar and began singing another song drunkenly and badly off-key. "The next gal I met was Lucy May Jones; Ole Lucy wasn't much but skin and bones; Big Adam's apple and long straight hair; My pappy looks better in his underwear."

Tillie giggled and Ben took another shot of whiskey.

Tobe entered the parlor from the street. The room was crowded with patrons and eight of Maud's sporting gals. Most of the customers were glancing with irritation upstairs at Ben's wailing. In one corner of the room, next to a small makeshift stage, was a sign that read:

DIRECT FROM ENGLAND
The Queens Player, Archibald Brimely
Presents
SHAKESPEARE'S
"ROMEO AND JULIET"

There was a derby-decked piano player in a white shirt—with red garters around his upper arms and complete with a black vest—sitting at an upright piano against a wall near the stage, playing accompanying music for the performance.

The Shakespearean actor stood on stage, profile to the audience, dressed like a lovely woman. The actor was obviously disturbed by Ben's singing, but continued like a true professional. "Wilt thou be gone? It is not yet near day," as Juliet.

Ben wailed the end of a stanza.

"It was the nightingale, and not the lark, that pierced the fearful hollow of thine ear," she continued as Ben hit a high note.

Brimely briskly changed sides to show his other profile made up as a man.

"It was the lark, the herald of the morn, no nightingale. Look, love, what envious streaks..." He noticed Tobe watching and tensed for a split second.

Tobe motioned him to continue, but louder, which he did without missing a beat. Tobe then moved to the stairway, all the while encouraging the occupants of the parlor to greater activity, and cautiously began slipping up the steps as Boot crawled on his belly behind him. Tobe stationed himself close against the wall to one side of the door in order to stay out of the line of fire should Ben start shooting through the door. He could easily hear Ben singing. Boot cocked his head to one side.

"Then I met a little gal named Carrie Lou White; Her figure it was awful and her face was a fright..."

Outside, John L. crept across the balcony and stood up beside the green trimmed window, his back to the yellow painted clapboard wall. He could hear Ben start the next verse over the accomplished actor down in the parlor.

THE NATIONS

"...Well if all they gotta offer is Amy Sue Brown; Gimme old Abe Lincoln in a calico gown."

Ben and Tillie commenced to laugh, but were stopped abruptly by loud pounding on the four-panel door and Tobe's shouted warning, "Larson! Come out with yer hands up! This is Marshal Bassett!"

Ben grabbed his pocket pistol, spun around and threw a shot at the door.

Tobe flattened himself quickly against the wall, and two more of Ben's shots blasted a second and third hole through the door paneling, tearing long splinters out of the thin dry wood. Boot covered his head with both paws.

Ben jammed his hat on his head, snatched up his guitar and gun belt in one hand and his pistol in the other. In a drunken stagger, he headed for the window. He pulled up, smiled and held a lone finger to his lips. "Shhhh." He blew a parting kiss to Tillie and flung the sash open.

Downstairs, the actor continued his performance as Juliet. "O, now be gone; more light and light..."

"So long, Sugar Cake," Ben stuck his head out of the window, but failed to see John L. in the shadows. He started climbing out the window when John L. suddenly swung his shotgun in a chopping arc, knocking Ben's pistol from his hand.

"Then window, let day in, and let life out," the actor as Juliet continued downstairs.

Ben fell out onto the balcony, dropped his guitar, then wobbled to his feet, swung his gun belt and jerked the shotgun out of John L.'s hand.

"Farewell, farewell! One kiss and I'll descend," the actor said as Romeo.

John L. managed to pick up the shotgun, brought the buttstock around quickly and connected solidly with the side of Ben's head. The blow turned Ben a backward somersault off the balcony and face down onto the muddy street with a splash, his hat landing beside him.

John L. dropped to the street and yelled to Tobe, "Out here, Marshal! I got 'em!"

Maud and the group of citizens that were present earlier came back into the street and converged on John L. as he stood over the unconscious Ben.

Upstairs, Tillie jumped from the bed, ran to the window and peered out into the rain while Brimely, downstairs, unaware of what had been going on, continued with his show.

"Methinks I see thee, now thou art so low," as Juliet.

John L. rolled Ben over with his foot. Blood streamed from a gash on the side of his head.

"As one dead in the bottom of a tomb. Either my eyesight fails or thou lookest pale," as Juliet.

Tillie gazed anxiously down into the street.

"And trust me, love, in my eye so do you. Dry sorrow drinks our blood. Adieu, adieu!" as Romeo.

THE NATIONS

She turned away from the window with a look of anger.

Tobe emerged from the parlor house, followed by Boot, to join John L., the patrons, sporting girls, a large black bouncer/servant and the wide-eyed actor.

"So that's Ben Larson," Tobe said as he looked down while Boot sniffed at Ben's face.

"Yeah...don't look so fearsome now, does he?" John L. opined.

"They never do, son...When they're stretched out thataway."

At that moment, Tillie emerged from the front door screaming like a banshee. She had thrown on a robe, but neglected to tie it. Tobe and John L. turned to see who was making such a racket.

"Benny! Benny...Oh, God! You killed him! You killed him! You bastard!"

Tillie began to wail away at John L. with her tiny fists and feet, screaming all the while. John L., in self defense, grabbed her in a bear hug. "Whoa, whoa, Tillie, settle down...hey...Hey!...Stop it now, hear? He ain't dead...Just busted his head open!"

Tillie still struggled, but was starting to calm down when Nellie Ruth ran up, clad only in her flannel night gown and lime green chenille robe.

"What is going on?...John L., just what are you doin' with *that* woman?"

John L. pushed Tillie into the arms of the very large black bouncer from the parlor house. As the transfer was made, Nellie Ruth slapped John L. hard enough to clabber milk.

"But...but...Nellie Ruth...I was...just...you don't...I mean...we...she...you...I...You know!" he babbled.

Nellie Ruth turned and looked very condescendingly at Tillie, still being held horizontally with one arm around her waist by the big man. This look set Tillie off again; she kicked the air, clawed at the black man and screamed at Nellie Ruth.

"Hush that woman and git her outta here!...John L., we'd better put the shackles on 'em," Tobe ordered.

Maud came over to help calm Tillie while Nellie Ruth, now ignoring John L., rushed over to Tobe. John L., happy to see that he was no longer the object of either Tillie's or Nellie Ruth's wrath, at least for the time being, ran off to get the shackles.

"Daddy? Are you all right?" Nellie Ruth asked as she noticed Ben on the muddy ground, gasped and averted her eyes. "Oh, how horrible! Is he..."

"No, honey. Just unconscious. Now go on back to the house..."

"Marshal, look! Here comes a Tumbleweed Wagon!" exclaimed Maud as she pointed up the street when a nearby flash of lightening momentarily lit up the downtown.

The rain had slackened to a light drizzle for a while and everybody watched the wagon as it rolled down the street, mules at a trot. Nellie Ruth glanced around to look for John L., now that she understood the situation.

138

John L. hurried back out of Tobe's office with wrist and ankle shackles and immediately began to shackle the still unconscious Ben. When he finished, Nellie Ruth walked over to him. "Are you all right? I'm sorry...I didn't realize what was happening. Can you forgi..."

"Nellie Ruth! Git off the street in that gown. Ain't you got no modesty?"

With a snort of disgust, she slapped him again and stomped off. "I take back the *sorry* part," she said over her shoulder.

John L. rubbed the side of his face as Tobe, who had been close enough to hear the exchange, walked up.

"Boy, there is two ways to argue with a woman...and neither one works."

Tobe and John L. helped Ben Larson to his feet. He was still dazed and shook his head to clear the cobwebs.

"Wouldn't do that much, Larson, just makes that gash bleed more...Take him over to Doc Thacker's, John L. I'll be along directly."

"Yessir."

John L. hustled Ben off as the Tumbleweed Wagon pulled up to a stop near them and Bass and Jack climbed down. In the back of the covered wagon the prisoner was still asleep—a skinny, seedy-looking character with a scraggly beard, dressed in a ragged black suit and a battered old high hat.

"Bass Reeves and Jack McGann. Butter my butt and call me a biscuit...It's good to see you," Tobe said as he stuck out his hand, first to Bass and then to Jack.

Farmer,Stienke

"Howdy, Tobe...good to see you too," said Bass as he grabbed his hand.

"Well, kiss a fat baby. That's Ben Larson!" Jack said as he noticed who John L. was leading off.

"Shore is. If'n you boys had gotten here five minutes earlier, you could have helped us take him," Tobe said as he grinned.

"Don't 'pears as if you needed any," Bass offered.

"Reckon we done fair-to-middlin'."

"Tobe, we got a prisoner here we need to lodge in your jail 'till we git ready to pull out of-the-mornin'." Bass said as Jack was unfastening the tailgate. The prisoner is still asleep. Jack stepped up into the bed of the wagon and unlocked the ankle shackles from the two inch thick trace chain stapled to the bed.

"That there is Horatio T. Budlow...better known as 'Preacher'. Used to peddle the gospel. Now he peddles whisky," said Bass.

"We've howdied," commented Tobe.

"All right, Preacher. Wake up!" said Jack as he shook Preacher's leg.

"What? You are releasing me?" The old man said, as he blinked his eyes and sat up from the water-tight Yankee wagon bed—so manufactured by northern wagon makers to allow the wagon to float like a boat if deep water had to be crossed.

"I guess not...You can sleep in the jail tonight," said Jack as he helped him to his feet.

"Praise be to the Lord...To be freed from this chariot of the devil for a few hours."

Bass supported Preacher as he climbed down from the wagon and then was joined by Jack to escort him to the jail.

"Got another prisoner for you besides Larson…Colored man we picked up this afternoon," Tobe said as he led them inside his office.

Thirty minutes later, Ben Larson, head bandaged and lying on a cot in a cell, stirred, sat up and looked around in a state of confusion.

Jed Neal and Preacher Budlow were in an adjoining cell—Preacher was fast asleep and Jed lying on a bunk, just staring at the ceiling. Bass, Jack, Tobe and John L. were sitting around the Marshal's office drinking coffee. It had begun to storm violently again, the lightning repeatedly flashed through the window glass and the thunder boomed and rolled as it echoed through town.

Jack flinched at the lightning. "Damn,…hate lightnin'…I mind Judge Parker'll dance'n Irish Jig when he learns we're bringin' in Ben Larson…and I will see him hang fer what they done to Hank."

"Just hope you can git the murderin' little snake to Fort Smith before his brother finds out you got him," said Tobe as he poured himself another cup of warmed over coffee.

"You think they might try to jump us?"

"Is a pig's ass pork?" Tobe replied as he sat back down.

"Who all is in the Larson gang?" asked Bass.

"Well, 'cordin' to the dodgers…Kell Brophy and Irish Buck Strong from Missouri…"

"They used to ride with the James boys," interrupted Jack.

Tobe nodded and continued, "Then there's the half-breed, Comanche Bob Miller and a natural born killer named Johnny Hawkins." Tobe paused and then said, "Think you and Bass could use a little help...just in case."

John L. jumped up eagerly. "I could ride with 'em! Like to kill me a few of the long-ridin' sons-a-bitches."

"John L., if you're gonna ride for the Judge, you'll have to learn that the object is to arrest 'em, not kill 'em. Not only do you not git the two dollars fer servin' the warrant, but it will cost ten Yankee dollars to bury 'em...Feller could go in the hole thataway," Bass cautioned.

"And if the whole Larson gang was to jump us?"

"Then God help 'em...'Cause we're gonna defend ourselves," replied Bass.

"John L.'s a good hand to have around, Bass. He just ain't learnt you can't kick a fresh cow pie on a hot day," said Tobe with a straight face.

"Aw, Tobe...Have too."

Bass and Jack suppress their grins, almost.

"And I 'spect I'd better come along, too...Meby we ought to deputize those two Choctaw Lighthorse that are still in town."

Bass nodded his agreement. "Well...we're gonna git some sleep. We'll start early-of-a-mornin'."

"I'll walk with you far as the hotel...John L., the night jailer ought to be here purty soon. Then you can take off," said Tobe.

"Yessir...'Night, Marshals," John L. replied as the marshals donned their slickers and hats and headed to the door.

THE NATIONS

The young deputy leaned back in his chair and propped his muddy boots up on the corner of the plain pine desk. He pulled his Single Action Army Colt out of his rained soaked holster and began to wipe it down with an oil soaked cotton rag.

"Hey, there!...You! I'm taking to you, law dog pup!" Larson called out.

"Shut yer trap. Prisoners ain't allowed to talk to Deputies."

"You the coward that clobbered me when I wuzn't lookin'?"

"I said, shut your face, Larson!"

"At least you know the name of the man that's gonna kill you."

***

CHAPTER SIX

SAND SPRINGS
DAYBREAK

The sun was just coming up in a crystal clear sky as Bass and Jack walked the prisoners out of the office. It was still chilly and damp, considering the almost all night rain storm. John L. led Tobe's California sorrel as well as his own chestnut Morgan saddle horse from the stable to tie to the rear of the wagon.

Tecumseh Moore and Lyman Jackson, the two Choctah Lighthorse now deputized as Deputy US Marshals, rode their Indian horses down the street toward the wagon while Tobe rolled up the canvas bonnet. A small group of early rising citizens were gathered out of curiosity. Jack unlatched the tail gate, hopped up in the bed, helped Jed up and then proceeded to fasten his shackles to the trace chain. Bass led Horatio Budlow up to the wagon, but Preacher hesitated.

"Oh, this abominable wagon! Verily, verily, it was built in purgatory."

"No time for sermonizin', Preacher. Git in," Bass ordered the scraggly old man as he pushed him up into the wagon where Jack started to work securing his shackles to the chain.

Tillie—in a plain gray cotton day dress with a high collar—hurried along the boardwalk toward the wagon as Tobe was bringing Ben out. The outlaw was sullen. There was part of a white bandage that just showed out from under his black hat that still had dried mud on it. In the corner of his mouth dangled an unlit hand-rolled cigarette.

"Where is my guitar? Ain't leavin' without it."

"Don't see as you got any say-so in the matter, sunshine," John L. said as Tobe walked the hobbled bandit toward the wagon.

Tillie ran up, but John L. blocked her path. "Keep her back, John L....I don't want her anywhere near him," Tobe ordered.

"I only want to tell him good bye!" Tillie said in protest as she stamped her tiny foot.

"Then say it from there," said Tobe as he shoved Ben up into the wagon.

Jack pushed Ben down on the thirteen-inch wide bench on the opposite side from Jed and Preacher and then quickly began to fasten the leg-irons to the heavy chain stapled to the bed. Tobe raised the tailgate of the wagon into place and latched it.

"Benny...I'm sorry," she said.

"It's all right, Sugar Cake. I'll be back before you know it."

"Wouldn't bet the farm on that if I's you, hoss fly," said Jack.

"Listen Deputy, you and this flimsy wagon will never git me to Fort Smith."

"You might be right, sweet-cheeks. I'd just soon ventilate you as not...So don't push it."

"John L., git my rifle and shotgun and a couple boxes of ammunition," said Tobe.

"Yessir," John L. said as he wheeled back into the office.

"All right, Tillie. Tell him good bye and then git on away from here," Tobe instructed.

She glared angrily at Tobe and then turned to Ben. "Good bye, Benny, Good luck!"

"So long, Sugar Cake!"

"Now then, skedaddle!" Tobe said as he gave her a gentle shove.

"All right, all right. Don't push," she said as she moved off down the boardwalk, looking over her shoulder. She stopped at the mouth of the alley and stood looking back at Ben.

Inside the Marshal's office John L. had a rifle and a shotgun in one hand, Ben's guitar and a small ten pound flour sack with several boxes of ammunition in the other as Nellie Ruth put her hands on his shoulders.

"John L....I'm really sorry about last night. I...I guess I just sorta jumped to conclusions...I didn't mean to slap you...Did it hurt?"

"Naw…Well, maybe just a little…I'm sorry too…You're not gonna stay alone, are you?

"No, Molly wants me to stay out with her at the ranch."

"Good."

"Now you be careful, you hardheaded nitwit…and look after Poppa…You hear me?"

Suddenly, she rose up on her tiptoes and gave him a quick, fleeting kiss. He blushed, ducked his head and headed out the door. Nellie Ruth followed after him.

Tobe walked up to Nellie Ruth as she came out of his office door after John L., and gave her a fatherly hug. "You take care now, Honey…You're stayin' with Molly 'till we git back, right?

She nodded and hugged Tobe again. Unnoticed behind Tobe, Tillie still stood at the mouth of the alley. John L. headed toward the wagon and held up the guitar. "Marshal, what do ya want me to do with this?"

"That's mine. Give it here!" shouted Ben

Bass took the rifle, shotgun and sack of ammunition and put everything in the weapons jockey box. He looked around at John L.

"Marshal? Should I give it to him?"

Bass frowned and said, "Well, I dunno…"

"Now, Marshal, it is liable to be a long, borin' trip and you upstandin' gentlemens of the law might need some entertainment."

"I reckon it's all right, John L. Don't see as how it could do any harm," Bass relented.

John L. grunted and handed the guitar to Ben, who grinned broadly. He set it against the bench beside him while Tobe picked up Boot, set him in the driver's seat and then he and John L. climbed aboard the wagon and settled themselves on the seat with Boot in the middle. Bass mounted his line-back dun gelding, followed by Jack on his sorrel and they joined Tecumseh and Lyman as outriders.

Tobe picked up the ribbons, snapped them at the team of four mules with a "Giddyap."

Boot added a quick bark and the wagon started in motion down the street. Bass and Jack jogged out just ahead of them on point with Tecumseh and Lyman trailing behind.

Nellie Ruth waved apprehensively as the wagon slowly moved past. "John L....take care of yourself, hear?"

Tillie still stood in the alley, forlornly staring after Ben who sent her a significant expression as he took the unlit cigarette from his mouth. Tillie saw his expression and her face wrinkled up in an effort to understand. Ben led her attention down to the cigarette by lowering his eyes to it. She followed his gaze and suddenly comprehended just as Ben casually flipped the cigarette away in her direction. It landed practically at her feet. She glanced around surreptitiously, dropped her small purse to the ground and then bent over and quickly scooped up the purse and cigarette at the same time. She turned away several steps into the alley, glanced back over her shoulder, unrolled the smoke, read what was written on the inside of the paper and then quickly hurried away.

WOODED ROAD
LATE MORNING

Tobe and John L. rode on the driver's seat—Tobe handled the reins. Boot now trotted beside the team while Bass and Jack rode out in front, about ten yards ahead, one on each side of the narrow road. Tecumseh and Lyman rode alongside the wagon. Jack let go a stream of tobacco juice at a lizard sunning itself on a rock beside the road and missed.

The three prisoners in the back of the wagon were being jolted roughly by the hard, bouncing bed as the wagon rolled over ruts and rocks. Ben looked at the black man, Jed Neal, sitting across from him on the other bench with undisguised hatred. Jed had not paid any attention to either Ben or Preacher—he was lost in his own thoughts.

"Hey, African." Jed didn't respond. "You...nigger!...I am talkin' to you."

Jed started from his reverie and just looked straight at Ben's eyes with no expression.

"What are you doin' here with us white men?...It's bad enough I gotta nigger marshalin' over me in this Godforsaken wagon, but I gotta sit down wind of one too?"

Jed stared at Ben for a moment and then calmly said, "I didn't do nothin'." He turned away from Ben and continued his gaze at the trees just showing their spring buds as they passed slowly by.

"That's what they all say...All the cowards, that is."

Jed turned back to Ben. "It is the truth. They think I killed a man, but I was only tryin' to help him."

"Sure you was. You look guilty to me, darkie. You just don't have the guts to admit it. Well, I ain't afraid to tell what I've done..." Ben began to shout. "You hear me, Marshals? I'm confessin'. I'm a killer! I have killed all over the Nations!..."

Bass and Jack dropped back even with the wagon. All the marshals and the Lighthorse reacted with silent contempt to Ben's shouted confessions.

"...Fourteen men to be exact. You hear me? Fourteen I've put away...Two of 'em were marshals!...And one of them was black as the ace of spades. 'Course I usually don't count niggers, 'cept that'un was totin' a badge."

Jack let fly an angry squirt of tobacco juice.

"Hear me, boy! I would not boast about such deeds," offered up Preacher Budlow.

"Why not, old man? I ain't scared....Wanta know why? 'Cause they'll never git me nowhere near Fort Smith."

"I was not thinkin' of that part, boy. I was referrin' to your immortal soul. 'Thou shall not kill'..."

Ben waved his hand impatiently at Budlow. "I know, you crazy old coot. I heerd all that hogwash before!"

"...In the Book of Genesis, it says, 'Whosoever sheddeth man's blood, by man shall his blood be shed; for in the image'..."

"I said I had heerd it! My Maw used to spout that stuff," Ben retorted.

"'But those things which proceedeth out of the mouth come forth from the heart and they defileth the man'...Matthew..."

"I don't give a good God damn where it is from! It's hogwash! Go piss up someone else's leg."

Preacher lifted up his eyes to the heavens. "Lord Almighty, did you hear that? This miserable sinner with bloodstained hands does not know what he is sayin'. Close thy ears, Lord, if you don't mind, so that thou won't have to listen to his blasphemin' talk."

Ben raised his own eyes in mockery. "Hey! Lord Almighty, up there. You gonna listen to this hypocritic old fool? If he's so good, ask him what he's done to be ridin' in a Tumbleweed Wagon...Ask him that, Lord."

"Beware, you young fool. You are temptin' the wrath of the Almighty. I am warnin'..."

Ben held a finger to his lips. "Shhhh. Shush up, old man. He's agonna ask you about it." He pointed to the sky with his shackled hands and then cupped his right hand behind an ear. "Listen!"

Preacher was suddenly caught up in Ben's spell and cast wild eyes toward the sky. He momentarily forgot the situation and expected to actually hear the Lord speak. After a moment of this, Ben resumed his sarcasm. "Huh?...I'll be danged. The Lord don't say nothin'." He shrugged. "Reckon he don't hear us...Maybe he was asleep." Ben snapped his fingers. "Say, that's it, Preacher! I'll bet he was takin' a nap." He threw back his head and laughed long and loud.

"Go ahead and laugh while you can, sinner! Purty soon you'll be dancin' at the end of Maledon's rope. Then you won't be laughin' so hard."

"And now that the preacher has finished his sermon, let us all sing hymn number ninety-three," Ben taunted in mock ministerial tones.

He picked up his guitar and began to sing an irreverent parody while Jed and Preacher glowered at him. "Bringin' in the thieves - Bringin' in the thieves. That's what this wagon's doin', Bringing in the thieves." Ben started laughing again.

Jack spit another stream of amber-colored juice.

Bass looked up and pointed up in front of the wagon. "There's the cut off."

Tobe pulled up on the reins with a "Whoa, there," to the team and brought the wagon to a halt. In front of the four mules about fifteen yards was a small weathered painted wooden sign placed at the fork in the road. The sign bore an arrow pointed to the north east and the inscription in dark green paint:

2 MILES TO LOGAN'S POST

And beneath that, another arrow that pointed south east and the words:

120 Miles to FORT SMITH

At the end of Fort Smith had been poorly added in red paint:

and HELL

"Think I'll ride over and ask a few questions. Logan or his wife generally know 'bout everythin' that's goin' on in this neck of the woods," said Bass.

"I see you. Want me to come along?" offered Jack

"No…better stick with Tobe…John L. and Lyman can come with me. We'll catch up down the road."

John L. climbed down, walked to the rear of the wagon, untied his horses' rope halter, slipped the bridle on and mounted. Jack tied his gelding to the now vacant iron ring bolted to the end of the sideboard, walked up to the front, and then clambered in the seat next to Tobe.

"Want me to handle the reins for a spell, Tobe?"

"Don't mind if I do, need to git down and water a tree 'fore we move on, though."

"Shake it mor'n three times and you're playin' with it."

"Past that stage…Almost," Tobe said as he chuckled and walked over to the tree line.

"Glad you said *almost*…scared me for a second," Jack said as he watched Bass, John L. and Lyman ride off down the Logan's Post Road.

OUTLAW HIDEOUT
ARKANSAS RIVER
AFTERNOON

All the Larson gang was present, save for Ben. Buck, Kell, Bob and Johnny were seated around a dilapidated table playing poker inside the out-shack. The dugout was notched into the side of a hill—the front wall had been built with prairie sod and a rough cut pine front porch covered with cedar shakes added. Inside, whisky bottles—some full and others derelict empties—were scattered about the dirt floor. Filthy glasses were in abundance. There were hand-made rope bunks and cots on one side of the big room with shelves holding an assortment of seal-tights and put-by mason jars of pickled peaches, watermelon-rind preserves and speckled butter beans on one wall and a pot-bellied stove in a corner. Wes paced the floor in the center.

"Have a drink, Wes, and relax before you wear out a good pair of boots," Kell said from the table.

"Kell's right, Wes. Ben'll be along," Johnny added.

"Aye, it'll not be the first time the lad's left his brains in his trousers," said Buck.

"No…But, by God, it'll be his last. Oughta geld the hardheaded little…" Wes stopped, cocked his head and listened as he heard the distant sounds of a horse galloping.

The others heard it too. Wes crossed to the hinged grease paper window, swung it open and looked out to see Tillie riding fast toward the cabin. Wes turned from the window.

"That ain't Ben," he exclaimed as he moved to the door and stepped out on the porch.

His companions emerged from the cabin to stand beside Wes as Tillie galloped up and slid her horse to a stop right in front of the porch. She had changed from her feminine town attire and had adopted a working man's clothes, with wool riding pants and a tan canvas jacket. Her long blonde locks were pulled back in a single braid.

"Which one of you's Wes Larson?" she asked as she fished a small piece of paper from her jacket pocket.

Wes stepped down from the porch and removed his hat. "At your service, miss. Who might you be?"

"I'm Tillie. Benny sent me. The laws taken him in Sand Springs last night," she said as she handed Wes the cigarette paper note.

Wes unfolded the thin paper and read outloud, "Tell Wes what happened, you know where…Damnnation!…Wouldn'tcha know it…"

"They're takin' him to Fort Smith in a Tumbleweed Wagon," Tillie interrupted.

"The devil and Tom Bell. If'n they git him up before the hangin' Judge, he's a gone goslin!" said Kell.

"How many of 'em was along?" Wes asked.

"Six…four marshals and two Lighthorse." She unbuckled the money belt Ben had taken from Blue and handed it to Wes. "Here's the money belt Benny was carryin'."

Wes took the belt, inspected it and looked at her strangely. "This all there was in it, miss?"

"Look, I may not be a choir singer in the church, but I ain't no thief!"

Wes pulled out some folding money from the belt and handed it to Tillie. "No offense intended…Here's for yer trouble."

Tillie looked at the money and said, "No thanks…I did this for Benny." She tried to hand the money back.

"Keep it…Did you hear anything else in town?"

Tillie paused for a second. "Oh…don't know that it means anything, but…Marshal Bassett told his daughter to stay with Miz Allgood until they git back."

Wes nodded. "Now git on outa here, and watch yerself. This country's full of owlhoots."

She looked quizzically at Wes and then spun her horse on his heels and rode away. Wes glanced around at the others.

"Saddle up..."

GROVE OF TREES ON A HILL
NEAR THE OUTLAWS DUGOUT

Tillie stopped under a bare Bois D'Arc tree at the top of a nearby hill and was watching Wes and the rest of the outlaws. She could see him talk to the others after they had saddled up. Comanche Bob and Johnny spurred out in one direction, Wes, Buck and Kell left in another. Tillie decided to follow Wes and his group. She eased her horse down the hill and stayed well back of the outlaws as she followed their trail.

LOGAN'S POST

Bass, John L. and Lyman rode up to Harvey Logan's trading post on the bank of the Verdigris River. There were a couple of flat bottom barges and a birch bark canoe tied to the dock. The barges were loaded with barrels, hides, crates of chickens, two pigs and wooden boxes of various trade goods.

"Logan gets new supplies," observed Lyman.

"Probably the first barges to get punted upriver since last fall. Folks in the area are most likely runnin' short of flour, salt pork, coffee and the like," concurred Bass.

"Ding dang!" exclaimed John L. "That's what I forgot...Arbuckle. Tobe's gonna have a conniption he don't get his mornin' coffee. Reckon we can buy some from Mr. Logan?"

"'Spect so, got'ny coin? Logan don't take foldin' money," said Bass.

John L. dug in his vest pocket. "Got three silver dollars."

"Hell, that'll buy enough coffee for the next six months. Tell him you just got two. Doubt he'd sell any less'n that."

They pulled up rein in front of the post and started to dismount when Logan stepped out on the porch drying his hands on a cotton towel made from a flour sack.

"Bass Reeves! What brings you to my neck of the woods? Or should I say who?"

"It is who, Harvey. Lookin' for Otho Burkhalter and Boone Finley."

"Ohoyo Ithana!" Logan called over his shoulder.

An attractive Native American woman came out onto the porch. "What, Harvey? I am making bread."

"Bass this is my new bride, Ohoyo Ithana..."

"Woman who knows," interupted Lyman. "She is Choctaw... Shee-ah, Ohoyo Ithana. Tapena Humma."

"Shee-ah, Red War Club," she said.

"My Christian name is Lyman Jackson."

"And mine is Sarah Gaines, now Sarah Logan."

"The marshal is seeking Otho and Boone," Logan said to Sarah.

"They were here yesterday. Bought supplies and Otho mentioned they were going to camp out at the hot springs for a few days. I 'spect they're still there, soakin' off the winter, marshal."

"Much obliged, Sarah. Oh, this pup needs to buy some Arbuckle," said Bass.

"You old enough to drink coffee, boy?"

"Yessir! But, it's for Marshal Basset back to the wagon."

"Well, yer in luck, son. Just unloaded a couple of cases...How much you want?" Logan asked.

"'Bout five pounds, I reckon. Got two silver dollars."

"That'll just cover it. Sarah, get the boy his coffee."

In a moment, Sarah came back out with a five pound cloth sack of Arbuckle coffee beans and traded the sack to John L. for the two dollars.

"Thank you, ma'am."

"You are welcome, boy." She turned to Bass. "Marshal, they know there's warrants out on them...Take a caution...hear?"

HOT SPRINGS

Bass, John L. and Lyman rode up from the back side of the hill and stopped on the crest, half concealed by a clump of brush. Bass took a pair of battered brass binoculars from his saddlebags and squinted through them down into the hollow below. "There they are. Right where Logan's bride told us they would be...in the hot spring."

He handed the glasses to John L., who focused the binoculars for his eyes and could just make out two figures in the small rock enclosed spring—a circular enclosure only fifteen feet across. Steam was rising all around them, both were apparently nude.

"You really think that's them marshal? So much steam, all I can make out is two men."

"It is. I'd know Otho's shoulders anywhere. Kinda square, don't you see?"

"Yeah, well, looks like we caught 'em with their pants down...So to speak," he said with a laugh as he handed the glasses back to Bass.

"Ya'll wait here. Goin' in alone," Bass said as he dismounted and handed his reins to John L.

"Aw, Bass..."

"Do as I say...I know one of these boys and if I go down alone, I can talk to him...You watch the horses. Lyman, you watch my back."

Bass started off in a crouched position on foot through the trees. John L. climbed down with a disgusted look, leaned against a walnut tree, pulled a piece of jerky from his pocket and tore off a chunk with his teeth. He held all three horses with his other hand while Lyman moved off down the hill at an angle behind Bass to some brush nearer the creek.

Otho and Boone were splashing in the waist-deep water, the steam rising all around them. Bass stealthily slipped up toward the bank of the springs—he kept as many trees and large bushes as he could between himself and the outlaws. As he neared the bank, he glanced down at the rocky ground. At his feet were two piles of clothing and boots. He reached his foot out and kicked aside some of the clothing to reveal two gun belts, holsters and pistols. He glanced around and saw their horses tied close by next to some bedrolls, a smoldering fire and cooking utensils for the camp they had set up. The outlaws continued to enjoy the warm water. Otho ducked under, vigorously scrubbed his medium length hair with his finger tips and then came out of the water face up and smoothed his hair back.

"Damn, this shore feels good, don't it, Boone?"

"It does, it does. Think my ass is startin' to wrinkle up like a prune, though."

Bass eased down to the bank and squatted quietly at the water's edge. Otho caught the movement, turned to see Bass and then Boone did likewise.

"What the...! Well I will be a razorback hawg, if it ain't Bass Reeves. How the hell are you, Bass?" Otho said as he flashed Bass a genuinely friendly grin.

"How are *you* doin', Otho?"

"Wells'r, was doin' fairly good...til' you snuck up on us." He paused. "You still ridin' fer the Judge?"

"'Fraid so."

Otho jumped and flinched, then rubbed one leg. "Ouch!...The daggon minners in this spring try to eat a feller up...You carryin' paper on us, air ye, Bass?

Bass took warrants from his coat pocket and waved them. He was still grinning.

"Thought so...Wells'r, it looks like, as th' feller says, *you caught us bare-handed*...handed, that is. The only guns we're wearin' right now, you're out of range of."

All three men laughed.

"Looks that way," agreed Bass.

Otho flinched again from the minnow bites. "Bass, how is that sweet mama of your'n?"

Bass looked down at the water for a moment then said, "She died a few years back, Otho."

"Oh...I am purely sorry...I had not heard."

Bass puts the warrants back in his coat pocket as he said, "Don't 'spect as how you could have. Sorta bein' on the move as you been."

"Many was the time she taken a peach switch to my bohunkas as soon as your'n...'Peers as tho it taken better on you than it did me...I really loved that old black woman."

"She loved you too, Otho."

Otho started wading toward the bank. "Come on, Boone. I reckon we had better git dressed 'fore the minners carry us off."

Boone waded out after him.

Bass remained kneeling as he gazed thoughtfully into the creek. He picked up a small rock and chunked it into the water.

"Bass, mind tossin' us our clothes?" asked Otho.

Bass stepped over toward the outlaws' gear resting on the ground behind him.

Boone and Otho suddenly bent down for an extra pair of guns hidden behind some rocks at the edge of the pool and come up with them in their hands.

Otho shouted a warning, "Protect yerself, Bass!"

Both outlaws started shooting in Bass's direction. Clouds of gray gunsmoke filled the air. Bass dived for the ground, bullets chipped bark off a pecan tree branch right over his head. He rolled over quickly, drew his hogleg, and fired back at them.

Lyman started to sprint through the woods toward the spring—stopped and fired a shot. Boone caught Lyman's slug in his leg, howled in pain and ran off through the brush with Lyman following close behind.

Otho fired again. Bass rolled to the opposite direction as a bullet buried itself the ground right beside him, kicking up dirt. The lawman quickly snapped off two more rapid shots at Otho. The outlaw jumped sideways as soon as Bass pointed the long barreled Colt his direction and avoided the first shot. The second drilled him hard in the midsection and spun the naked man around completely. Otho fell out of sight behind some low bushes. Bass paused, and then he got slowly to his feet.

John L. hitched the horses to the tree, drew his pistol and moved forward in a crouching run down the hill toward the hot spring.

Bass eased over behind the bushes where Otho was laying. He lowered the hammer, holstered his pistol, leaned over, helped him to a sitting position against the trunk of a tree and knelt down. Otho was holding his hand over the wound just below his chest. There was a considerable amount of blood spurting out between his fingers. He lifted his hand up briefly and looked down at the wound. He groaned with pain and fear. "Oh...God...!God a'mighty!"

"Take it easy, Otho."

"Bass...You done punched a awful bad hole in me. I'm bleedin' like a stuck hawg!"

"Dammit all, Otho! Why in the hell did you throw down on me? You know I don't miss!"

"...Yeah...." He paused while he tried to get a breath. "...and I never could hit a bull in the ass with a broom."

"Then why, Otho?...Why?"

Otho reached up with his other hand and grabbed Bass's coat and pulled him closer. "Bass...I just couldn't bear...bear the thought of...goin' to Fort Smith in that...that Godforsaken wagon...I just couldn't bear it."

John L. moved cautiously through the woods. He stopped, cocked his head to listen; heard nothing. He looked around and then moved cautiously on through the brush down to the spring.

"Bass?..." Otho said weakly.

"Uh huh?"

"Don't...don't wanta be buried nekked...nekked as a jaybird...will you...will you put my...clothes on me...before you...before...you..." He took one last breath, released his hold on Bass's coat, sighed slowly and Otho Burkhalter's life on earth ended, his eyes stared sightlessly at the sky through the bare tree tops. Bass gently put out his hand and closed his friend's eyes.

Down the small creek a few dozen yards, Lyman came upon Boone sitting naked on a rock in the edge of the water bleeding from the bullet wound in his thigh. There was no more fight left in him. Lyman took the pistol from his hand and stuffed in his gunbelt. He helped Boone to his feet and directed him back up the creek toward his clothes and then to where Bass was kneeling beside Otho.

John L. walked up and stood beside Bass, staring down with a quizzical look. Bass's eyes were full of tears as his glanced up at John L. and Lyman and then turned away.

"Once...Once a long time ago, when...when we were kids...Otho saved my life...I was crossin' a creek bigger than this'n...when the...the log broke...If he hadn't pulled me...out... out of the water..."

John L. turned away and kicked at a piece of rotten wood. Lyman just stood there with a knowing expression.

WOODED ROAD

The wagon lumbered along the rough road with Tobe at the reins. Jack sat beside him on the seat and Boot was riding in the boot next to Tobe. Their saddle horses were tied behind by rope halters and Tecumseh was riding ahead of the wagon.

Jed was lying curled on the jostling bed asleep and Preacher dozed, his chin on his chest. Ben gave each of them a furtive glance, and then he stealthily picked up his flattop guitar and began to fumble with the underside. He looked up again and then slid open a secret compartment, took out a small Remington double-barreled derringer and quickly slipped it inside his shirt beneath his waistband. Then with a smug smile, he flipped over the guitar to play. "Hey! You badge-pushers up there. You wanna hear some more music?"

Tobe and Jack exchanged glances of annoyance and neither made a reply. Ben's shouted question awakened Preacher and Jed.

"I figured you was just dyin' to hear me play again," he said as he started strumming.

BANK OF A STREAM

Wes, Kell and Buck knelt beside the crystal clear spring-fed creek, filling their canteens while resting their horses. Wes struck a phosphorus match on his britches and touched the flame to the end of a skinny dime-store cigar.

"How long you think it will taken to ketch up with 'em, Wes?" asked Kell.

"Sometime of a mornin', I 'spect. Ain't no need to hurry. No sense in ridin' our horses in the ground."

"Aye, it would put us in a bit of the trouble," agreed Buck.

"Course, we'll have six spare horses after we kill those four marshals and two Lighthorse," offered Kell.

"Point," agreed Wes with a knowing grin.

***

CHAPTER SEVEN

CAMP BY A STREAM
DUSK

Tobe squatted at the fire, preparing to put on some coffee. Jack just finished shackling Ben's feet to the front wagon wheel. Jed and Preacher were already shackled to the larger back wheel. Tecumseh was off in the near woods gathering more dead branches for the campfire.

"Now you don't think I'd go runnin' off just before supper time, do ya?"

"You'd better be glad Tobe is in charge here, Larson. If it was left up to me, I wouldn't give you didly-squat to eat."

"I git the feelin' you don't like me much, Jack."

Jack ignored the remark, but fired a squirt of tobacco juice at Ben's hand that was resting on the ground beside the wheel.

Ben quickly jerked his hand back just in time to prevent it from being splattered by the obnoxious fluid. The smile dropped from his face as he glared at Jack.

Tecumseh walked back into the campsite with a large armload of dead-fall and piled them a few feet from the fire for easy access.

"This should get us through supper. I will gather more later."

"'Preciate it," said Tobe as he added a few sticks to the fire and then put a handful of fresh ground coffee beans in the pot set on a flat rock close to the flames. "Boys, the Arbuckle's on and purty soon we'll have some beans. Jack, why don't you and Tecumseh see if you can bag us a varmint fer stew before dark. Boot...go help 'em."

"We'll give it a shot, Tobe...*Shot*, ya understand." Jack grinned at his own joke as he picked up his Winchester—he, Tecumseh and Boot started for the woods.

Tobe opened the poke sack from the wagon, removed a small cloth bag of coarse lumpy salt from down at Grand Saline, Texas, added a few pinches, and then cut a couple of hunks of sowbelly from the slab to add to the beans hung over the fire in a large cast iron pot.

Ben watched the others disappear into the dense woods and then started rubbing his head. "Marshal?"

Tobe looked around back at Ben. "Yeah? What is it now?"

"Feels like this hole in my head is commencin' to bleed again."

"Ain't much I can do 'bout it 'cept meby change the bandage."

"That might help."

Tobe got up from stirring the beans and started across to Ben; got even with the wagon tongue and suddenly remembered he'd better take precautions. He slipped his revolver out of its holster and laid it on the dead grass, just out of Ben's reach. Then he moved on to the outlaw, knelt over him and began to examine his head. "Why, yer head ain't bleedin'…"

Suddenly, Ben brought his hand up, jammed the nickel plated derringer he had palmed from his shirt into Tobe's midsection—the old lawman stiffened as he felt the gun against him.

"Bat an eyelash, old timer…just one eyelash, and I'll send you straight to hell," Ben hissed.

"Where in Sam Hill…?"

"Never you mind. Do what I say if you wanta stay alive. Now…real slow and careful…slide that shooter over here…with yer foot."

Tobe slowly stood and moved back away from Ben, reached out with his foot and slid the pistol over within his reach. Ben scooped up the Colt, tucked the derringer back in his waistband and then cocked the hammer on the .45.

"Do not do it, Boy. The eye of the Lord is on you," Preacher spoke up when he saw what Ben was doing.

"Shut up, you crazy old bastard!" He turned back to Tobe. "Now, Marshal…ease back over here and unlock these irons…And don't git feisty."

Tobe removed the keys from his vest pocket, stepped over and unlocked the ankle shackles from the spoke of the wheel, and then unfastened the wrist manacles. Ben stood up, moved away from the wagon and closer to Tobe's horse, tied securely beside John L.'s and the mules on a picket line strung between two trees.

"This here is more like it. 'Course, I'm gonna have to take yer yella-colored horse...But, then you'll not be needin' it no more, 'cause dead men cain't ride."

He slowly raised the gun to eye level, pointed directly at Tobe's head, and grinned sardonically.

Jed glanced around frantically for some way to help. He spied a rock, about the size of an apple, partially buried near his feet.

"You look a little peak'ed, Marshal," Ben taunted the lawman. "Say hello to Jesus."

. Suddenly, Jed hurled the rock, striking Ben squarely between the shoulder blades, staggering him. Ben dropped to one knee, and then rose unsteadily. He whirled around to face Jed, his whole body shaking with rage. "You dirty nigger!"

Tobe quickly shouted, "You fire a shot, boy, and Jack 'n Tecumseh will come arunnin'...You forgit 'bout them?"

"No, I ain't forgot. I'll pick them off 'fore they know what's happenin'," Ben said as he aimed Tobe's pistol at Jed's head and pulled the trigger.

Jed threw himself sideways as best he could, just as Ben squeezed the trigger. The bullet burned a path across the black man's neck just below his left ear. Gunsmoke drifted across the campfire as Jed frantically strained at the chains binding him tightly to the wagon wheel. His eyes grew wide with fear as Ben cursed, cocked the gun again, slowly, deliberately.

"Damn you black bastard! Die, nigger!" he screamed as he touched the trigger.

A shot suddenly rang out from the far side of the clearing. The Single Action Colt was torn violently from Larson's hand and spun away crazily. Ben screamed out in pain, doubled over, dropped to his knees and grabbed at his right hand. Tobe lunged forward and jerked the derringer from the outlaw's waistband, and then slammed him to the ground, and hovered over him resolutely, holding the cocked .41 rimfire against Ben's temple.

"Shoe's on the other foot now, ain't it? You scum suckin' little pig! Give me one reason. Just one reason, and I'll give up the $2.00 to Bass and Jack my own self!"

At the edge of camp, Bass stood beside a tree with his '73 Winchester resting against the trunk, a tendril-like wisp of smoke still drifting up from the barrel. He levered a fresh .44-40 round into the chamber before he lowered the rifle ever so slightly and moved cautiously forward. John L. and Lyman entered the small clearing behind him with the wounded Boone Finley.

Ben was curled up in pain on the ground. He removed his left hand that had been wrapped around his right and discovered his trigger finger was missing—he panicked. "You ruint my hand!!...My fanger's gone...You shot it off...God damn you all to hell!"

Preacher suddenly started cackling with glee and clapping his hands happily like an excited child. "Retribution, God's retribution...Hallelujah! '...and with what measure ye mete, it shall be measured to you again'...Matthew seven, one and two..."

Bass interrupted Preacher's sermon, "How is Jed?"

Jed sat up. "I'm all right, Marshal. Just scratched my neck."

There was a shallow bloody wound along the left side. Tobe took a bandanna from his pocket and tied it around Jed's neck.

"I'll kill you, Marshal! I'll kill you for this...If it's the last thang I do, I swear to God, I'll kill you!" Ben screamed at Bass as Jack, Tecumseh and Boot came running into camp.

"What in hell is goin' on!?" Jack asked.

"Aw, Ben got a bit sassy, and Bass blowed one of his fingers off," Tobe said somewhat nonchalantly.

Jack walked over to Ben and looked at his hand. "Good, by God...Now we'll not have to listen to anymore of that damn guitar pickin'."

"You too, Jack. I'm gonna watch you squirm before you die!"

"Why, the boy is still brash...How you gonna do that with yer eyes all bugged out from the squeezing of the noose?...All you'll be adoin' is squealin' like a pig under a gate," Jack retorted.

"There ain't gonna be no noose around my neck! You'll never git me to Fort Smith!"

"Larson, listenin' to you is like wipin' yer ass on a wagon wheel..." Jack said as he turned away from Ben. "...There just ain't no end to it."

Tobe picked up Ben's guitar and started to examine it. He walked over to the others, holding the guitar. "Looky here.

171

Here's where the wormy little snake hid that derringer. This is why he was so all fired hot to have his guitar."

Jack took the guitar from Tobe to look at the hidden compartment. "Well, slap A'nt Gussie in the face," he said and then calmly walked over and swung the guitar against a wagon wheel, shattering it into kindling.

Ben reacted with silent, trembling rage.

"There, now he'll hide no more little shooters in it."

Ben's hatred for Jack was suddenly forgotten when he looked back down at the bloody stub of his finger. He held the injured hand and started whimpering, "Ain't nobody gonna do nothin' for me 'fore I bleed to death?"

Bass took him by the arm, yanked him to his feet, led him back over to the wagon, and seated him, none too gently, on the ground by the front wheel. "You ain't about to bleed to death...yer too blamed mean," he said as he secured Ben's feet to the wheel again and knelt beside him to inspect his hand—he pulled his last spare bandanna from his vest pocket. "Jack, give me a little of your 'bacca."

"Damnation, Bass! You wanta waste some of my chaw on that pig slop?"

"Better than havin' to bury him later and not get the warrant money."

"Still a waste, if you ask me," Jack grumbled as he pulled his Bowie knife from his belt, cut a small chunk from his plug of Brown's Mule and pitched it to Bass.

Bass put it in his mouth, wallowed it around a minute, spread it over Ben's stub of a finger and wrapped the bandana around it, tore the end and tied a knot.

Tobe walked over and retrieved his Colt from the grass. He wiped the smear of blood off on his pants and examined it closely. A frown appeared under his white mustache—the trigger was sheared off flush with the top of the trigger guard. "Damn, Bass. You shot my trigger smooth off!"

"Had you rather I not taken that shot, Tobe?"

"Didn't say that, but what in hell am I gonna use for a shooter?"

"Grab Ben's from the weapon's jockey box. He just donated it."

"That'll do," Tobe responded.

Ben opened his mouth to object, but Preacher suddenly shouted excitedly, as he took a small object from Boot's mouth. He was laughing crazily and dancing around in a small circle next to the rear wheel where he was still chained next to Jed. "Hey, looky! Looky! Looky! I found it! I found it! Looky here!

"What the devil you talkin' about?" Tobe asked.

"The finger, Marshal…The gore-spattered finger from his wicked hand. The blood of innocent men was on that hand and now his own blood is on it. Retribution. Divine retribution! Boot was gonna make supper of it."

Tobe, with a look of mingled nausea and disgust, grabbed the grisly object. "Gimme that thing, you half-witted old reprobate," he said and hurled the finger into the fire.

"Wait! What're you doin'? You cain't burn it up!" Ben screamed.

"Why not? You don't need it no more," Tobe answered.

"You cain't do it, I tell ya! It's wrong! It's unholy!"

"You're a fine one to talk about unholy," Jack countered.

"But it ain't right to burn up part of a man!" Ben pleaded.

"What would you do? Bury it and have the Preacher conduct funeral services?" asked Jack.

"That's it! We should hold services and pray for it. And for the rest of yer rotten carcass too! Because soon, you're gonna be burnin' just like it is, in the everlastin' fires of Hell! Praise be to God!" Preacher yelled.

"Shut up! You ravin' old fool!" Ben yelled back.

"The Good Book says: 'Fear him which is able to destroy soul and body in Hell'."

"Shut up! I am warnin' you, old man! Shut up!"

Bass interrupted, "That's enough!"

"That is what I say. You're both beginnin' to turn my stomach. And whether the rest of you want anythin' or not, I'm fixin' to eat," said Tobe as he squatted beside the fire, picked up the coffee pot and poured himself a cup.

Jack grabbed up a blue graniteware plate, a wooden handled fork and shoveled himself some beans into it from the cast iron pot. Bass grabbed three more plates, filled them and carried them to Jed, Preacher and Boone and then came back and got one for himself. John L. turned away with a sick look on his face while Lyman and Tecumseh pick up plates also, dished up some beans and move over to their blankets to sit.

174

"Ain't hungry," said John L.

Bass grinned as he watched John L. walk quickly away toward the bushes. In a moment, they all could hear him throwing his guts up.

Tecumseh turned to Lyman. "Young white man upset over little thing."

Lyman laughed at the thought. "It is not as if the finger ended up in our beans. Perhaps I will never understand the white eyes."

After darkness came, everybody had finished eating. Bass was sitting beside Jed—both were nursing their evening coffee from some battered tin cups. Only the night sounds of crickets, an occasional owl and the first frogs coming out of hibernation down at the stream could be heard.

"Jed?…Tobe told us what you done…I just wanted to thank you," said Bass.

"A man either does right or he don't, Marshal."

Both men paused in retrospection, and then Bass asked, "Where did you come from, Jed?…I mean, where was home?"

"Fannin County…Texas, sir. Bonham is the county seat."

"Just across the Red, ain't it?"

"Yessir, I was born on the Neal place. That's how I got my name."

"I heard of a Colonel George Neal in the war."

"Yessir, that was him. I was with him at Chickamauga as his body servant…we got separated'n ain't seen 'em since. I hear tell he got bit by his dog and died of the hydrophoby last year."

Bass hesitated then asked, "Where was you headin'…when you got picked up?

"Waldron. Waldron, Arkansas…My wife 'n me got a farm there."

"Any children?"

"Yessir, six,…five boys and a girl…I shore miss 'um." Jed paused and then asked, "How 'bout you, Marshal, where're you from?"

"Well, born in Crawford County, Arkansas on the Reeves plantation. I sorta took off during the war when I heard about the freein' of the slaves and came over into the Nations. Lived with the Seminoles, then the Creeks for a while. Met my Nellie Jennie and homesteaded some land over near Van Buren, Arkansas…We got us ten chil'ren, five boys and five girls. Got offered a job of work marshallin' fer the Judge 'bout ten years back after trackin' for a spell. Been doin' it ever since."

"Ten children? Reckon I got me some ketchin' up to do!"

They are both silent for a moment, each occupied with his own thoughts. Then Bass spoke again, "You know, Jed, you don't look to me like the kind of man who could kill…for one little ol' finger ring."

"Marshal, I know the evidence is mighty strong against me…but God as my witness…I did not kill that man. He was already shot when I got there, I was just tryin' to help him."

"Well, I always figger a dog that ain't killed chickens, don't run…I'll help all I can."

"But this Judge Parker…"

"Jed, I know the Judge personal. He's a stern man and a fearsome man in some ways...but he's got feelin's. And he's fair...Now, best git some sleep...How's yer neck feel?"

"Aw, it's fine, Marshal. Like my daddy used to say, 'Had a worse place on my lip and never quit whistlin'."

Bass chuckled.

After a moment, Jed spoke back up, "Marshal?...How is it they is coloreds...that's marshals?"

"Wells'r...some folks think that because a man looks different that he is different...But, here in the Nations, a man is judged by the way he does his job....'Night, Jed."

"Night, Marshal."

Bass got up and walked toward his bedroll over by the fire. Jed lay back on the ground, pulled his wool blanket up to his chest and with his head pillowed on his hands, stared up at the western sky where the stars looked like distant camp fires scattered through the night.

MOLLY ALLGOOD'S HORSE RANCH
MID-DAY

Molly Allgood's ranch was a modest but very neatly kept place consisting of a simple whitewashed clapboard house, built in the dog run style with a full front porch. A red barn with a matching bunkhouse were built behind the house, next to two privies—the larger being a two-holer. Beside the barn stood a set of corrals made rough cut local pine, and a round breaking pen was constructed out of cedar posts set close to discourage green broncs from trying to run through the slats. Inside the seventy foot diameter pen, a couple of hired hands were trying to snub a two year old painted mustang to the deep-set center cedar post. The gelding was bucking wildly against the woven grass rope, his nostrils flaring as he breathed deeply. One man had a flour sack and was attempting to blindfold the mustang to calm him down.

Molly Allgood was hoeing crabgrass weeds from her wheel chair near the front steps of her house. Built on the edge of the porch near the steps was a three-foot wide seesaw ramp, to which were attached several graduated gear wheels and a crank. The quick yard work complete, she rolled backward onto the ramp and began to turn the crank with her good left hand.

Nellie Ruth exited the screen door, wiping her wet hands on her apron. She watched in silence as Molly cranked the ramp level with the porch and rolled backwards onto it. "I declare, that contraption never ceases to amaze me."

"Right clever, ain't it. Reckon I got my inventiveness from my Pappy. He was always dreamin' up some newfangled doodad...like my convenience. Sure beats those two-holers in town that are a pure source of consternation for someone in my situation.

"Molly, you are truly a remarkable woman."

"Ain't I though?" Molly said as she spun the chair around, reached out with her left hand and held the screen door open.

Nellie Ruth grasped the back of the wicker chair and rolled Molly into the twelve foot wide dog run down the center of the house. The kitchen was located at the far end of the dog run in the well built home. As in most homes of the time, the dog run served also as a parlor with couches and chairs along the sides.

"You know, child, all that life demands from a body is a little gumption and a willingness to spill some sweat," Molly said as Nellie Ruth rolled her into the kitchen

"I guess so. But if I was in a wheelchair...I don't know if I could deal with it...'Course, if it was the Lord's will that I..."

"Aw, Lord's will, my fanny! Folks blame the Lord for ever'thin'. It wasn't the Lord's fault I got crippled. It was that tom-fool husband of mine...God rest his soul."

Molly rolled up to the big chrome trimmed black wood-burning stove with an overhead bread warmer and reached for a steaming coffee pot. She poured some into a heavy porceline glazed mug on the table. "When it come to horses, Walter Allgood didn't know beans from barley...And speakin' of beans, hand me that jar from the cupboard."

Nellie Ruth obeyed her, then set a pan and colander beside the bean jar. Molly uncapped the jar and poured some of the beans into the pan, began sorting them for rocks as she talked. "That day before we started to town in the buggy, I warned Walt about that blamed skittish mare...but, he wouldn't listen. Oh, how he loved that animal! She was a high stepper and he liked to show her off."

Molly paused a moment to examine a handful of beans before dropping them in the colander. "What happened?"

"Oh...Well, we were nearin' the bridge over Crawford's creek..."

Suddenly, Molly and Nellie Ruth heard the sounds of a horse galloping up.

"Miz Allgood. Miz Allgood! It gonna happen! It. gonna happen!" Sky, a young Indian hired hand, shouted from outside.

Molly set aside her work. "What in tarnation?" she said as she spun around. Nellie Ruth came up behind to push her back down the dog run to the front door.

Molly and Nellie Ruth emerged from the house, as Sky swung down off his pinto, happily excited. He was leading Molly's horse with a special belt built in the saddle.

"What is it, Sky?" Molly asked.

"The sorrel, ma'am! She fixin' to foal! Down to the creek pasture."

"Well, bless Paddy! I want to be there!"

"Yessum, thought you would."

Sky climbed the steps to the porch, lifted Molly from the wheel chair, carried her to a dapple gray mare and set her in the saddle. She belted herself in as Sky slipped her feet into the oxbow stirrups.

"Nellie Ruth, honey, would you draw some water and cut some ham hock for the beans? The boys are gonna be hungry after fightin' that string of broncs all day."

"Go on. Don't worry about a thing." Nellie Ruth shook her head and smiled as she watched them gallop away, clods of mud flying off the horse's hooves. "A truly amazing woman. Truly amazing."

She opened the screen door and walked back to the kitchen where she picked up a four gallon white porcelain bucket with a red ring around the top lip from the drain board and headed toward the back door. She walked to the hand-dug well and set her house bucket on the short wooden bench next to the covered rock-lined well. She moved the wooden well bucket to the middle of the well shaft, lifted the center cover and released the rusty metal cog on the crank gear, letting the bucket fall twenty feet to the water below. The bucket quickly half filled itself with water and turned upright.

Nellie Ruth cranked the L shaped metal handle attached to the three inch diameter roller set across the well shaft—winding the rope up neatly in a tight spiral. When the bucket cleared the opening, she pulled the rope over to the side and poured the two gallons of clear, cold water into her house pail. Then she dropped the well bucket back down for another trip.

No sooner had the bucket splashed down when the sight of two strangers riding in through the ranch main gate attracted her attention. Comanche Bob and Johnny Hawkins, leading an extra saddle horse rode up at a gentle lope smiling. She smiled back, thinking they might be friends or acquaintances of Molly's, or just travelers in need of some water. They pulled up just feet away from the petite young woman, swung down and tipped their hats curtly.

"How'do, ma'am," said Johnny.

"Afternoon. What can I do for y'all?" asked Nellie Ruth.

"Just git on the horse, Ma'am."

"What?…Just who are you anyway?"

"Do like we say, lady, if you know what is good for you," Commanche Bob said.

"Now wait just a minute! If I holler, a dozen hands will come arunnin' with..." she said as Johnny moved beside her.

"And they'll wind up dead...Right here," Bob interrupted.

"He's right, ma'am...Best you git on the horse," added Johnny.

"But, I can't ride like this!" she said referencing her full, ankle length skirt. She glanced frantically over her shoulder at the horse pens, and then back at each of the grinning men. Her hand made contact with the partially filled house bucket. Bob reached out to grab her by the arm, but Nellie Ruth swung the pail hard, hitting him in the groin dropping him to his knees and splashing the few inches of water up into his face. He grunted, and before Johnny could get react, Nellie Ruth swung the near empty metal pail up between his legs, where it thunked loudly from the solid contact. Johnny grabbed at the bucket much too late, his hands only served to hold it there after she had released it and turned to sprint to the barn. He looked quizzically at Comanche Bob, who watched in confusion as Johnny's eyes crossed and he fell to one side, striking his head against the rock wall around the well.

Nellie Ruth held the front hem of her skirt up several inches as she ran as fast as her shapely legs would carry her. She looked quickly back to see Bob pull a dazed Johnny to his feet and the two men staggered painfully after her. Inside the barn, a block and tackle hung low from the central rafter supporting the hay loft. She grabbed it and ran to the base of the wood ladder leading up to the loft, climbing two of the ladder's twelve steps before she stopped. Bob and Johnny hobbled into the barn only scant seconds later.

Nellie Ruth released the block and tackle as the two tried to get their eyes adjusted to the light conditions inside. Comanche Bob turned as the movement of the heavy block and tackle caught his attention. He almost succeeded in moving out of the way, and only got a deep cut across his eyebrow and a couple of three inch long scrapes to his face as he was spun around and went down hard. Johnny reacted just in time to catch the wood and iron assembly full in the face. His nose was bloodied and he had lost an upper front tooth before ending up flat on his back.

Nellie Ruth contemplated climbing the ladder to the loft for a brief moment. Then she realized there was no route of escape from up there. She spied a rack of four-up harness hung at the side of the barn. With her adrenaline pumping, she ran to the rack, lifted the wagon traces up, and ran back over to the unfortunate Bob and Johnny and slung the spaghetti like harness on top of both men. The two struggled to stand as they further entangled themselves on the seemingly endless leather straps.

"I thought Wes said she was a slip of a thang'n wouldn't be no trouble," said Bob as he tried to untangle himself.

"He lied," Johnny added as he finally crawled free of the mess.

Nellie Ruth hurried to a find a hiding place at the rear of the barn. She reached the square wooded chicken feed bin and lifted a lid, only to find it full to the top with dried ear corn.

"There she is!" Johnny yelled as he wiped the blood from his eyes.

He helped Comanche Bob back to his feet and the pair moved cautiously toward the cornered woman.

She responded by grabbing the dried ears of feed corn and throwing them at Johnny and Bob as hard and fast as she could. "Git outta here! You trash leave me alone!"

Bob and Johnny ducked and dodged, sometimes successfully, other times not, and then eventually separated to try to outflank her. Johnny saw his opportunity when she turned to throw at Bob and dove at her legs, tackling her into a massive pile of hay beside the corn crib. Nellie Ruth started kicking, biting and slapping him as hard as she could until Bob arrived to help.

"Dang! She's like trying to stuff a momma bobcat in a sack!" cried Bob.

"Grab some of that twine over yonder!" Johnny yelled, trying to hold Nellie Ruth down with sheer body weight.

Bob grabbed a length of hay twine, and tied her feet together while Johnny held Nellie Ruth's arms, then he tied her hands together in front. Suitably restrained, Bob threw the young woman over his shoulder and limped his way outside and back over to the horses.

"Now, you little hellion, you can ride or I can tie you on like a sack of taters...Yer choice," said Bob as he sat her on the ground.

"I'll ride," Nellie Ruth said defiantly.

Comanche Bob swung up into the saddle. "Cut her loose, but be careful."

Johnny pulled out a pocket knife and very cautiously cut her bindings. Bob took control of the reins of her horse as Johnny lifted her to the saddle, and then hopped aboard his own mount. Bob smiled as Johnny gingerly opened his mouth and felt for the hole where a front tooth had been.

"You look like hell, Johnny-boy."

"Just wait'll you look in a mirror, half-breed."

COUNTRYSIDE
DAY

Bass, John L. and Tecumseh were trotting their horses side-by-side along a well used road. They slowed up and moved over to the edge to let a four-up freesco road grader pass. Bass tipped his hat at the Indian operator sitting on the metal seat centered over the seven foot blade, who nodded in return. He reined his horse back to the somewhat smoother road and as they rode under some trees, they pulled up.

"We better rest the horses for a spell. Let 'em graze," said Bass.

They dismounted, ground tied their horses on some nearby winter rye and cheat grass and hunkered under the tree.

"I hope we done the right thing, leavin' the wagon again," John L. offered.

"Jack and Tobe ain't pilgrims. Plus they got Lyman."

"I reckon…Still, if the Larson gang was to…"

"Don't go borrowin' trouble, son. The gang prob'ly don't even know we've got Ben. 'Sides, I got other warrants to serve.

185

Soon as we pick up Neely McClaren and Myra Maybelle Shirley, we can head back."

"A woman? We got papers on a woman?" John L. asked incredulously.

Bass nodded. "You prob'ly know her better as Belle Starr."

"Belle Starr? They call her Queen of the Oklahoma Outlaws! I heered tell that she rode with the Younger brothers and the James boys...Robbed trains and such."

"Cain't git no proof of that."

"Then wha'd she do?"

"Larceny of two horses, accordin' to the warrant."

"Well, I swan. Never heard tell of a woman horse thief afore. Which one we gonna try and pick up first?"

"Neely lives just up the road a piece."

"How do you know he'll be to home?"

"I understand he is a Choctaw farmer and home is where he would be this time of year, ain't it, Tecumseh?"

"Choctaw farmer no different than white farmer...He has got fields to tend to and get ready for spring plantin'."

The McClaren farmhouse was a modest, frame structure with run-down out buildings scattered about and an open rock-rimmed well in the front yard. The main house had been white-washed at one time, but the sun and rain had left it looking worse for wear. There were a half-dozen wagons and one horse buggies parked around it with another eight saddle horses tied to hitching rails—and a gathering of about fifteen people, including seven or eight small children. The people were all simple farm folk, some white, some Indian and a few blacks, the careworn women in cheap dresses and most of them wearing poke bonnets.

They gathered around the porch and the yard with that strange, hushed attitude peculiar to places where death has just visited. From somewhere inside, came the sound of women weeping and sobbing over the rhythmic cadence of the Choctaw death chant. In dramatic contrast to the weeping inside, the children laughed as they romped around the yard in a never ending game of tag.

Bass, John L. and Tecumseh approached their horses at an easy trot. They rode up beneath a massive old hickory tree where an old farmer with a full white beard and a weathered, seamed face that resembled oak tree bark, stood alone, whittling on a piece of wood.

Bass dismounted. "This the McClaren place?" he asked the farmer.

"Yup."

"Someone died, did they?"

"Neely's Papa...Yesterd'y," the old man replied.

"Sorry to hear it....Neely about?"

"Yonder, on the porch. I'll fetch 'em fer ya," the farmer said as he turned and walked toward the house, leaving Bass and John L. to exchange uneasy glances.

As the farmer spoke to Neely McClaren on the porch, they both looked back at the Marshals. Neely, a slight built half Choctaw Indian around thirty-five with close cropped hair, nodded to the old man, patted him on the shoulder and stepped off the porch. His eyes were red from crying and he was wiping his nose on a old blue paisley print bandanna. He was dressed in faded bib overalls, worn brogans and a patched chambray shirt. As he walked up he noticed the badge on Bass's vest. "How'do. I am Neely McClaren."

Bass extended his hand. Neely shook it firmly.

"I am Deputy Marshal Reeves...This here is Deputy Patrick and Choctaw Lighthorse Moore...Sorry 'bout yer Pa."

"Good of you to say so, Marshal...Yesterd'y mornin', he tripped over a stone and struck his head on...on a plow share...It fetched him dead..." Neely said as his voice cracked and he began to cry anew.

Bass merely shifted uncomfortably and glanced at John L., who dropped his head and looked off. Neely regained control of himself. "I 'spect as you are carryin' paper on me, ain't you, Marshal?"

"I am." Bass removed the warrant from his inside coat pocket and held it up. "Accordin' to witnesses, about a month ago you robbed a store over in Ada. When Captain Moon of the Chickasaw Lighthorse come on you commitin' the crime, you fired on that officer, inflictin' a severe head wound. Captain Moon is now blind and will never see another lick...Which makes it rough on his wife and eight young'uns." Bass paused. "Did you do it?"

Neely shows an expression of genuine remorse. "Yess'r...It was me that done it."

"Why, Neeley?…What did you want to take and do a thing like that for?"

"I needed the money, Marshal, to feed my family…and I did not know where else to git it." He stopped and took a breath. "God as my witness,…I would give my right arm if I hadn't shot that officer. He yelled at me and got me all nettled and…I reckon I just spooked." Neely leaned his head against the tree and began to sob deeply.

Bass again looked uneasy. John L. showed little sympathy and responded with a look of contempt. Tecumseh showed absolutely no emotion.

Bass laid his hand on Neeley's shoulder. "Neely?"

Neely looked up at Bass. "Yess'r?"

"I'm gonna give you a break…If you will give me somethin' in return."

Neely looked at Bass with a puzzled expression. "What could I give you, Marshal?" He waved his hand at his surroundings. "I ain't got nothin'."

"Yes…Yes, you have. You've got somethin' the poorest man on the face of this earth has…and worth more than all its gold."

"What is that, Marshal? I don't understand," he said, still puzzled.

"Yer word, Neely…You can give me yer word."

"Sir?"

"You give me yer word you will come in and give yerself up at Fort Smith within the next two weeks…"

John L. reacted with a look of shock and amazement that Bass could be so trusting with an outlaw. A hint of a smile on crossed Tecumseh's face.

Bass continued, "...and we'll ride away from here right now."

Neely could hardly believe his ears. An expression of relief and gratitude flowed over his features. He began to cry again.

"I figure you need a few days to git yer paw buried and kinda git yer chores caught up about the farm here."

Neely replied in a cracked voice, "Yess'r...could use a few days."

"Well? What about it? Do I have yer word?"

Neely extended his hand to Bass. The two men sealed the bond with a firm handshake.

"Yess'r, Marshal. I will be there. You can depend on it."

Bass mounted up with John L. still regarding him as if he had lost his mind. They reined around and rode off, leaving Neely standing beneath the tree, gazing at their retreating backs. His tear stained face a picture of emotional gratitude.

Bass, John L. and Tecumseh jogged along back the way they came, at first silently for a while.

"You really trust him, Marshal?...You willin' to take the word of a criminal?" John L. asked in wonder.

"He ain't no criminal, son, just a hard-scrabble farmer who made a bad mistake. And now he's sorry as hell about it."

"And you honest-to-God believe he'll turn hisself in?"

"I'll bet my badge and commission on it," Bass replied.

"Young white man does not understand. Neely gave word. Neely mother Choctaw, she teach him much honor...Without honor, Choctaw just well be dead," Tecumseh spoke up. "There no jails in Choctaw Nation. When a Choctaw commits a crime, which is rare thing, the tribal council will pass sentence and the guilty is to show up at a certain date, on his own, for punishment...even if that punishment is death. Such is the honor of the Choctaw."

"How far is it over to Sam Starr's place, Tecumseh?" Bass inquired.

"Two hour ride, I 'spect."

"Well boys, let's get it done," Bass said as he untied the cloth poke sack from his saddle horn. He pulled open the draw string and grabbed a couple corn doggers—a hand sized patty made of corn meal, hot water and salt, pan-fried in bacon grease—and tossed one to each of the other men. "This will do 'til we get back to the wagon." He plucked another one out for himself and stuck in between his teeth while he tied the sack securely back to the horn.

Tecumseh led the three riders on game trails through a thousand acre wooded area located south of the Starr home place. They came out of the thick timber less than a quarter mile from the fenced in front yard of the small frame house. John L. gazed curiously at the white picket fence as the three pulled up in front. "This place looks like it belongs in town. You sure you got the right one?"

"Samuel Starr is Cherokee. His wife, Belle, white. She bring white ways with her."

All three dismounted, ground tied their horses, and stretched out their backs. Tecumseh walked over to the gate, lifted the latch, and held the small gate wide for Bass and John L. to enter the well kept yard. Bass reached the door first and knocked loudly, then stepped back one full pace.

"You expecting trouble, Marshal?" John L. asked.

He grinned back at the young deputy as he shook his head. "Screen door swings this way, boy," as he pointed to the hinges.

"Oh," John L. sheepishly replied.

In a moment, a hand moved the lace curtain slightly from a front facing window, then footsteps could be heard approaching the door. A medium built man pulled opened the door. "Can I help ye?"

"You be Samuel Starr?"

"Who's askin'?"

Bass pulled his coat aside to show the Deputy US Marshal's badge afixed to the left of his vest, then reached inside the coat to pull out the papers pertaining to this visit. "I got a warrant for Myra Maybelle Shirley...So, I'm gonna ask you once more. You be Samuel Starr?"

"You be Bass Reeves, I take it."

"Last time I checked."

"Figured as much when you three rode in. To tell the truth, you boys are 'bout two days late."

"How so? Did she light out when she heard we were comin'?"

"No sir, just the opposite. When she heard it wuz you a carryin' papers on her, she went over to Muskogee and turned herself in to Marshal Bud Ledbetter."

"That a fact?" Bass looked at him curiously. "I'll wire the marshal when I get to the next town. Much obliged," he said as he touched the brim of his hat.

With that said, the lawmen worked their way out to their horses and mounted up. Starr watched them ride off, and then headed back into the house.

John L., almost busting with enthusiasm, looked over at Bass. "If that don't beat all! Can you imagine? It's almost like going fishin' and have the fish jump outta the water on the bank before you bait the hook!"

Tecumseh looked at him as if he had lost his mind. "Young white man think we go fishing?"

"No! 'Course not. Just tryin' to make conversation 'bout how Bass Reeves' reputation rides out ahead of him. People far 'n wide in the Territory know he don't tolerate no bullcrap. They don't want Deputy US Marshal Bass Reeves on their tail...Haw!"

Bass just shook his head and grinned, slightly amused by the day's event.

***

CHAPTER EIGHT

WOODED COUNTRYSIDE

The road cut across the verdant landscape like a reddish brown ribbon through the rolling pine covered hills of eastern Indian Territory. Tobe had control of all four reins, comfortably driving the wagon with his forearms resting easily on his thighs. Jack sat beside him, cradling a Greener side-by-side. Out front, by almost fifty yards, Lyman rode point, his eyes and ears taking in every tiny movement and noise. Boot jogged alongside him, occasionally stopping to check a scent he had detected beside the road or to mark his territory.

"What got you in the marshalin' business, Jack?" Tobe asked.

"Aw, well,...when the war was over, since I didn't know much about beeves, I figgered the only things left I was qualified for was to go on the scout as a road agent or be a law…like my older brother, Hank…Just decided I would rather be on the back side of the chase as the front."

"Ain't it the truth…Hank was a good man…Haw up there, Ted!…I dunno why, but I don't like the way things feel," Tobe said as he pulled back on the brown leather straps and looked around nervously.

"How's that?"

"Just what I said…Got a uneasy feelin' along the scruff of my neck. Be glad when the boys git back."

"They'll be back soon as they check out the McClaren and Starr places," Jack said reassuringly.

"Shore wish they'd hurry every chanct they git. I'm gittin' the fidgets."

"Tobe, I really think if the gang was gonna do anythin', they would of done it by now…They prob'ly don't even know we got 'im."

Tobe grunted, scowled at Jack and glanced uneasily at the wooded countryside. He clucked at the mules and snapped the reins lightly over their rumps. They began slowly walking down the road again.

In the back of the wagon, Boone checked the bandage over the wound in his thigh. Preacher had his old worn leather bound Bible open and a pair of tarnished brass-framed spectacles perched on his nose and was mumbling to himself as he read the Scripture. Jed was watching him out of boredom.

Ben was sitting, angry and sullen—nursing his throbbing maimed hand and staring out the rear of the wagon, tirelessly scanning the horizon behind them for any sign of his rescuers. Once, for an instant, he thought he saw something in the distance. He perked up, before he realized it was just a couple of deer moving through the trees and slumped back into his dark mood. Preacher continued to mumble. Ben shot him a couple of annoyed glances before he finally exploded. "Old Man! How long you gonna keep up that infernal mumblin?" Preacher didn't respond. "Hey! Old fool. I am talkin to you!"

Budlow finally looked up, peering over the top of his Ben Franklin style glasses. "I heered you, you evil-hearted whelp of Satan!...I aim to go on readin' just as long as it pleases me and the Almighty."

"Leave him alone, kid, where you and me are goin', we're gonna need all the salvation we can git," Boone warned the younger outlaw.

Ben looked over at Boone with hatred, snorted in disgust and returned to his horizon scanning. Preacher resumed his murmurous perusal of the Scriptures. The heavy wagon continued to roll inexorably down the rough, rutted road. Ahead of the wagon, there loomed a large stone protruding several inches from the ground. The front iron tire over the felly rim passed over it, lifting the wagon and letting it down with a vicious jolt. Preacher was bounced violently on the hard wooden seat.

"Wretched wagon of Beelzebub!" The rear wheel struck the same rock, delivering another teeth-jarring jolt. Preacher turned his eyes heavenward. "Ill-begotten carriage of Lucifer!...Oh, Lord, this wagon is mighty hard on a man's bony south end. We would beseech Thee, O Great and Generous Father, to give us a few miles of smooth road...If it be thy will, ya understand, Amen."

Wes, Kell and Buck, sat their horses on a wooded hill about a mile away from the wagon as it bounced slowly along. Buck had Wes' binoculars pulled up tightly as he scouted the countryside. "The cailín Tillie said they was six laws with that wagon. But I only see two marshals and a Lighthorse, Wes Larson."

"Wes, this is a lead pipe cinch...Like shootin' turtles with a buffalo gun," added Kell.

"Be partic'lar you boys don't hit Ben with a wild shot...Let's go," Wes said as he led the others obliquely down the hill to set up for an ambush ahead of the wagon.

From two hundred yards away, an exhausted Tillie sat on her horse watching Wes and the others ride down the hill, taking care to keep themselves shielded from the wagon. From her different vantage point she also could still see the wagon. Instead of following Wes, she reined downhill directly toward the wagon in the distance.

Tobe rubbed the back of his neck again and glanced around at the woods and the Potato Hills on both sides of the road. "Consarn it! I wish I was shed of this bad feelin' I got."

"Plague take it, Tobe! I wish t'hell you'd hush...Damned if you ain't got me plum edgy now...Cain't drive a nail in my ass with a hammer," Jack said as he, too, looked around.

In the back of the wagon, Jed reached down and rubbed at his ankles where the shackles had started to rub a sore spot. He stuck his fingers down in his boondockers, grabbed the top of his yellowed socks and tried to pull the thin material up between the iron and his leg with little success. Preacher put away his Bible and glasses, took out a small round tin—just a little larger than a spool of thread—of Garrett Snuff, removed the lid, tapped a measure into his lower lip and replaced the tin in his vest pocket. Boone, who had been asleep, suddenly woke up and looked around.

Ben was sitting in a relaxed position with a suspicious grin of satisfaction on his face. Tobe and Jack were silent and thoughtful, as they rode through the shadowy woods with a hill on both sides of the road. Jack reached into his lower vest pocket, took out his deer-skin pouch, unrolled it, cut a piece off his plug of Brown's Mule and wedged it in the side of his mouth, between his cheek and gum.

The silence of the idyllic forested Potato Hills was abruptly interrupted by gunfire from the bushes and trees on the right side of the road. Lyman was knocked backward from the saddle by a shot to the chest. He hit the ground behind his horse, rolled up to one knee, drew his weapon and was hit twice more. The mortally wounded Lighthorse went down for good.

Tobe was hit in the right arm just above the elbow while another just grazed his ribs. He grunted and slid off the seat out of sight into the boot. No sooner was Tobe hit, than Jack, now exposed to the gunfire, was grazed on the shoulder. He drew his gun and dropped low in the boot beside Tobe for cover.

Jed, Preacher and Boone all scooted down on the floorboards back in the wagon for protection. Ben, with a grin on his face, dove low for his own safety.

"Great jubilee!" yelled Preacher.

Up in the boot, Jack asked, "How bad you hit?"

"Flesh wound, arm. You?"

"Graze. Gotta get to the weapons box."

"Don't try it. All the shootin' is comin' from that side."

From his protected position behind a foot-thick fallen dead tree, Wes fired repeatedly at the wagon, jacking the old Winchester's lever rapidly as a cloud of oily gun smoke drifted over him. The distinctive smell of burnt sulfur hung in the still air. Forty yards away, Kell kept a close eye on the inert body of the Indian lawman he had dropped—his rifle sights still aimed at the bloody smear on the dead man's jacket. Once he was certain the man was no longer a threat, he cut back through the trees to rejoin Wes and Buck. He took up a position standing behind a mature pine, safe behind its trunk.

Buck leaned around a much smaller tree and snapped off another shot from his Smith and Wesson Schofield revolver. The .44 caliber round ricocheted from the top of the wagon seatback, and screamed off into the heavy timber on the north side of the road. He pulled the trigger again only to have the hammer drop on a fired case. In the excitement of the ambush, he had failed to count his rounds, but quickly reacted to his predicament while he leaned his back firmly against the tree trunk. He pressed the frame lock on the Smith and Wesson as he grabbed the barrel and pushed it down forcefully. The frame pivoted open, ejecting the soot-covered spent brass hulls onto the pine needle litter between his worn boots. He fumbled in his coat pocket for a handful of shiny new rounds and quickly dropped three into the upturned cylinder. He jostled with three other rounds to re-grasp them from the rimmed ends, completed the loading process and snapped the frame closed. It only took a few seconds—he thumbed the hammer back until it locked at full cock and leaned around the trunk to send another round down at the stationary wagon.

Jack took advantage of the brief lull to bail out over the left side of the wagon. A shot rang out as he cleared the sideboard and splintered one of the seven yellow-pine bows that supported the canvas bonnet. He hit the ground, rolled, and then scrambled to his feet and took refuge behind the thick front wagon wheel. His heart beat wildly as he flipped open the loading gate on his Colt and dumped the still smoking empties out on the reddish dirt roadway. Jack pulled six .45 rounds out of the leather loops sewn into the back of his belt and stuffed them, one round at a time, into the waiting cylinder. He slapped the loading gate closed and sprinted to the rear of the wagon, where he stuck his head up and quickly took an aimed shot at Buck's head barely sticking out from behind the tree. The round was off the mark only slightly, but sheared off a fist sized chunk of bark before it sent Buck's hat flying.

"Sumbitch!" Buck yelled as he ducked back behind the trunk, tree splinters were stuck into his left cheek. He looked down at his damaged hat, but decided not to try and retrieve it right then.

Kell snapped off two rapid rounds at the marshal, but both went slightly high as they whizzed mere inches above Jack's head. Jack ducked down and reloaded again. He touched the side of his jaw where a bullet from the first volley had left a short gash. Red blood coated his fingertips. *Damn, that was way too close.* He noticed Boot laying close to the ground in between the rear wheels, his paws placed over his nose. An idea came to him. "Boot! Go find John L.!"

Boot looked up at Jack, cocked his head to the right.

"Go! John L.!"

Boot instantly sprinted from under the wagon and ran back down the road, dodging spurts of dust from bullet strikes fired by both Kell and Buck. Jack sprang up and fired at Kell and then again at Buck. They ducked for cover as Jack dropped down and checked on Boot. The red and white border collie was still sprinting down the road and was quickly out of range. Jack reloaded and searched the terrain for a way to flank the ambushers.

The team lunged in terror, but Tobe had the reins wrapped tightly several times around his left forearm. He pulled off his red wild rag bandana and, holding one end of the folded piece of material in his teeth, made two wraps around the injured arm with his good left hand. Tobe tucked the free end under the end held firm in his teeth and tugged it taut.

"How you doin', Tobe?" Jack yelled from the back of the wagon.

"Hangin' in there, pard. You?"

"Just glad these jackasses cain't shoot no better'n they can...Jed, how are you boys in the wagon?"

"Nobody hit back here, Marshal," Jed answered as he looked about without getting his head too high.

"Say yore prayers, badge man! My brother'n 'em gonna leave both of ya'll to the buzzards a'fore this day's done!" a reinvigorated Ben Larson hollered out.

"Shut up!" Boone yelled as he kicked Ben with his good leg.

WAGON TRAIL

Bass, John L. and Tecumseh were easy loping along a narrow dirt road several miles away. They heard the sound of distant gunfire, reined up and stopped for a moment to listen.

"Hey, ain't that shootin'?" asked John L.

"Rifles and handguns," added Tecumseh.

"That'd be just about where the wagon would be, I make it...Damnation!" exclaimed Bass.

"That's Boggy Slough between here and there! No way we can get through," said Tecumseh as he pointed in the direction of the shots.

"Gotta go around, then. Lead the way Tecumseh."

They heard more firing just as Boot charged out of the woods about fifteen yards up the trail and stopped. He barked twice at John L. and wheeled back the way he came, ran a few feet, stopped again and looked back over his shoulder at the lawmen. They all exchanged excited glances.

"I suggest we follow Boot! He's a hellova lot smarter'n most people I know!" yelled John L.

"I agree," concurred Bass. "No question he wants us to follow."

The lawmen spurred their horses away, following after Boot as he ducked back into the brush and headed toward a nearby ridge. They rode hard, whipping and spurring their mounts to top speed, zigzagging in and out and around brush. Tecumseh led the way leaning low over his saddle to duck under the branches. Bass and John L. spread out behind Tecumseh to avoid the dangerous whipping limbs as the Lighthorse tore through the trees hard after Boot.

He led them down into deep gullies, their horses sliding on their haunches, and up the sides of hills and splashed across narrow shallow creeks, instinctively seeming to know to stay away from the wet swampy area. Occasionally, Boot would find a game trail that made the going easier, but it was too often short-lived.

The gunfire grew louder as the lawmen pushed their horses to their limit. Tecumseh momentarily lost sight of Boot, but in a short moment, he would appear from the woods, give a quick bark, turn and head off again. Each of the lawmen had removed their hats and stuffed them under the gullet of their saddles to keep from loosing them in the thick woods. Their hair was full of twigs and their arms and sides of their faces were covered in scratches. All three horses were lathered and showing signs of flagging, but there wasn't an ounce of quit in any of them as they lunged up the next hill.

THE TUMBLEWEED WAGON

Tobe cocked his pistol and took a poorly aimed shot with his left hand at a puff of smoke coming from Wes' position. His slug smacked into the log a yard from the outlaw's head.

Scarcely a hundred yards away, Tillie observed the battle—torn by her emotions. The love of her life was lying just out of eyesight in the back of that damnable wagon. Finally she could stand it no longer—she spurred her horse down the hill and onto the roadway a short fifty yards from the wagon. She closed the distance quickly, riding hard and whipping the tired mount's shoulders with the poppers on her reins. Tillie pulled up hard and dismounted, even before the horse had come to a complete sliding stop—drawing a set of elevens in the dirt. She tumbled headlong into the road a few yards from the wagon's tailgate.

"Girl, get down! dammit!" Jack yelled as she scrambled to her feet. He got up to intercept the desperate fallen angel.

Wes fired once as he caught sight of Jack again. The bullet tore a ragged hole in the back of Jack's hat brim. Kell fired low into the road and worked the lever quickly for a second shot just as Tillie came into view from behind a cedar tree growing alongside the road. Jack reached out and snagged Tillie around the waist as she struggled to sprint past him and climb into the wagon.

"Benny, Benny! No!...No!" she cried out as she flailed at the marshal.

Her momentum spun them both part way around. Shots rang out from Kell and Buck up on the hillside. Two bullets meant for Jack tore into Tillie's back, the impact sent both sprawling to the ground. Tillie gazed into Jack's eyes with a look of shock and surprise. Her mouth opened as if to say something, but no words ever came. She simply collapsed and rolled off his chest and into the dusty road.

Jack was stunned, but only for a moment, when more shots poured out of the cover on the hillside and tore into the dirt inches from him. One shot ricocheted off a rock, and whined off, just over his head. Jack clawed his way over Tillie's body and scrambled up between the two frightened horses tied to the end of the wagon. He grabbed the top of the tailgate, hoisted himself over it and flopped inside, landing beside the shackled Ben. He grabbed the outlaw's hair, yanked it back hard and jammed the muzzle of his pistol under his jaw. Tobe fired another round, this one at Buck. It just clipped his right ear and cut a small crescent in the outer edge. Almost out of breath, Jack inhaled deeply before he called out in strong clear voice that echoed though the Potato Hills. "Larson!...Stop shootin'!...You hear me?...I said hold yer shootin'!"

"I hear you!" Wes called back.

Jack looked at Ben, who was no longer full of piss and vinegar. He could smell the fear in the smaller man.

"Call off this here fuss and clear out! I've got my shooter against yer brother's head and I'm fixin' to turn it loose and splatter what little brains he's got all over this wagon!"

Wes turned on his companions angrily, "Idiots! Now see what you've gone and done! You fools was shootin' like washer women!...You ignernt bastards shot the girl!"

Jack angrily prodded Ben deep under the jaw with the muzzle of his gun. "Go ahead....you worthless piece of shit...You tell 'em!"

"Wes! Wes! Do like he says...He'll kill me!" Ben yelled, his lower lip quivering.

Wes hesitated, trying to think of some other way to save the situation.

"Larson? You hear what he said? Gonna count to three...One!" Jack yelled.

"I hear!" Wes replied as he reluctantly put his gun away. "All right, Marshal! You tak'n this pot...We're pullin' out!"

Kell looked over to Wes in amazement. "We ain't gonna give up, air we?" he whispered.

Wes shook his head and motioned for the others to follow him. Crouched low, they moved off through the brush toward their horses.

Inside the wagon, Jack lay still, his gun still under Ben's jaw, waiting. Tobe crouched low in the boot, listening.

From up on the hillside, Wes called down, "Sit tight, Kid! We'll be back!"

Jack looked at Ben's face as he heard the message from his brother. A slight smile came to Ben's lips, but it disappeared quickly as Jack twisted Ben's face towards his. "Tell you one thing, *kid*. If'n they do come back...by God, yer chances ain't worth a three cent shin plaster."

The three outlaws ran unseen up to where their horses were tied. Wes untied Kell's horse.

"What are you fixin' to do Wes?" Kell asked.

"You'll see."

Wes then untied Buck's horse and slapped them on their rumps with his hat, sending them off in a gallop. The pair of horses disappeared in the dense cover of woods. Kell and Buck stared at Wes as if he's crazy and exchanged confused glances.

"But that's gonna leave us with only one horse among'st us!" Buck protested.

"What do you mean one horse? There's two good ones tied to the back of that wagon."

Kell and Buck suddenly grasped Wes's plan. He motioned for them to follow him back down toward the Tumbleweed Wagon.

Jack kept his pistol trained on Ben's head as he listened to the sound of horses galloping away. Satisfied the outlaws had departed—he hopped out of the wagon on the right side and opened up the weapons jockey box. He withdrew a '76 Winchester and levered the action partially open see that it was loaded.

Jed and Preacher raised their heads cautiously and slowly peered out over the side. Ben smirked at them as they peeked out. Then, suddenly in a whimsical mood, he pointed his left finger. "Bang-Bang!" Ben said and then laughed.

His actions startled Preacher and he ducked back down frantically. Ben continued to laugh hysterically at his joke. Jed and Boone gave Ben icy stares. Jack, turned, and looked angrily toward the back of the wagon. Tobe rose up from the boot and was inspecting his wounds. Jack saw the movement and looked back to the front of the wagon.

"You gonna live?" he asked Tobe

"'Spect so...too far from my heart."

No sooner had Tobe's words left his mouth when a shot rang out and a slug dug into the side of the wagon just an inch from Jack's head.

Tobe ducked back down and Jack sprinted to the brush at the side of the road.

"Yee-haww!" Ben let out a yell.

Tired of being a stationary target, Jack took to the offense, firing up at the three outlaws and using cover to try to close the distance. The three had trouble tracking him. Jack fired off a round that creased Kell's rib cage and left a painful gash. All three fired in unison.

Bass, John L. and Tecumseh, following along behind Boot galloped up to the edge of a small clearing in the woods. Quickly, they dismounted, tied their horses to some limbs and started off through the brush, with rifles at the ready. Boot followed behind.

Jack exchanged fire with the bandits as Tobe tried to keep up a crossfire. The outlaws fired back as he ran dry in his Winchester. He tossed the rifle to the ground, used a tree trunk for cover while he pulled out his handgun. Jack's pistol clicked empty after two shots. He holstered it and then drew his shoulder pistol and continued to blast at Wes and the gang.

Coming down the hill behind the Larson gang, Bass, John L. and Tecumseh finally caught sight of all three men firing away. John L. took aim and started to pick Wes off. Bass slapped John L.'s rifle down.

"I want 'em alive." Bass said, and then fired his rifle into a tree limb above Wes' head. He fired a second time, closer—the bandit trio whirled around to look behind them.

"Give it up! You're covered!"

The outlaws hesitated a moment, and then commenced firing up the hill and scrambling to get away.

Bass, John L. and Tecumseh started shooting at the three running men. Jack and Tecumseh targeted Buck simultaneously. He took a rifle and pistol round from each side and spun to the ground, face down. Wes and Kell, fired wildly in the direction of the marshals, and then began to run frantically through the woods. All four lawmen continued to shoot at the fleeing pair until they disappeared in the brush.

Wes arrived first at his horse and mounted—Kell swung up behind. He spurred the horse repeatedly as the two rode away, crashing through the brush in their panic to escape.

"Doggonit, Marshal! I had him dead to rights," John L. complained bitterly.

"I know, son. I know…I sure hope I don't come to regret not letting you kill him."

John L. closed and secured the tailgate of the wagon two hours after the three rode in to the rescue. He gave a hard look at Ben who was back in the wagon, locked down again after the bandage was changed on his hand.

Bass motioned Jack and Tobe off to one side. The two injured lawmen both wore makeshift bandages—Jack, on his face and Tobe on his shot-up right arm and a larger one wrapped around his ribs. Up the road some forty yards, Tecumseh was stoically standing guard, a well worn Winchester rifle cradled in his arms.

"Have a seat, gentlemen," Bass said as he took a knee, then sat down on the gray winter killed grass.

Tobe grunted in pain as he got himself seated across from Bass. Jack sat beside Tobe, looking on as Boot circled the three, then crouched close to the town marshal. Boot licked Tobe's hand sticking out of his cotton sling. A stony seriousness masked Bass' emotions.

"Jack, I want you and Tobe to do something for me."

"What is that?" Jack asked.

"Ride on ahead to Muskogee, see if Bud Ledbetter or any other deputies are there and…"

"Not likely," interrupted Jack.

"We ain't leavin' you and Tecumseh alone," Tobe snorted.

"We got a chance to git this whole bunch, if we git some help. 'Sides, y'all ought to see a doctor 'bout them wounds," Bass countered.

"I guess not…Been hurt worst than this and it never stopped me before…ain't startin now. We ain't leavin'…period," Jack said with an air of finality.

"You stubborn jackasses! I can do just what you did. Long as I have a pistol to Ben's head, they'll not try anything. Now, dammit, go for help!"

"We'll do no such a dad-blamed thang!…We'll be in Muskogee t'morrow, so until then, we're stickin' together…The discussion is over!" the older Tobe replied. He struggled to his feet, turned on his heel—leaving Bass to shake his head and mutter to himself.

John L. was standing nearby looking down at the marshal. Bass glanced toward him as if he was going to say something, but John L. spoke first, "Huh uh…Don't look at me!"

Bass, resigned to the situation, walked over to Lyman's grave beside Tillie's and Buck's and placed Lyman's hat on the makeshift cross. Jed was leaning on a shovel.

Preacher read from the Bible. All had their heads bowed. "It is sown in weakness; it is raised in power; it is sown in a natural body; it is raised a spiritual body." Preacher closed the Book and lifted his eyes heavenward. "Almighty God, our Gracious and Forgivin' Father, we commit this spiritual body, the soul of this thy humble servant, Lyman Jackson, to thy great and lovin' mercy and we would beseech thee not to judge him too harsh. If he sinned from time to time, forgive him Lord. And if, every now and then, he made a mistake and arrested one of thy innocent servants such as the one who speaks to you now…Wells'r, just overlook it Lord and understand that he was doin' the best he could. So, be patient and go easy on him, Lord. "And go easy on Tillie, this poor lost child of sin, Lord. She had a heart of pure gold and accepted all who came to her for solace. This fallen angel, this daughter of misery and this sister of joy, accept her to thy bosom…If it by thy will, ya understand…Oh, and Lord, thou will also be receivin' this ne'er-do-well, Buck Strong, don't know nothin' 'bout him, but here he is anyhow, if you don't mind, ya understand. Amen! Yehoa-bia-chee, Tapena Humma!" he added in the Choctaw language for Lyman, meaning *Go with God, Red War Club*.

"Amen," repeated Bass and Jed.

They all turned to go back toward the wagon and Boone leaned over to Preacher to whisper. "Preacher, that there was mighty powerful, I would 'preciate it if you was to say a few words over me after the Judge is done."

"I would be proud to, son. The Almighty forgives all."

BANK OF STREAM

Comanche Bob, Johnny Hawkins and Nellie Ruth rode up to the stream and dismounted. The three horses moved to the water and began to drink without encouragement. Johnny untied his canteen and walked upstream from the horses and filled it. Before he took a drink, he offered it to Nellie Ruth. "Would you like a drink, miss? No sense in getting your dress muddy."

"Thank you."

She took the canvas covered canteen and drank heartily. While she drank, Bob, who was kneeling by the horses filling his own canteen, watched her lustfully, through narrowed eyes. Her waspwaisted dress accentuated her femininity and made him desire her even more. Johnny took the canteen from her after she finished.

"Thank you," Nellie Ruth said as she blotted her lips on the dainty handkerchief she had kept in the apron that was now rolled and tied up behind the cantle.

Johnny drained the canteen. Bob looked at Nellie Ruth's lips and instantly was jealous of Johnny. He wanted to have the chance to taste those lips himself. Johnny refilled his canteen as Bob drank his fill and then followed suit. Johnny then tied his canteen back on the saddle horn and dug some brass binoculars out of his saddlebags. Bob watched Nellie Ruth closely as she twisted to and fro at the waist, attempting to work the knots out of the days ride. His reverie was soon broken.

"Bob, watch that the horses don't drink too much water. Foundered horse ain't much good...and keep an eye on her. I'm going to see if I can spot Wes and them from the top of the hill."

"Won't let her out my sight. Take that to the bank," Bob said as Johnny climbed the steep ridge above the spring-fed branch. In a couple minutes, the slightly rotund outlaw was out of sight beyond the scrub brush and mature elm and oaks. Bob forgot about the horses and leered as Nellie Ruth knelt by the water. She dipped both of her hands into the clear cold water and splashed it repeatedly on her face, washing the trail dust away.

Then she lifted the edge of her long skirt and dried her face. As she did so, one trim ankle was exposed and Bob didn't miss it. He looked hungrily at Nellie Ruth, but she paid him no mind. She stood up and started to turn away.

Up on the top of the rocky ridge, Johnny scanned the distance through the binoculars. As far as he could see, there were no horses or wagons visible. He rolled the knurled center focus to bring the image into tighter focus. Slowly, he turned and checked another section of countryside until he was sure there were no people in the circular field of view.

Down at the stream, Bob moved closer and grabbed Nellie Ruth by the shoulders, spinning her to face him.

"What are you doing?" she exclaimed before she placed her hands on his chest. She pushed him and jerked away.

"You sure are purty...Purty as a wildflower, I have to say," Bob said as he reached out and grabbed her by her wrist.

"Keep away! Take your filthy hands off me!"

He hung on tight and they scuffled violently as she frantically tried to protect herself. She slapped at his face with her open left hand as he pulled her closer for a kiss. He parried and blocked the blow, grabbing her arm above the elbow. She managed to push off from him one more time, but the entire shoulder of her dress was torn away. Bob yanked her back by the firm grip he still has on her right wrist. She stumbled back toward him—he wrapped his right arm around her waist and threw her onto the soft ground beside the creek. He fell on top of her, his body weight pinning her down completely. Bob kissed her roughly on the mouth as his right hand released her wrist and slid across her chest, groping at her breast. Nellie Ruth screamed loudly and flailed at him with her free left hand. She clawed at him, bit him on the lip and tried to kick him off of her—without success. He ignored her feeble attempts to dislodge him and released her right wrist. His hand slid quickly up to her jaw, where he pressed her mouth closed and her head back to prevent her biting him again.

"Regular wild cat ain't ye? We'll just see how much fight you got left when I's finished!"

His fingers dug into her left breast as he lowered his face to her neck and licked it. Her left hand clawed at his back, and then slid down to his waist. Suddenly, she felt the smooth handle of his revolver and yanked it free of the stained leather holster. Her fingers wrapped around the grip of the gun and swinging it with all her might, brought it down across the right side of his head with a sickening *thud*. He moaned in pain and rolled away from her. She dropped the gun and scrambled up in panic.

Johnny had seen the start of the attack from the ridge top and rushed down the steep hill at breakneck speed, stumbling and sliding until he reached the stream. He arrived as Nellie Ruth fell to her knees and broke into hysterical sobs.

"What's goin' on here? Are you all right, miss?

She could not answer, only sob uncontrollably.

"Ohhh," Bob moaned as he sat up, blood streamed down over the side of his face and ear. He reached for the source of the pain and withdrew his hand to see it covered in blood. "God dammit to hell!" Bob staggered to his feet and grabbed for his sixgun. The fact that it was not there enraged him further. "You worthless bitch! I swear, I'm gonna kill you this time!"

His left hand produced a Bowie knife out of his belt sheath and he started toward Nellie Ruth in a rage. Johnny moved in from the side and grabbed his wrist, restraining him with much effort.

"Use yer brain, Bob! Wes'll put a bullet between yer eyes. You know how he is about women!" Johnny shouted as the two wrestled just feet from the distraught woman.

Bob hesitated for a moment, then gradually began to cool off and gather his wits. He put away the knife, untied the bandanna around his neck and began blotting the blood from his head. "Looky what she done to me, Johnny!"

"You was botherin' her, wasn't you?...You're lucky she didn't take yer damn fool head off."

Johnny picked up Bob's gun and handed it to him. "Here...And git them horses away from that water! They had enough...that's all we need, a couple of foundered horses!"

He put the binoculars back into his saddlebags and turned to Nellie Ruth. "It's all right now, miss...Come on, lets go."

She began to calm down and slowly stopped crying. Johnny held his hands cupped together about knee level. She stepped into his hands and he hoisted her up into the saddle. Nellie Ruth wiped the tears from her eyes on the torn sleeve of her dress, found the stirrups for her feet and glared at Bob as he and Johnny saddled up. He glared back. The three rode back up the creek embankment and onto the road in silence.

MARSHAL'S CAMPSITE

In a flat meadow with a small meandering creek flowing through the middle, the five lawmen had decided to make camp for the night. The four mules and their horses were long tied to a picket line stretched tight between two small cottonwood trees only thirty yards downstream from the wagon—there was plenty of grass.

Bass, Jack, Tobe, John L., Tecumseh and their four prisoners finished their meager supper. Bass laid aside his plate, took out a pipe and lit up. Jack sopped up the last of the bean gravy from his plate with a corn doger—laid the tinware down and took a bite of tobacco from his plug. "Well, they left us alone the balance of the day...What do ya reckon they're up to?"

"No idee...But they are gonna have to make their move by t'morrow. Ain't about to let us git to Muskogee, where we can git help."

John L. looked out past the small circle of firelight, straining to see what might be lurking on the darkness beyond. "They might try to jump us tonight...with us around this fire."

"Firelight's tricky...guess who we're gonna bed down close to the fire?" Tobe countered.

"I see you, Tobe." Jack stood up and headed for the skillet. "I'll clean up this mess and take first watch."

Bass shook his head. "You stood first watch last night. I'll take it tonight."

Jed looked around the campfire at the weary lawmen. The riding and constant threat of attack had begun to take a heavy toll. "Marshal, I would be glad to clean up the supper things...if you'll trust me out of these irons long enough."

Bass and Jack exchanged looks of uncertainty.

"I ain't gonna try to run away...Give you my word...Man to man."

Ben couldn't believe his ears. "His word! What good's the word of a nigger?"

Bass shot a look at Ben. "Jack, unlock his shackles."

Jack dropped the skillet next to the fire and walked over to the front wheel of the wagon and freed Jed from the irons.

"Now, ain't that a fine howdy-do! One nigger special treatin' another," Ben grumbled.

Jack turned to Ben with blood in his eyes. "Larson, I don't see no niggers! I see a Deputy United States Marshal and a prisoner who has got somethin' you'll never have...and that's honor!...Now shut yer damn mouth or I'm gonna tear yer head off and spit in the hole."

He fired a dark stream of juice in Ben's direction. Ben jerked his foot out of the way, but not in time to keep it from being splattered. Preacher cackled with glee.

"That's the ticket, Marshal! Hee-hee-hee! Spit on 'em...Drown the varmit!"

"Shut up, you old lunatic."

Preacher continued to laugh and point at Ben, who angrily hurled his utensils aside, rolled over with his back to the others.

Boot trotted over and picked up the discarded tinware in his mouth. He took it to Jed and dropped it at his feet before he sat down beside the black prisoner. Jed patted Boot on the head and scratched him behind the ears. "Got yourself a good dog, Marshal Bassett. Ain't ever day a man finds a dog like that."

"Actually, Jed...he adopted me."

Miles away in another flat spot along the road, Wes picked up a cup and was filling it from the coffee pot set next to a two-foot wide campfire. Kell was tearing off a hunk of flat bread warmed in the empty skillet. Wes was about to take a swig of the steaming java when the sound of hoof beats approaching caused him to set aside the cup and reach for his gun. He flattened himself into the short dead grass and Kell drew his pistol, and then retreated back into the darkness away from the firelight. Eventually, three dark figures on horseback became recognizable as Johnny, Bob and Nellie Ruth riding in. Wes stood up as they reined to a halt and stepped off their horses.

"What the devil tak'n you so long?' Wes demanded.

"We...we had a hard time finding this place," Johnny sheepishly replied.

Wes doffed his hat to Nellie Ruth. "No reason to be afraid, miss, nobody's gonna hurt you. T'morrow, we'll let you go."

She regarded the man's attempt at chivalry with as she sarcastically replied, "I must say...That is very gentlemanly of you."

Wes noticed in the flickering light that something was amiss. "How did her dress git torn, Johnny?"

"Well...uh...You see, Wes..."

"That one there!" Nellie Ruth angrily shouted as she pointed to Bob. "He attacked me!"

Bob was quick to his own defense. "That's a lie, Wes. Naturally she didn't want to come...so she put up a little fuss..."

"He's the one who's lying," Nellie Ruth shot back

"You gonna believe her, Wes?"

"What happened to yer head?" Wes asked as he eyed the bloody bandanna on Bob's head.

"Bumped it on a low-hangin' limb."

"I hit him with his own gun," Nellie Ruth added proudly.

Bob squirmed as Wes eyeballed him. "Listen, Wes, that ain't the way..."

Suddenly. Wes lashed out with a vicious backhand that sent Bob's hat flying, staggered him backward and knocking him to the ground. "Don't you lie to me! You've always been too handy when it come to grabbin' women...Next time, Johnny'll git the honor of buryin' you...You got that, half-breed? You'll show this young lady the same respect you would yer own sisters...or answer to me!"

Bob nodded glumly. Wes turned back to Nellie Ruth, "We already got you a nice soft bed made up yonder under that tree, miss. You go ahead and turn in whenever you like."

Nellie Ruth looked at Wes strangely, perhaps with a small bit of attraction, then turned away and headed toward the improvised bedroom. Set up under the trees, the enclosure consisted of some saddle blankets hung from ropes to serve as walls for her privacy. She disappeared behind the blankets with a final curious glance at Wes.

Johnny looked around and saw only one horse. "Where's Buck?" he asked curiously.

"He won't be ridin' with us no more," was all that Wes said.

Johnny looked at Wes with a puzzled expression as the outlaw leader turned away. Just then, Nellie Ruth screamed.

Wes drew his pistol and sprinted back toward her makeshift room in the trees. He threw the saddle blankets aside to find Nellie Ruth curled up on the corner of the soogan with her back up against the tree. She had been preparing for bed, dressed now only in her camisole. She was frozen with fear and could only point to a large dark and hairy tarantula as it crawled toward her bare foot. Wes reached down and swatted the spider into the brush with his bare hand.

"Are you all right, miss?"

He reached down to help her up as he holstered his shooter. She wrapped her arms around him, still shaking. Wes gently stroked her hair, trying to calm the frightened eighteen year old woman. He pulled her closer to him and embraced her gently. After a moment, her breathing slowed as Wes continued to gently stroke her hair. Nellie Ruth lifted her head back and their eyes met. He was smitten with the raven haired beauty. She gazed up into his compassionate eyes and reacted to his warm smile. Wes softly kissed her forehead, her eyes, nose, cheeks, and her chin and finally moved to her already parted lips. The gentleness turned to ardor as a small flame became a raging prairie fire. Nellie Ruth returned his passion with equal fervor—they devoured each other with their kisses. Wes moved from her mouth toward her slender neck, covering every square inch with tender kisses. Her hands explored the groove down the middle of his back as his hands begin to unbutton her camisole. He started to kiss her shoulders and then moved downward toward her breasts. At that moment, Nellie Ruth was consumed by her passion and she sighed deeply.

It was the sigh that brought Wes back to reality. He gently pushed her away, holding her at arms length for what seemed like an eternity. "It ain't right."

She caught her breath and looked at him incredulously. "Coming from you?"

They looked at each other for a long moment, before Wes stood up and leaned on the tree with his outstretched hand. He turned his head upwards and gazed at the millions of stars in the clear western sky. "I couldn't live with it..."

Nellie Ruth rose beside him and put her hand on his shoulder. Wes could not look at her. "...and neither could you, missy," he said as he abruptly turned—and without a backward glance, lifted the blanket aside and walked back to the campfire.

Nellie Ruth sat down on her bed roll, pulled a blanket over her and settled back. For a moment, she lay there, gazing up at the star-speckled sky—a single tear trickled down her cheek.

***

CHAPTER NINE

PRAIRIE
EARLY MORNING

The wagon creaked as it rocked and twisted down the shallow
slope of the long grade. Other than the steady rhythm of the
mules as they plodded down the dirt road, the remote terrain
was quiet. Not even a bird chirped. Bass and Jack rode on either
side the wagon, uneasily scanning the countryside for signs of
trouble. Tecumseh was at point, his rifle at the ready, lying
comfortably across his thighs. Young Deputy Patrick held the
reins loosely, his eyes searching the open grass for assailants.
Tobe sat beside him nursing his wounded right arm, wincing as
the motion of the wagon bounced the arm out slightly allowing
it to fall painfully back into contact with his ribcage.

Ben, in the rear of the wagon was growing increasingly impatient—his nervousness obvious to everyone, and the injured hand pained him more than ever as it throbbed with every beat of his heart. He searched the horizon with eyes that were beginning to betray his desperation while Boone watched him contemptuously.

Tecumseh saw movement in the distance and raised his left hand to signal to the marshals. John L. pulled the team to a halt as Jack pointed ahead, following Tecumseh's gaze. A lone horseman rode up from a shallow swale on the right side of the road and stopped in the middle, holding up a stick with a white rag attached to it as a flag of truce.

Bass fumbled for his binoculars for a moment, and then adjusted them to show the distant horseman clearly. "That there is Kell Brophy."

John L. hopped out of the wagon, levered a round into his Winchester and leveled it at the horseman as he rode closer—keeping him in his sights at all times. Jack called over to Bass on the far side of the wagon. "Keep me covered, Bass, I'll ride out and see what he wants."

Bass shook his head. "Let him come to us. Don't get us spread out."

Jack remained stationary, but pulled his rifle from the scabbard. Kell rode in slowly, smiled and lowered the flag. He nodded briefly as he passed Tecumseh. "Mornin', gents."

"Keep both hands on yer saddle horn, if you don't want me to punch yer ticket," Jack said as the dry crusty scab on his face wound pulled and reminded him of their last encounter.

Kell twisted his body around in the saddle so that his empty holster could more readily be seen. "Ain't armed, Marshal. See?"

Bass looked derisively at the outlaw. "What do you want?"

"Wes wants to make a deal."

"We don't make deals."

"I think you oughta better hear it first, Marshal...Wes wants to make a swap...Our prisoner for Ben.

Bass exchanged glances with Jack. "Yer prisoner?"

"I think you know her...Marshal Bassett's daughter?"

Tobe and John L. shouted in unison "Nellie Ruth?" Tobe's eyes bored a hole in Kell. "You slop swilling pig...if you've harmed my child...."

"Easy there, Marshal. Nobody's touched her," Kell blurted as he raised his hands.

John L. applied more pressure on the Winchester's trigger. "You stinkin', yella-spine'd...I oughta put a bullet..."

Jack swung his horse in front of John L. to block him. "Not yet, boy."

"Hold it now, Marshal. It wern't my idee," Kell pleaded.

"Nellie Ruth?" Bass said as his energy suddenly drained from him—a deep tiredness settled over his features.

"Here's something Wes said to give you."

Kell tossed Bass a small gold heart-shaped locket. John L. ran around the back of the wagon and took the locket from Bass. He pressed the tiny catch and opened it—inside was a picture of John L. on one side and Nellie Ruth on the other.

"What is it, John L.?" Tobe called out.

"It's the locket I give Nellie Ruth for her birthday. She was wearing it the day we left."

Tobe climbed down painfully from the wagon and asked John L. to show him the locket. He hung his head when the familiar piece of jewelry hit his hand. "Oh, Lord God."

"Wes says he'll give you ten minutes to make up yer mind," Kell said matter-of-factly.

"Don't need ten minutes....But it is goin' to be done my way," Bass shot back.

"How is that?" Kell asked.

"You go back and tell Larson...when you wave that white flag, I'll start Ben walkin' from here. At the same time you release the girl. We'll have Winchesters aimed at Ben's back, so there better not be no trick shufflin'."

"I'll tell 'em," Kell said as he whirled and headed back toward the other outlaws at a gallop.

Bass and Jack dismounted from their horses—Jack jerked off his hat and slammed it on the ground. "I'll be brass plated and double rectified!"

"We've got no choice! It's Nellie Ruth!" John L. pleaded.

"Hells bells! I know that, boy! It's just the thought of bringin' that little snake this far just to have them win the game like this...It's enough to make a man tak'n up the drink!"

Bass said nothing. He walked to the rear of the wagon and lowered the tail gate.

In a small grove nestled by a nearby creek bed, Wes, Nellie Ruth, Bob and Johnny were waiting under the trees. Wes turned at the sound of a horse approaching fast. Kell came into view as he crested the hilltop and approached at a full gallop. He pounded up to them and dismounted—a broad smile across his face.

"Did he agree?"

"Just like you said, Wes."

Wes turned to Nellie Ruth. "I tol' you I would turn you loose this mornin'…and I always keep my word. 'Course, what the marshal don't know is…I would have let you go anyhow."

The two shared a long poignant glance.

"Thank you," she said softly. Her actions and the related passions she felt from the previous night still conflicted her.

Bass climbed into the wagon and unlocked the leg irons from Ben. Jack stood right behind them with his rifle trained on Ben's forehead.

As Bass keyed the lock on the manacles around his wrists, Ben cracked at the Preacher, "So long, Preacher! Give my regards to Judge Parker…Read him a few lines of Scripture and maybe he won't hang your bony little ass!"

"You think you are so all-fired smart, do ye? 'Woe unto them that are wise in their own eyes and prudent in their own sight!'"

Ben threw back his head and laughed a mean, nasty laugh. "Hallelujah!"

Bass pushed Ben out of the wagon and marched him out past the lead team. He gave him an angry shove that sent the outlaw sprawling. Ben shot him a murderous look and scrambled to his feet.

"It ain't over between you and me, nigger! Not by a long shot. You owe me a finger!"

"Don't push it, boy. You ain't out of the woods yet. 'Sides, you are welcome to come back and try me...any ole time."

In the distance, several riders appeared as they rode up from the depression some three hundred yards away. Kell rode out in the forefront and waved the flag attached to his rifle. Bass waved his hat back at the riders who continued until they were a hundred and fifty yards out where they pulled their horses up.

Wes looked at Nellie Ruth. "Go ahead, miss. You are free."

Nellie Ruth dismounted and began walking.

Bass gave Ben another shove. "Go, git outa here."

Ben started out, but turned around and continued walking backwards. He pointed at Jack before he started his trash talk. "Jack, I ain't forgot that you owe me one guitar. I'll see you one of these days and give you a third eye."

"I guess not...You could not hit me with a handful of seed corn, boy. We burned up your trigger finger! Remember?"

The words inflamed the young sociopath. He pointed his left index finger at Jack and made a mock pistol with his thumb. "Pow!" he shouted. "Right in the forehead!" Ben laughed.

Kell watched as the two converged. He remembered something important. "I checked the law dogs out like you asked, Wes. Two of 'em are shot up. Not fatal, but the girl's pappy is wearing a sling on his right arm. One of the Federals is shot in the face and wearing a bandage."

Wes smiled. "That means they won't be so all fired up to follow us when we have Benny back."

Ben turned around, he and Nellie Ruth walked slowly toward each other with at least 100 yards separating them. Ben strutted arrogantly along, a triumphant smirk on his face. The four lawmen watched intently, their Winchesters trained on Ben.

The outlaws waited anxiously as they sat mounted, watching closely—their guns at the ready in their hands. Nellie Ruth and Ben moved steadily toward each other, closing the gap to only thirty-five yards between them. As Ben drew nearer to Nellie Ruth, he flashed her a big grin. He swept off his hat in a mock gesture of courtesy and bowed at the waist.

"Mornin' to you, Miss. Out for a pleasant stroll, air ye?"

She tossed her chin up haughtily and fixed her gaze straight ahead, intending to ignore Ben completely. As their paths converged, she was prepared to march right on past him when he stepped over to her, grabbed her forcefully and began wrestling with her for a kiss. She tried to defend herself by punching him with her small fists.

"Take your hands off me, you murderin' trash!"

John L. reacted with furious rage. He bolted forward, his Winchester already at his shoulder. "That son of a bitch!"

Tobe reached out and snagged John L.'s vest with his left hand and restrained him.

"Let me go!" John L. demanded.

"You're gonna get her killed! Hold yer water, boy!" Tobe countered.

Ben finished planting a firm kiss on her tightly pursed lips. Nellie Ruth clawed until she broke free—pushed him away and gave him a resounding round house slap across the cheek and eye that staggered him. She broke and ran toward the wagon.

Ben took off his hat and swung it happily in the air. "Ye haw!" he yelled as he began to run the last seventy-five yards to his brother and the gang. The pain in his hand forced him to hold his right arm across his upper chest and steady it with his left. Otherwise, every step was one of agony.

Nellie Ruth ran to up John L. and fell breathlessly into her boyfriend's arms. He wrapped his arms around her and pulled her tightly to his chest.

"Nellie Ruth, Honey! Are you all right?" John L asked as he held her at arm's length where he could see her face.

"They didn't hurt me..." she cried as she looked for Tobe. "Daddy! You've been wounded!" She tore away from John L. and ran to Tobe. "Oh, Daddy! Does it hurt bad?"

Tobe grinned wryly. "Never heard of anything hurtin' good, girl...but, it'll be all right. Especially since you're safe."

One hundred and fifty yards away, Wes dismounted just before Ben reached the group. Ben finally let go of his aching hand and grabbed for a rifle in Wes's saddle scabbard.

"Gimme a gun, Wes!"

Wes spun Ben around and slammed him to the ground. "Damn you, Ben Larson! You've done messed up enough for right now!"

"I'm gonna kill me a couple of yella-dog marshals!"

"Will you shut up a minute!"

"Wes, looky what they done to my hand!" Ben pleaded as he held up the throbbing appendage.

Wes looked at the bloody bandage, and then extended his left hand. Ben grabbed it and was pulled upright.

"Lemme see that hand," Wes groused.

"We ain't got time! They'll get away!"

"Stand still!" Wes ordered. He peeled the bandage aside slightly, peeked at the wound and grimaced. "Hell's fire and damnation!"

Kell, Johnny and Bob crowded around to take a look and reacted with sickened expressions. The hand was swollen twice normal size with bright crimson around the finger stub—pus seeped from the obvious infection and streaks of red fanned up his dirty forearm. Wes ripped Ben's sleeve open and pushed it back.

"Look at them red streaks up yer arm...You got the blood poisonin'. I seen this in the war. We gotta git you to a doctor, pronto," Wes admonished his younger brother.

"They's two or three good ones in Checotah. Old Doc Weber, fer one," Kell offered.

Ben shook his head defiantly. "We can tend to that later! Right now them marshals are sittin' down..."

"We'll tend to it now! You wanta lose that arm?" Wes shouted.

"Well...no, 'course not...But what about them marshals?"

"We can settle their hash another time. Now mount up, damn you!"

Ben saw there was no sense in trying to argue the point. He climbed aboard the chocolate brown mare Nellie Ruth had ridden. The five reined their horses in the direction of Checotah.

Back at the Tumbleweed Wagon, Tobe was holding Nellie Ruth with his good left arm. Jack stood, silently gazing off after the outlaws who were visible on a rise a quarter mile away. Bass gazed bitterly at the same sorry sight. John L. leaned his Winchester down against the wagon wheel. Boot came over to Nellie Ruth happily wagging his tail. He stood on his hind legs and walked upright the last four feet to her. She dropped down to her knees and hugged Boot while he kissed her face.

"Oh, Boot, I missed you too," she said as Boot jumped down and spun around in a circle three times.

"Boot, you'll have to walk along side. Won't be room for all of us in the seat," said Tobe.

Boot barked his okay.

"Come on, honey, let's get you up there," John L. said as he pointed up at the wagon seat. He took her left arm, Tobe grabbed her right and the two strong men lifted her up to the wagon step.

"Up you go, baby girl," Tobe said.

John L. handed her his rifle, and then climbed up beside her.

He set his rifle against the inside of the boot and reached back down to help pull Tobe aboard. The three watched helplessly as the five outlaws slowly disappeared over the small rise in the distance.

Bass inhaled deeply as a stirring of emotions rose inside of him anew. His broad mustache curled itself into an inverted U shape as a deep frown appeared on his oval face. "I will be damned if I am gonna just stand here and let 'em git away!"

Jack looked over at his fellow marshal. "They headed straight south. Bet a dollar they're goin' to Checotah to a doctor."

John L. took his place on the right side of the wide wagon seat. He looked down at Jack questioning what the older man had said. "Checotah?...Why Checotah? We ain't more'n four hours from Muskogee."

Bass walked purposefully around the team to his horse and mounted up. "They're afraid of runnin' into Marshal Bud Ledbetter in Muskogee...John L., you stay with Tobe and Nellie Ruth. We'll try to rejoin you before you git to Sallisaw."

"Oh, no! I ain't missin' a chance to put a bullet in Ben Larson!"

He climbed down from the wagon and started for his horse tied up at the rear.

"Now John L. Patrick! You listen to me..." Nellie Ruth said resolutely.

He paid her scant attention. "You'll be safe with Jack and yer father."

Jack looked toward Bass, who shook his head. Jack cut John L. off before he made it to his horse. "John L., my old daddy used to say, 'Boy, if you want to best a man, first git him mad'....And son, you're too damn mad to go. You'll git one of us or yerself kilt."

Jack reined his horse around and nudged his spurs into his flanks. Bass and Tecumseh followed.

Nellie Ruth was incensed. She called after them as they broke into a steady lope. "You're fools, all of you! At least git yourself some help!"

John L., likewise, was still visibly angry. He yanked his hat off and slapped it against his thigh in frustration, sending red dust flying off his pants. He watched the three of them ride out until they dropped below the falling terrain leading down to the creek just two hundred yards south of their position. Reluctantly, he tugged his hat down to his ears, climbed back aboard the wagon and took his seat next to Nellie Ruth. He lifted the four traces and glanced back south one last time.

"Those three had better look for some kind of luck while they's at it. They're gonna need it."

He clucked twice and snapped the reins over the four mules. The wagon lurched ahead.

"Hold up boys," Bass said to Jack and Tecumseh. The three reined back their mounts as they approached the crest of a rise. In the distance, their quarry was topping another much longer rise almost a mile away. "See no sense in lettin' em know we are on their trail. They's headin' in straight line fer Checotah."

"I see that, but what's your plan? You gonna let them so far ahead that they will get in and out of town before we get there?" Jack shot back as he let fly a stream of tobacco juice and wiped clean his mustache on the back of his hand.

"Not likely," Bass said. "We're gonna let 'em think we are on the way to Muskogee with our prisoners. Meby have a chance to catch 'em all in one spot."

Jack looked up at the sun's position. "Hope you're right, Bass. Don't fancy trackin' those copperheads after dark."

A few minutes passed and the Larson gang cleared the distant hilltop. Jack brought his stirrups gently to the sides of his horse and urged the copper sorrel back into motion.

John L. glanced across at Tobe. He didn't like the man's color, as he appeared more pale than usual. Tobe had not complained, but the younger man could tell he was hurting by the way the older man closed his eyes from time to time—the clench in Tobe's jaw muscles gave him away. Nellie Ruth leaned on John L.'s shoulder, exhausted from her ordeal. The sun was still high and John L. guessed it was close to 2 PM when the first signs of civilization came into view. Coming out of a bend, a large Federal style frame house with dark green shutters was situated just a hundred yards off the road. A split rail fence kept the milling cattle out of the well manicured yard surrounding the imposing house. A red barn and several outbuildings accentuated the ranch, owned by a wealthy cattleman who also owned the local bank. In the distance, some three-quarters of a mile, a half dozen church steeples rose up above the trees. One

Catholic, others Southern Baptist, Methodist, Church of Christ
and one Presbyterian, the churches competed for the souls of
Muskogee's five thousand residents.

"Comin' into town, Tobe. How you makin' out?"

The marshal's eyes flew open as he responded to the news.
He blinked twice and wiped the trail dust from his lids with his
left hand. "Got to admit it's a pleasurable sight. This wagon seat
done wore out its welcome a ways back."

Nellie Ruth squeezed John L.'s arm and smiled sweetly at
him. He transferred two of the reins to his right hand, reached
around her and pulled her tight to him. In the back of the
wagon, Boone, Jed and Preacher sat up in anticipation of the
stop, hoping for a chance to get out of the infernal wagon, if
only for a while.

CHEROKEE NATION
MUSKOGEE

John L. pulled up beside the US Marshal's office, set the brake
and looped the reins around it. He hopped off the wagon and
tied the lead mules up to the round metal ring set into the
limestone curb with their lead rope. Passersby stopped to gawk
at the three prisoners. John L. pointed at one young tow-headed
boy.

"You there! Go inside and fetch Marshal Ledbetter. Got a
wounded law officer here!"

"Yessir!" the boy replied as he ran to the office door and
flung it open wide.

John L. moved around to the left side of the prisoner wagon and reached up to help Tobe descend.

"Umm!" Tobe groaned as the wounds sent pangs coursing through his arm and side.

Boot came close and whined until Tobe got his feet securely on the red brick street. Tobe then stood erect to help Nellie Ruth down from her perch. "Watch your step, little one."

"Daddy, you are hurt too badly. Let John L. do it."

He reluctantly stepped back and allowed her to jump into her boyfriend's arms. John L. caught her around her handspan waist and lowered her gently to the ground. She looked up at him and batted her eyes.

"My, but don't you get stronger every day."

He looked at her questioningly. She had never been that fired up about throwing compliments his way.

"I'll see about a doctor for your daddy and Boone. Then we got to get you a hotel room and a ticket home after we git somethin' to eat."

Just then, a burly no-nonsense man with a Deputy US Marshal's badge walked from around the back of the wagon. He looked into the wagon at the three prisoners, then shifted his gaze to Tobe and John L. "I'm Bud Ledbetter, Deputy US Marshal assigned to Muskogee. Who might you be and where in hell are the men assigned to this here Tumbleweed Wagon?"

"I'm Sand Springs town Marshal Tobe Bassett. My deputy is John L. Patrick. We rode with Bass Reeves and Jack McGann to help bring in Ben Larson."

"Larson? He ain't in there!" an obviously perturbed Ledbetter said as he pointed his thumb at the wagon.

"Not anymore," Tobe replied glumly. "Long story."

"All we got is time, marshal. This here must be yore daughter, Nellie Ruth," Ledbetter observed.

"How did you know who I was?" the pretty young woman wondered.

"Woman named Allgood, from over your way sent us a telegram yestidy. Said you was kidnapped. That a fact?"

"Yes it is. They used me a hostage to trade for Ben Larson."

The big man's face showed his displeasure as he mumbled, "Damnation." A poker player he was not. His mind raced as he tried to connect the dots. "So, they grabbed you to trade for Ben. Bass and Jack are trailing him and the gang, I take it?"

"Them and a Choctah Lighthorse named Tecumseh Moore. They think the Larsons 'er headed to Checotah fer a doctor. Ben had a finger shot off," John L. added.

"Ain't no laws in Checotah…Three against six…not smart. Kinda surprised at Bass."

"They's only five of 'em, now. Killed Irish Buck Strong in an ambush. That's where Tobe got hit. Ya'll got doctors in town?" John L. asked.

"'Course we do. Let's get you over there to a good one. I see one of your prisoners has an injured leg. May as well bring him along."

Tobe handed the keys to John L. who lowered the tail gate and climbed aboard. He turned back to Ledbetter as he unlocked Boone's shackles from the heavy chain.

"Marshal, you want to put these other two in yer jail while we are in town? I don't 'spect we'll be leavin' till Tobe gets stronger."

"Go ahead and bring 'em down, too. We already got 'nother one waiting inside for Bass. Belle Starr turned herself in a couple of days ago. Said she heard it was Bass Reeves had papers on her...scared to death of that man...Cain't say as I blame her none. Gonna give me a full house, though." Ledbetter hollered out to his jailer inside the one story red brick building, "Wilson! Out here and give this man a hand!"

A slightly built man with a limp emerged from the jail, carrying a sawed-off double-barreled shotgun. Jed and Preacher followed his directions as they filed into the drab looking structure.

"Marshal, where's a good place to eat? We're pretty famished,'" asked John L.

"Buttermilk Pie Restaurant next door to the Cattlemen's Hotel 'cross the street. Betty Mae Killpatrick will make you throw rocks at yore grandma's cookin'," Bud said.

"Thanks, Marshal. Tobe, that's where we'll be when the doc gets through with you," said John L.

"Want us to order up something for you, daddy?" Nellie Ruth asked.

"You bet, Honey, you know what I like and see if she's got some steak bones for Boot...Oh, and be sure to add 'bout half of one of those buttermilk pies..."

"I know...your favorite."

John L. took Nellie Ruth by the arm and led her through the bystanders across the street toward the Buttermilk Pie Restaurant.

"This way," Ledbetter said as he motioned for the shackled Boone to move down the raised wooden side walk. He and Tobe walked side-by-side behind Boone as he limped ahead. The marshal turned his head to Tobe and spoke plainly, "Now, Doc Cooke is as good as it gets, leastwise here in Muskogee. His office is over in the next block. If he cain't fix it...it jes cain't be fixed."

"I apreciate it, Marshal. Not as young as I used to be."

Ledbetter smiled for the first time since they met. "Reckon none of us are, Tobe. But I'm pleased to finally get to meet you to your face. I've heard tell of you. Any friend of Bass is a friend of mine."

MUSKOGEE, OKLAHOMA
DECEMBER, 1909

The fresh-faced reporter flipped another page over in his notebook and started a new one. "Bud Ledbetter..."

"James Franklin Ledbetter, we all called him Bud. Later on, he was one of the Four Guardsmen of Oklahoma, as they were known," said Bass.

"Four Guardsmen?...Oh, right."

"Deputy Marshals Bill Tilghman, Heck Thomas, Chris Madsen and Bud Ledbetter. Four of the finest lawmen I ever knew. It was you reporter types that hung the moniker of the Four Guardsmen on 'em. They never cared much about that kind of folderol. I knew Tilghman and Ledbetter the best, Heck and Madsen come along later...Sure could have used Bill and Bud when we trailed the Larsons into Checotah. But it wadn't to be. We were goin' into harm's way and we knew it...Just didn't see we had any choice..."

***

CHAPTER TEN

CHECOTAH
CREEK NATION

Just after three-thirty in the afternoon, the Larson gang came into view of Checotah. The small town was located in McIntosh County, at the spot where Interstate 40 is now crossed by US Highway 69. Named for Samuel Checote, the first chief of the Creek Nation elected after the Civil War—Checotah was a bustling small farm town.

Horses were standing hip-shot at hitching rails, with a dozen wagons, drays, buckboards, and buggies parked along the street. Eight-foot wide boardwalks ran the entire length of the main street on both sides. Between every third and fourth hitching rail was a six-foot long, two-foot deep wooden water trough, set close to the boardwalk.

Wes slowed his horse from a trot to a walk as he gave instructions to the other men, "Johnny, you and Bob ride in slow and don't start no trouble. Find a doctor and hitch your horses outside his office. We'll ride in a few minutes later. Keep your eyes open and your mouths shut…Are you hearing me?"

"Got it, boss. Me and Bob will check it out good," Johnny assured him. "No problems, right?" Johnny looked at Bob hard. Bob nodded vigorously.

The two nudged their mounts faster and pulled away from the rest of the gang. Kell, Wes and Ben pulled up a hundred yards from a one-room log house on the northern outskirts of town. Wes let his horse lower his head to graze on some winter cheat grass along side the road.

"How you a doin', baby brother?" Wes asked.

"Dammit, Wes, how many times I gotta tell you not to call me that? A yard of cock and a bucket of balls and you still call me *baby*!"

Wes laughed. "Guess the infection ain't got down there!"

Kell chuckled at the joke as he watched Bob and Johnny circle their horses and pull up to a peeled rail hitching post. From the distance they could see the two casually casing the town for any signs of lawmen. Checotah didn't have a town marshal and Eufala was the county seat where the county sheriff would be. Wes occasionally glanced in their direction and returned to looking nonchalant.

A Native American woman with a colicky baby wrapped in hand woven blankets walked out of doctor's office as Johnny pretended to adjust the latigo on his saddle girt. He noticed the doctor—a slim younger man with a handlebar mustache and wearing a white doctor's coat—when the man held the door open for his patient. He couldn't hear exactly what the man said to her as she left, but Johnny assumed it was merely a cordial parting salutation or additional instructions for her baby. Johnny turned to look at Bob who was searching the town for suitable female companionship. "Sawbones is a young one. I seen him when that woman left his office yonder. Ol' Doc Webber must'a kicked the bucket."

Comanche Bob turned quickly and looked at the office door, which by that time, had closed completely. He did catch sight of the Indian woman walking past with the baby in her arms. He tipped his hat and smiled, but the woman took one look at his scratched and bandaged head and recoiled visibly. Johnny laughed.

"Told ya you wuz a sight."

"Shut yer trap!" Bob snapped back.

Inside the Heaven's Waiting parlor house, two doors down from the doctor's office, a rather chubby piano player in a black derby with a starched white shirt and black arm bands began banging out his rendition of "Buffalo Gals" on a tinny stand-up.

"Sure could use me a beer and a chaser," Bob said wistfully. He leaned out into the street to try to catch sight of any of the sporting girls near the parlor's windows.

"Not now, breed. Wes said stay put and keep outta trouble. That's 'zacley whut we are gonna do if I gotta shoot you myself."

"Tell me agin why I joined up with you?" Bob grumbled as two more young ladies walked past, headed for the general store on the other side of the doctor's office. He pointed at the one tall young red-headed girl in a calico dress and powder blue crinoline blouse. "Now that there is the one for me!"

Johnny just shook his head and looked up to see Wes and the others riding in slowly.

The trail had been easy to follow. The Larson gang had made no attempt at hiding their tracks, figuring the lawmen, shot up and undermanned as they were, would not make a play on the numerically superior group. They were wrong, but the seasoned lawmen did not aim to ride helter-skelter into an outlaw ambush.

Whenever the three caught sight of the men they followed, they had dropped back until the five had disappeared over the gently rolling terrain. The grassland was interspersed with stands of mature post oak and in many places, cedar or pine. Wildfires that often scorched the prairie in the dry season kept lower growing brush to a minimum. In the days past, the plains Indians would routinely fire the prairie to burn off the old mature grass, keep the cedar trees at bay and make fresh green grass available to their main food supply, the buffalo.

Eventually, the trail entered a mature stand of pine trees tall enough to withstand the grassfires that burned in the sparsely populated land. Bass, Jack and Tecumseh spread out and rode in single file, exercising caution as they carefully passed through the woods surrounding the outlaw's trail to Checotah. In the lead, Tecumseh, by far the best tracker in the trio, pulled up and dismounted.

"How long ago?" Bass asked the Lighthorse as he checked the texture on the horse droppings in the trail. The Indian wiped his fingers off on his boots.

"Thirty minutes...Forty-five at most. Turds still a bit warm inside. Horses need rest. Moving slower now and draggin' feet."

"And how far to Checotah?"

"Not far...Two miles meby," he said as he forked his saddle.

"Still got plenty of daylight," Bass said as he nudged his horse onward.

MUSKOGEE
CHEROKEE NATION

Tobe left the doctor's office with a fresh bandage and his arm in a sling and looked for the restaurant the doctor had also recommended. A block down to the left he spied a hand painted sign perpendicular to the wooden one story building, proclaiming the Buttermilk Pie Restaurant in large blue letters on a white background. He crossed Commerce Street and approached the front door of the eatery. He reached for the knob and turned to Boot. "You stay outside Boot, I'll bring you something in a bit."

Boot cocked his head, sat down and watched as his master entered. Tobe spied John L. and Nellie Ruth at a nearby table covered with a red and white checkered linen table cloth and moved toward them. The proprietor looked up from wiping a table off and turned to Tobe as he started to pass by her.

"That your dog at the door, Marshal?"

"Yes, ma'am. He's my best friend. Name's Boot."

"Shouldn't oughta leave your best friend outside," she said with a wink.

"Oh. Well, I wasn't sure that dogs were allowed..."

"I can tell right off that your Boot is a well mannered dog, so you just bring him on in. He's welcome."

Tobe glanced at her. "You'd be the owner, Betty Mae Killpatrick, I take it?" Tobe asked.

"You take correctly, Marshal."

Tobe grinned, turned back to the door and opened it. Boot just sat there, his head cocked again.

"Come on in, son. The nice lady says yer welcome. Go say thank you."

Boot quickly entered, padded directly over to Betty Mae, sat down and raised his right paw. Betty Mae bent over, shook Boot's paw and he kissed the back of her hand.

"Well, my...I knew you had manners. I bet you'd like a nice big steak bone and a bowl of milk, wouldn't you?"

Boot woofed, wagged his tail and made two quick circles and sat back down.

"Be careful, Betty Mae, you know what Mark Twain says: 'Pet a dog and you've got an all day job,'" offered Tobe.

She laughed and said, "I don't mind." She turned and headed toward the kitchen.

Tobe headed over to John L. and Nellie Ruth's table.

"Steak and fixin's be out in a few minutes, Marshal," said John L.

Tobe pulled up a chair and sat down. "Feel real guilty about feedin' my face when Bass 'n them 'er headin' in harm's way...Shoulda stayed with 'em."

"I got the impression Bass Reeves is not a man to argue with, Daddy," said Nellie Ruth. "Besides, we had to get you to a doctor. That wound needed treatin' before infection set in."

"I know...still don't set well."

"The doctor give you anything for pain?"

Tobe reached in his coat pocket and pulled out a small green bottle. "Give me some Laudanum. Said it would take the edge off whilst we're travelin'."

Nellie Ruth nodded.

"Looks like we'll have an extra passenger in the Tumbleweed Wagon when we pull out," offered John L.

"If we pull out...I still think they're crazy, goin' after those killers with just the three of them," countered Nellie Ruth.

"Well, all I can say is, with those three against the five in the gang, I still wouldn't want to be in the Larson's boots," said Tobe.

CHECOTAH
CREEK NATION

Johnny and Bob leaned against the hitch-rail in front of the doctor's office. A sign hung from the porch over the boardwalk proclaimed:

Dr. H. N. Carson, GENERAL PRACTITIONER.

Johnny rolled a smoke, while Bob picked at the scab on his head where Nellie Ruth had smacked him with his own Colt. "You reckon the doc'll have to cut off Ben's hand?" he asked Johnny as he looked back at the office.

"Dunno. They been in there a long time."

"That there would be a shame, him being right-handed and all."

"Reckon so. It's his own damned fault for not waitin' 'til we got there to spring him."

"I know, Wes is really pissed off at the boy for it."

Johnny nodded, and then brought the cigarette up to his mouth to lick the paper and suddenly saw something that excited him greatly. His jaw dropped, as did the cigarette, to the ground. "Oh, shit fire!"

"What?" asked Comanche Bob.

He looked at Johnny who tilted his head twice in quick succession back up the street.

Bass, Jack and Tecumseh were riding slowly, line abreast. Jack was in the center, with Bass and Tecumseh spread out, covering the entire street, watching alertly. All three had their rifles out and resting across their thighs.

Johnny whispered to Bob, "Quick, tell Wes."

Bob turned and took two steps toward the office door. It suddenly opened, and Wes, Ben and Kell emerged from the doctor's office. Ben had a clean fresh bandage on his hand and carried a bottle of tonic the doctor had prescribed.

Wes was smiling. "You see now, Kid? It is a good thing I made you come to..."

Bob rushed up them, held up his index finger to his lips to shush them to silence. All three looked curiously at him until Bob pointed with his thumb extended over his shoulder. Wes and the others glanced up the street.

"What?" Wes demanded before his eyes locked on the imposing figure of Bass Reeves riding closer on his lineback dun. "Son of a bitch!" he said in a low voice.

Ben reached over and drew his Colt from his holster with his left hand. He blurted out as he fumbled with the grip, "Them damn laws!"

Wes glared at his younger brother. "Damn you, Ben!"

Bass, Jack and Tecumseh all heard Ben's remark and scanned the crowded street, quickly spotting the five bandits. All three lawmen jumped off their horses and swatted them on the rump.

"Clear the street!" Bass yelled as he searched for cover.

The unsuspecting townsfolk looked around to see what the commotion was about. The lawmen's horses thundered down the busy thoroughfare.

Ben had difficulty cocking the single action with his off hand. The pain in his shooting hand felt like molten fire when he tried to fan the hammer back. He dragged the hammer against his gun belt bringing it to full cock, aimed at the fast moving Bass and pulled the trigger. The blast of the .45 Colt resounded off the wood framed building and echoed down the street. The bullet whizzed past Bass and buried itself into the red and white painted pole mounted outside the barbershop on the other side of Front Street.

Women screamed and horses reared up from the sound of gunfire. Two horses snapped off their reins from the hitch rails and ran down the street in panic, nearly trampling a couple crossing to the Blue Bird restaurant. Bass and Jack both dove to the ground, returning fire. Spectators scattered in every direction, fearing for their lives as bullets bounced off the hard packed dirt street.

Tecumseh raced for three young children playing in the street, scooped all three in his arms and sprinted into an open door way. He dumped them inside the haberdashery and moved back up to the edge of the door frame to get a bead on one of the outlaws. A pall of gray gunsmoke covered the boardwalk in front of the doctor's office as all five members of the Larson gang blasted away at Bass and Jack.

Bass rolled to his right, and then back left, as pistol bullets kicked up dirt on either side of him. He spied a freight wagon tied up ten yards away and made a snap decision to move to it for cover. He clawed his way to his feet and had lunged forward only three steps when a bullet knocked his left leg from under him. Bass went down hard and rolled over on his belly. He levered three quick shots from his Winchester at Kell, who was working his way down the boardwalk using horses for cover. His hurried shots went just wide of the mark. Wes fired two more shots at Bass—then his pistol ran empty. Jack glanced around wildly for cover, a shot kicked dirt in his face before it ricocheted up.

"Jack! Take cover!" Bass yelled.

Jack spotted a couple of barrels stacked on the boardwalk in front of Chick's Mercantile just thirty yards away. He scrambled to his feet, rifle in his hand and sprinted, but a shot from Ben caught him in the thigh, and rolled him. Ben awkwardly thumbed the hammer back on his Colt. He aimed at Jack's head as the marshal struggled to his feet.

"I told you what was coming to you!"

The hammer fell on a dud. Jack hobbled to the closest water trough and lay behind it.

"God dammit!" Ben shouted when he realized what had transpired.

Wes and Ben attempted to reload. Ben struggled with the badly infected hand while Wes tried to get back into the doctor's office. The young man had wisely barricaded the door with a chair once the shooting started. Wes ducked as low as possible and flipped open the loading gate and dropped the smoking empties to the boardwalk.

Bass crawled as fast as he could behind the wagon. Bullets splintered the yellow painted hickory spokes just above his head. He instantly was aware the Larsons still had a full view of him from their vantage points. He fired once at Bob, clipping the half breed inside his left arm, and then scrambled to his feet, and dove behind the closest water trough. He landed hard on the rough sawn planks of the boardwalk. Kell moved back toward his own horse, firing furiously at the lawmen.

Jack fired a couple of shots and moved for some barrels stacked on the boardwalk in front of the Checotah General Store. Bob fired at him, the bullet creasing Jack low across the back. Jack went down, but immediately scrambled up and dove behind the barrels in front of Montague's Hardware store. Bass found Johnny in his rifle sights. He squeezed off a shot, catching him in the left shoulder and spinning him around. Johnny slumped down behind the horses and yelled over at Comanche Bob, "I'm hit! Give me a hand, Bob!"

Comanche Bob panicked. The thunder of several rifle shots echoed off the walls—gunsmoke filled the air and burned his eyes.

"I'm gittin' outta here!" Bob yelled as he whirled and broke into a run down the boardwalk.

Bass led him with the front sight of his Winchester. He pulled the trigger and the hammer fell on an empty chamber. He ducked below the rim of the water trough as Wes fired a round. The slug dug into the two inch thick planks on the side, only inches above Bass' head. The marshal tossed the Winchester aside and drew his Colt. He took aim and squeezed off a shot at Bob. His bullet caught him right between the shoulder blades. Bob sprawled dead over a bench along the sidewalk.

Jack fired at Wes, who had moved down the boardwalk almost ten yards. He had a clear shot, but the horse tied to the railing reared up unexpectedly, snapping his reins. The round meant for Wes struck the terrified horse in the spine—it fell dead in the street. Wes fired a round from his Colt, barely missing Jack as it dug into a barrel of sorghum molasses, sending a stream of the thick black syrup running down the side of the oaken staves.

Jack quickly levered another round into his Winchester and caught Wes flat-footed behind the fallen horse. The brass front sight of the rifle glinted in the afternoon sun as he centered it on the outlaw's chest and pulled the trigger. The impact of the solid hit staggered Wes, who looked down at the dime sized hole in his vest. Wes glanced across the street at Jack, who fired another round that also connected. The impact of the second slug slammed him back against the whitewashed wall, spreading a bright crimson stain as Wes' legs gave out and he slid down to the walk.

Kell fired at Tecumseh, who ducked back inside the doorway to reload his pistol. The Lighthorse looked out again, he saw the injured Johnny crawl behind some feed sacks and take aim at Bass from his blind side. Ben was firing at Bass from behind some boxes and had Bass' attention. Without hesitation, Tecumseh holstered his six-gun and sprang from cover on top of Johnny. The slightly built Choctah knocked the gun from Johnny's hand. It slid off the boardwalk and down onto the street. Johnny managed to roll over and send a crashing blow to Tecumseh's face, but the smaller man fought on ferociously. He struck Johnny three times in the face as they rolled over and over down the boardwalk.

THE NATIONS

Kell aimed at the two, trying to get a clear shot at Tecumseh, but the melee was just too fluid. A near miss smacked into a nearby lamp post and caught Kell's full attention. He returned two shots at Jack, who was still kneeling behind the leaking molasses barrel across the now empty street.

Johnny rolled over on top of Tecumseh, got his left hand across his mouth and his fingers searching for his eyes. The bigger man pulled his knife and drew his hand back to strike. Tecumseh got his hand on to Johnny's to try to block as he bent his legs at the knees and worked his feet in closer to the bigger man's rump. With a blood curdling war cry, Tecumseh pushed his legs with all his might and sent the larger man flying back over his head. In a flash, he had his own knife out of its hand-tooled and beaded scabbard. He sank the blade deep into Johnny's midsection and twisted it. The outlaw's legs jerked several times—then he lay still, except for his boot heel tapping on the boardwalk in his death throes.

Slowly, Wes pushed himself up to his feet and stumbled his way down the boardwalk, bleeding badly. Bass crawled out from behind a water trough and fired at Wes, catching him through the belly. The bullet slammed him into the side of a building, but he kept stumbling ahead, crying out in pain. "Benny! Benny! Where are you?"

Faces of frightened citizens could be seen peering out of windows and around the edges of doors. The sound of constant gunfire had slowed considerably. Kell turned and swung his pistol at Tecumseh. Bass lying prone on the boardwalk caught the movement and snapped a shot at Kell. The heavy .45 ball tore into Kell's shoulder, shattering bone and causing him to drop his shooter to the plank walk. Kell spun around from the bullet impact and fell against a wooden canopy post. He grabbed at the wound instinctively, blood spurted from between the fingers of his left hand as he cried out, begging, "Hold it, Marshal!...I give up! Don't shoot!...I give up!"

Ben was only yards away, watching with contempt from behind the boxes. "You gutless bastard, you ain't about to give up!"

He swung his gun around and blasted Kell. The bullet hit him squarely in the chest, sending backward into a wall. He slid down to the boardwalk—dead.

Tecumseh leapt to the safety of the doorway, reloaded as fast as his fingers would allow and snapped off a shot at Ben. Unfortunately, Ben moved just as Tecumseh fired—the shot knocked a chunk of wood out of the box inches from his head. Ben rose up to fire back at Tecumseh.

Jack saw his chance and steadied his pistol atop the leaking molasses barrel and squeezed the trigger. The bullet struck Ben in the head. He grunted, then fell like a rag doll against the wooden boxes and wound up lying on his back, his legs on the sidewalk, his torso and head in the dirt street.

Suddenly, the silence was overwhelming and palpable. The gunfight was over. Bass got up to his feet amidst the cloud of gunsmoke. He took a few steps, favoring his left leg. Something didn't feel right, but he was in no pain. He stopped and looked down at his left boot. He lifted his foot and rotated it inward at the ankle. The left boot heel was missing. *Well I'll be damned.* Then Bass glanced at the holster on his right hip. There was a bullet hole through it, front to back. He stood for a moment, gazing about him at the mute testimony to the violence and carnage that had just ended.

Jack emerged from behind the barrels, limping conspicuously with blood staining his pants from the wound in his thigh. Wes continued slowly stumbling along the boardwalk mumbling unintelligibly. Tecumseh emerged from the doorway holding his pistol cautiously.

Excited townspeople converged on the scene, parting quickly to make room for Wes as the dying man stumbled past. They recoiled from him as if he were afflicted with leprosy, afraid to be touched by him, revulsion on their faces.

"What on God's earth is happening?…Who is he?" A woman asked pointing at the former gang leader.

"That's Wes Larson!" a man answered.

"The outlaw?" she asked.

"Yessirreebob! That's him!…Wes Larson, the outlaw! At least what's left of him."

A woman spectator quickly pulled her small child out of Wes' path as he stumbled ahead, not even aware of where he was heading. Two young boys in an alley, watching him stagger past them, glanced excitedly at each other.

"Did'ja hear that? Wes Larson! The bad man!"

They scooped up some small rocks from the street and began tossing rocks at him. Wes came to a halt, hanging onto a canopy post, so weak, he could barely stand. The small boys continued to pelt him with rocks. Some hit their mark, striking him in the head with considerable force.

Wes turned slowly toward them and spoke pleadingly, "Please stop...don't boys...please...please don't...don't hit me...no more...please..."

Ignoring his plea, with typical childish cruelty, the boys resumed their torment. Wes was struck again in the head by a rock. He shook his head in pain as the tears rolled down his face. Wes hung his head and cried,

"Somebody...somebody...please make 'em stop...please!"

A middle aged woman came up and grabbed the boys by the ears, leading them away. "Here, boys! Stop that!...Little hellions. Come away from there!"

Wes glanced around with a desperate, blank look on his tear stained face. He was obviously delirious. "Sis?...Sis?..Help me...Come help your little brother!"

His pleas landed on deaf ears. No one moved to help. He suddenly collapsed, sliding down the post, dead—his eyes staring sightlessly down the street.

There was not a single solitary sound for a long moment as the crowd looked on, stunned. They stood motionless, staring in fascination and horror at the dead man.

The marshals worked their way through the crowd. All three looked at Wes as he lay slumped against the post, a look of stoic relief on their faces.

"Had to happen sooner or later," Bass remarked

"Guess so," Jack agreed as he untied his bandanna from his neck and began to wrap it around his leg.

Just five yards away, a small boy poked at Ben's body with his finger. He pushed on Ben's head and it rocked gently to the side then returned to its previous position. Ben's eyes suddenly snapped open. The young boy jumped back and fell onto the seat of his pants—his mouth was open, but he was so terrified no sound uttered forth.

Ben was lying with blood oozing from a shallow wound across his temple. His eyes focused on the three lawmen standing in the street next to him. He brought his pistol to bear on the one nearest to him—it was Jack. He cocked the hammer slowly. "Here's that third eye, Jack..."

The hammer fell on an empty chamber. They were all empty. The lawmen were momentarily frozen in place. Then, in a flash, Jack drew his gun, cocking the hammer as it cleared the holster, his finger slid into the trigger guard as he thrust the gun forward and started to squeeze.

Ben stared down the barrel of Jack's pistol, hatred for the lawman oozing out of every pore in his body. He silently cursed his luck, running out of ammunition before he extracted revenge. His lip began to tremble. The harsh reality of his situation hit him like one of his own bullets. There was no one to left save him from the hangman now. Every one else was dead. "Go ahead!...Kill me!...If you got the balls!...I'm the one that gut shot yer badge-tot'n brother."

Jack stared at Ben for a moment, his jaw muscles flexed, and then his finger slowly relaxed on the trigger. He uncocked the hammer, holstered the weapon, limped over and kicked the empty six-shooter out of Ben's hand. He leaned over and stared down at the pitiful excuse for a human being. "I guess not...I'd rather see yer sorry jaybird ass hangin' from Judge Parker's gibbet...you wormy little bastard!"

Ben's eyes showed his dread and fear of being hanged. His body was racked with sobs and he began to cry like a child.

"Believe I will go over to the telegraph office and notify Marshal Ledbetter of what went down here and to have Tobe 'n them load up the wagon 'n meet us at Campbell's crossin' near Webber's Falls tomorrow," Bass said as he pulled out the handcuffs for Ben. "Yella always has a way of comin' out in a man," he said as he looked down at the blubbering excuse for a man. He snapped the heavy irons closed and yanked the wounded outlaw to his feet. "Here you go, Jack. Chain him to the lamp post till we git this mess cleaned up."

"My pleasure."

"Tecumseh, if'n you'd go find the undertaker and commission him to handle the bodies, I'd 'preciate it. We will need death certificates on all of 'em."

"Know man who does that work here. He married to cousin," the Lighthorse said and headed across the street.

Bass hobbled over to the lamp post and gazed at the bloody bandana Jack had wrapped around his leg. "McGann, you need to go over 'n see that doc 'bout yer leg 'n them other wounds."

"Aw, they'll be all right. Got my leg wrapped with…"

"Ain't open to discussion, Jack…Damn, if'n you ain't the most bull-headed thing on two legs…Shame that bullet didn't hit you square in the head…wouldn't be hurt atall."

Just then a small boy came up to Bass with a stacked leather boot heel sporting a bullet hole in one side. "Marshal, looky what I found up the street!"

Bass took the damaged heel and laughed. "Thought they got me for sure when that one hit. How'd you like to keep it for a remembrance?"

"Jumpin' Jehosaphat! Can I?"

Bass tousled the boy's sandy hair. "You bet, son. Stay on the right side of the law, ya hear?"

"Yessir, I promise!" he replied as he ran off to show his new prized possession to some other boys.

MUSKOGEE
CHEROKEE NATION

Tobe, Nellie Ruth and John L. were still seated at the table, all having coffee. Tobe was pushing the flat bottom of his fork around the saucer, packing up any crumbs left from his second slab of buttermilk pie when Marshal Ledbetter entered and approached their table.

"Well, Tobe, you look a site better," Bud said. "Mind if I sit?"

"Feel better, Marshal. Grab a chair. I'll get Betty Mae to bring you some coffee."

"Not necessary, she saw me come in," he said as he pulled out a chair, being careful not to disturb a sleeping Boot.

Betty Mae walked up with a white ceramic mug of steaming coffee and a blue china saucer with a very large slice of buttermilk pie. "Think Tobe likes buttermilk pie better'n you, Bud," she said as she set the coffee and pie in front of him.

"Anybody that didn't like your pie, I just might have to put in the hoosegow for bein' crazy," he said as he picked up his fork and cut a piece off the cream-colored delicacy. He followed the pie with a sip of coffee. "Damn, that'll cure what ails ya...pardon the language, miss."

"No apologies necessary, Marshal. I live with my father. Hear a lot worse than that," offered Nellie Ruth.

"Nellie Ruth," Tobe admonished.

"Well, it's the truth."

"Um-um, Betty Mae, you outdid yerself today," Bud said as he took another bite.

"Oh, go on with you," Betty Mae said as she swatted his shoulder with her towel and turned to Nellie Ruth. "Sweetheart, I noticed your dress was torn. Why don't you come with me? Got a daughter just about your age that's off to school in Denver...There'll be a dress back in her room she'll never miss."

"Oh, I'm sure I can stitch this up if I..."

"Don't be silly. Now you get up and come with me, child."

Nellie Ruth looked at Tobe, who nodded and she followed Betty Mae toward the back.

"Now there goes a fine woman," Bud said as he forked another piece into his mouth, and then reached in his coat pocket, pulled out a telegram and handed it to Tobe. "By-the-by, just got this from Bass."

Tobe took the paper from Ledbetter's hand and just stared at it for a moment.

"Ain't you gonna open it?" asked Bud.

Tobe slowly opened the telegram with some trepidation and started perusing it.

"You want to read that out loud, Tobe?" John L. asked.

Tobe looked up at John L. and began to read, "Caught up with Larsons in Checotah. Stop. All dead but Ben. Stop. Jack got flesh wound in leg. Stop. Meet us tomorrow at Campbell's Crossing with wagon. Stop." Tobe looked up at a grinning Bud Ledbetter.

"Read it on the way over," Bud said.

"I will be damned...They done it," Tobe said softly.

"Hot dang!" exclaimed John L.

"Bass Reeves, tough as they come. Know I wouldn't want to tangle with him...Jack neither, fer that matter," said Ledbetter.

"'Spect that's so. I know..." Tobe stopped in mid-sentence as he noticed Betty Mae and Nellie Ruth coming across the room.

Nellie Ruth's raven hair was freshly brushed and up on the top of her head and she was wearing a blue and white gingham dress that looked as if it were made for her. The blue of the dress matched the blue of her eyes perfectly. John L.'s jaw hung open.

"John L., close yer mouth, son...you'll catch flies," Bud whispered to him.

"Oh, my, my daughter...How does that poem by Wordsworth go?...'She was a phantom of delight when first she gleamed upon my sight; A lovely apparition, sent to be a moment's ornament'...or somethin' like that...But it don't do you justice, girl," Tobe said, mesmerized by his child.

"Didn't know you read poetry, Tobe," said John L.

"Wadn't raised in a barn, boy. Wouldn't hurt you none to try some of it yerself. I read poetry to her mama most every night." Tobe turned to Betty Mae. "Like to pay you fer the dress, Betty Mae. Don't look as if it come from the local mercantile."

"Nonsense, you'll do no such thing. It never fit my baby like it does Nellie Ruth...and that settles that," she said as she gave her head a quick nod.

"Well, why don't I show you folks over to the Cattlemen's Hotel and let y'all git some rooms. You'll need to be a loadin' up 'bout dawn-thirty...I'm sure you could use some rest," said Bud.

"Like to git up in time to git some of Betty Mae's breakfast," said Tobe.

"Have my feelin's hurt if y'all didn't," she countered.

THE NATIONS

"So we got to take a hot bath and rest up in a real bed that night at the Warwick Boardin' House there in Checotah. Jack's wound turned out to be a flesh wound, sore some, but not critical. Had a nice supper 'n breakfast over to Aunt Mae's Cafe. Tecumseh offered to watch over Ben in his room at the boardin' house...chained him to a bed post."

"Take it that Ben Larson lost some of his vinegar, then?" the reporter asked.

"You could say that." Bass paused and chuckled. "Scared to death of Tecumseh. Every two, three hours, he'd take out his big Bowie, feel of Ben's hair and just grin. Doubt that Larson got much sleep that night."

"What about your boot?"

"Oh...weren't nothin', found a saddlemaker who also cobbled some on the side. Built me a new heel in less than an hour. Good as new."

Abruptly the front door opened and a very attractive, woman with wide cerulean blue eyes in her mid-forties opened Bass's front door. She carried a wicker basket with a red and white checkered cloth covering the top. Her blonde hair was done up in a bun on top of her head and she wore a full-length forest-green dress that buttoned up to her neck.

"I brought your lunch...Oh, I didn't know you had company," she said.

The reporter immediately got to his feet.

265

"It's all right, honey, this is...What did you say yer name was again, son?"

"Hogy Carter, sir. I'm a reporter with the Oklahoma Daily News, out of Oklahoma City."

"Well, Hogy Carter, this here is my daughter, Mary Alice Reeves Chisholm, I call her Mame. Think I tol' you 'bout her. She's a school teacher down to the Muskogee High School. Teaches history and literature. She's the best they got."

"Oh, Daddy, that's not so." She held her hand out to Hogy. "How do you do, Mr. Carter. Are you doing a story on my father?"

"Yes, ma'am. I've just about filled up two notebooks. I may have about enough to write a book. Your father is an amazing man."

"Knowing Dad, I suspect he has been on the modest side."

"Yes, ma'am. I've had to pry much of it out of him," Hogy glanced at Bass and smiled. "Oh, what of your brother, Hubert?"

"He owns a dairy over in Arkansas, near the old home place. He has four children. Done well for himself."

"And speakin' of children...how're my grand babies, daughter?"

"They're all fine, Daddy. Little Bass finally got over the croup. I expect he'll be over in a bit to pester you."

"They live two houses down. Mame calls it pesterin', I just calls it lovin'," Bass said to Hogy.

"I'll go fix your tray, need to warm up the stew just a bit anyway. May I fix something for you, Mr. Carter?" Mame asked.

"Take some coffee, if you have it, ma'am."

"I can handle that. You go right ahead and continue with your interview. I'll be back out in a few moments," Mame said as she headed to the kitchen.

"Now, where was I?" Bass asked.

"Checotah, you had just gotten a new heel built for your boot."

"Ah, right. Well, so we tied all the Larson's horses in a string, like we did those the Trotters had, and mounted Ben on the lead horse. Figured it would be kindly hard to run off with four horses tied behind you. Then we headed out toward Campbell's crossin'..."

***

CHAPTER ELEVEN

CHEROKEE NATION
MCINTOSH COUNTY
CAMPBELL'S RAILROAD CROSSING

Nearly fifteen miles south of Muskogee and twenty miles east of Checotah where the road to Campbell crossed the tracks, Bass, Jack, Tecumseh and with Ben in tow, had just pulled up rein. Ben was shackled to the saddle horn and his horse was being led by Tecumseh with the four remaining horses of the gang behind him in the daisy chain.

"Looks like we beat Tobe 'n them," Jack opined as he gingerly stepped off his blaze-faced gelding. He had a white bandage around his thigh. His other bandages were underneath his shirt. The minor wound on his face he preferred to let air—thought it would heal better.

"They had a bit further to go, plus drivin' the wagon," said Bass. "Might as well go sit in the shade of those trees over there 'till the 111 comes along. 'Cordin' to the station master..." Bass took out his watch from his vest pocket, flipped it open and looked at the time. "...should be along in 'bout fifteen minutes."

Tecumseh handed Ben's lead rope to Bass, got down from his Appaloosa, knelt and placed his hand on one of the steel rails.

"Train nearly three mile away," he said as he stood back up.

"Thought you were supposed to put yer ear on the rail, Tecumseh," said Jack.

"Frost this mornin'. Ear might stick."

Jack aimed an amber stream of tobacco juice at one of the rails and watched as it frosted over when it hit. "Oh...right," he replied with a grin.

Suddenly in the distance came the sound of a train whistle.

"Yer right on, Tecumseh. Yonder she comes and a touch early," said Bass as he pointed to the smoke trail that just now appeared over the tops of the trees.

"Tecumseh, know."

Iron Mountain and Southern Railway engine number 111, a old wood burner from the era of the War of Northern Aggression—as southerners termed the Civil War that had ended some twenty years earlier, pulled a wood tender, two passenger cars, two livestock cars and a caboose. Coming around the gentle bend in the tracks, Jason Blackman, the engineer spied the four waiting at the crossing. "Those marshals are right on time. No sign of that wagon that is supposed to meet them," he said to the fireman.

The soot covered fireman wiped his brow with a dirty handkerchief and leaned onto the poker he used to move burning chunks of firewood around. "No skin off'n my nose. But if we have to wait long, it will play hob with the schedule."

"We git paid by the mile, Marvin, so don't you go gittin' yerself wrapped around the axle."

The engineer pulled back on the Johnson bar to throttle back on the locomotive. The lightly laden train began to immediately reduce speed for the planned rendezvous. As the train began to slow, the engineer sequentially bled off steam pressure. Bass and the others moved their horses back away from the track to reduce the possibility of their mounts spooking.

As the engine approached slowly, Bass nudged his horse up alongside the cab. "Ease 'er up with the caboose just past the crossin', if'n you don't mind. Gonna need to load up some spare horses in one of yer livestock cars," he shouted up to the engineer. "Then blow yer whistle…I 'spect the wagon ain't far off. Let 'em know we are here."

The engineer nodded and held up his thumb. Several travelers in the passenger car had their heads out the windows, anxious expressions on their faces until they saw the badge on Bass's vest. The relief was obvious. Train robberies had fallen off in the Territory somewhat, but still occurred on occasion.

When the train came to a complete stop, the conductor made the announcement to the passengers, "You folks can git out and stretch your legs a bit. We have to wait on some more passengers. Don't wander off too far...Hate to leave you behind."

The engineer gave the whistle two long blasts.

Two miles west of the crossing, John L. nudged Nellie Ruth. "Hear that, honey? Couldn't be more than a couple miles to the crossin'."

"That's good, sweetheart, 'cause this wagon is not my idea of a very good way to cross the country."

"Our ancestors made it all right."

"They didn't have a choice...Plus they weren't carrying a bunch of outlaws in the back."

Her father, Tobe, took another sip of laudanum. He set the bottle on the bench seat between his legs and pressed the cork down tightly to seal it off before he stuck it back into an outside pocket of his coat.

"How's the arm doing?" John L. asked.

"Still a might sore. Don't think I care to try to make it all the way back to Sand Springs if I had to sit this hard ridin' monstrosity another couple days."

"Daddy, you are gonna be all right aren't you? I'm not used to you carrying on like this."

"I'm not used to being shot up, if that's what you mean...I was a bunch younger when I got wounded in the war."

"Tried to teach him to duck, but you know what they say about old dogs and new tricks," John L. deadpanned.

"Boy, this arm will heal and you know what they say about paybacks."

Nellie Ruth eyed the two men in her life and smiled. "Don't make me get a switch after you two."

She snuggled next to John L. and leaned her head against his left shoulder. Boot trotted alongside the wagon and made frequent forays into the scattered brush to search for the scent of a rabbit or covey of quail. Tobe watched him for a couple minutes before making an observation.

"I bet that silly dog runs three miles for every one we travel on the road. He'll probably sleep all the way to Tulsa on the train."

"I'll be right behind him," added John L. "Didn't sleep well last night for some reason."

Nellie Ruth squeezed his hand then patted his left leg. "Me neither, honey. Me neither."

Thirty minutes later, the three spotted the six car train stopped just past the dirt road crossing that was headed east toward Webber's Falls then to Fort Smith. Four of the dead outlaw's mounts were being loaded by Tecumseh and a brakeman into the livestock car. The Tumbleweed Wagon rolled to a stop near the train. Passengers looked at the well known conveyance and whispered among themselves about the famous outlaw, Belle Starr, in the back.

Jack motioned to a couple curious onlookers. "Step back folks, don't need nobody getting hurt." He tied his horse to the back of the wagon and then limped up forward to assist Tobe descend from the bench seat.

John L. set the brake, stood up, stretched, climbed down and then reached up to help Nellie Ruth. "Come on down, honey, these here folks are waiting on us."

"Can't be done with this wagon any sooner."

"Tobe, got a little chore for you in Sand Springs, if you are up to it," Jack said as Tobe alighted on the gravel road.

"Surely, my pleasure. I may have to get my deputy to lend a hand."

"Simple chore, really. Got four horses and tack from the Larson gang. We get to keep the proceeds from the sale of confiscated or abandoned property. Helps pay off the funeral costs when we don't bring the wanted suspects in for trial."

"I'll make sure it gets done proper."

"You can wire us the money in Fort Smith. Keep ten dollars for your end of the deal."

"I'd shake on it, Jack, but this wing's a bit sore, yet."

"Don't mean a thing. A man of character don't have to prove it ev'ry day. I want to thank you and the boy for steppin' in when we needed you."

"I'll pass the good words on to 'im," Tobe said as he smiled and looked across to the other side of the wagon at his daughter and his deputy. "Think the boy grew an inch or two in the past week."

Bass stepped around the wagon, approached John L. and extended his hand.

"Son, we appreciate all you and Tobe did to help us out. I'll make sure the newspapers and the Judge hear about your service. You, sir, are a good man."

"Thanks, Marshall Reeves. I'm glad it worked out like it did for you and Jack. It was a real honor workin' with you. If'n you are ever are up our way again, drop in and say howdy. "

"That's a promise," Bass said as the two men shook hands. "Guess, we better tend to those prisoners. Trains have schedules, I'm told."

Bass picked up the reins to his horse and led it back to the wagon, followed by John L., where he untied the young deputy's horse and looped his horse's lead rope into the iron ring. He unlocked the tailgate and let it fall with solid *thunk* as John L. led his and Tobe's horses toward the cattle car.

Bass climbed up into the wagon, turned around and assisted the manacled Ben, who had been led over by Tecumseh, up into the bed. He sat Ben next to Preacher Budlow and shackled his ankle restraints to the heavy logging chain stapled down the center.

The outlaw's head and hand were bandaged and his chin hung despondently on his chest. Boone rode on the other side next to the new addition, Belle Starr. Bass moved to the front and unshackled Jed and then moved back to the rear to jump down.

"Marshal, you think the judge will go light on me since I give myself up to Marshal Ledbetter?" Belle asked as he moved past her.

"Don't know, Belle, he don't take kindly to horse thieves."

"But, I told you I found those horses."

"Yer odds on convincin' Judge Parker of that 'er slim at best. Didn't have yer brand on 'em, nor did you have a bill of sale. You dance...you gotta pay the fiddler, Belle...But it was a good thing I didn't have ta come lookin' fer ya."

Bass turned, jumped the three feet to the ground and reached back to give Jed a hand. "Jed, I never did believe you killed that drover, but I had to have proof...You understand?"

"Yessir, I understands."

"Findin' that money belt in Larson's belongin's...Well, that's proof enough."

"I wasn't worried, Marshal...A man either does right or he don't."

Bass nodded and grinned and then motioned to Jack who was holding the reins to a horse. He led the copper sorrel with three stockings and a sock up and handed the reins, his Henry rifle, a small leather pouch and other belongings to him.

"Jed, there's a good horse and saddle. Don't think Wes Larson will be aneedin' 'em nomore," Bass said.

"Thank you, Marshal. Now I kin ride back to Sand Springs and git Jacob."

"Jacob?" Jack asked.

"Yessir, Jacob is my mule."

They chuckled—Jed mounted and swung the horse around. "So long...meby I'll see y'all in Fort Smith. Thought I might apply for a marshallin' job." He held up the small brown leather pouch. "First, I gotta deliver this to Lorena Matthews down to

Gainesville. I give my word to a dyin' man...Ain't nothin' no stronger'n that."

"Man either does right or he don't...We would be proud to have you ride with us, Jed...We will put in a good word fer you to the judge," said Bass.

"I would appreciate that, Marshal." He rode up close to the wagon and leaned down. "So long Preacher. I'll remember you in my prayers."

"Thanky kindly. Good Lord go with you," Preacher said as he doffed his battered old top hat.

With a final wave, Jed rode away southwest toward Gainesville, Texas. Bass turned to Tecumseh.

"Tecumseh, reckon there ain't much to say but how much we 'preciate yer help and we're all terrible sorry about Lyman...Is there anythin' we can do?"

"No, Marshal. It falls to me to tell his family. Tecumseh was proud to ride with the Tumbleweed Wagon, the great wagon of the law, and to serve with you and Jack...Shee-ah! I go," he said as he wheeled his horse about and rode off south.

Bass waved his hat at the conductor to signal that the train could resume its trip. Then he helped Jack climb aboard the wagon and take the reins. Bass mounted up and, riding along side, waved back at Tobe, John L. and Nellie Ruth standing on the rear platform of the second passenger car as the train began to chug off with great belches of black smoke from the diamond stack. The engineer blew the whistle twice. Boot sat beside

Tobe—raised one paw and waved it at Bass and Jack as the wagon rolled off east from the crossing.

Preacher gazed wistfully after Jed's retreating figure. There was a small amount of moisture in his eyes—a dampness not all together attributable to his advanced age. Then he took out his tin of snuff and dusted a small portion into his lower lip. As he was about to settle his brass-rimmed spectacles on his nose, the wagon hit a large rock and the glasses bounced from his face and fell to the bed. "Drat this accursed wagon...Oh, Lord Almighty, hear me now. I don't mean to be always complainin', but this road is all fired rough and hard! If you will recollect, Lord, it is written in the Book of Isaiah that 'every valley shall be exhalted and every hill shall be made low; and the crooked shall be made straight, and the rough places plain.' Now, I don't mean to be a criticizing, Lord, but this is one stretch of road you musta forgot about. It is rough and it is bumpy and hard on the brittle bones and backside of thy weary servant. Could you smooth it out just a mite? I don't care a jot or a tittle how you do it; cause you know a heap sight more that I do about how to do things. But do it Lord!...If it be thy will...ya understand. Amen," he said as the wagon continued off toward the horizon and Fort Smith, Arkansas.

SAND SPRINGS
CHEROKEE NATION

The sun was low in the sky when the Number 116 engine from Tulsa, blew its whistle a quarter mile from town. Molly Allgood sat in her wheel chair on the passenger platform beside the station—looked up from her reading and closed the book. The red and black coal-fired engine pulled the tender, two passenger cars and a single cattle car ahead of a red caboose into the small station and chugged to a stop beside the platform.

The portly conductor opened the forward door to the first passenger car and stepped off the short stairs leading down to the wood planks. "Sand Springs! End of the Line! Everybody off!" he yelled.

Molly was excited as she looked for familiar faces to disembark. A pair of drummers—salesmen for a patent medicine company—got off first, followed by a school-age girl with a small bag made of carpet material with two leather handles. "Do you see them?" she asked Sky.

"No, ma'am...Not yet."

The engineer vented steam from the boiler, obscuring the view for a couple of seconds. Then the figure of a tall slim man appeared stepping down the steps on the other side of the steam cloud.

"Is that John L.?" she asked.

"Possible," grunted Sky as he watched the man turn and reach back up to the steps.

When the steam dissipated slightly, the hourglass figure of a young woman in a blue and white gingham dress was visible as she took the hand of the young man standing on the platform.

"It's Nellie Ruth...She's got a new dress!" exclaimed Molly.

John L. helped her down and turned back to the steps. Tobe carefully exited the train car to insure he didn't bang his injured right arm on the narrow door frame. His signature white mustache curled up in a broad smile as he gazed across the platform at Molly. Boot jumped down the steps and headed at a dead run toward Molly and Sky.

"I got it from here, son. Why don't you see to the horses?"

John L. turned and headed back to the stock car. Nellie Ruth slipped her arm in her father's good one as the two walked toward Molly. She was rubbing Boot's ears while every muscle in his body seemed to move at the same time, reveling in the attention. Molly gave Boot a final pat and started rolling her wheelchair without assistance—she closed the distance between the three.

"Nellie Ruth! I was so worried!"

"I'm sorry to give you such a fright. But the marshals took care of the Larson gang...forever," she said as she bent over and gave Molly a kiss on her cheek.

"That's welcome news...Tobe, honey, how's that arm?" she asked as she checked out the sling.

"No hill for a stepper."

"Ain't that just like a man? Can't even get a straight answer out...Girl! Is that what I think it is?" Molly asked as she glanced down at Nellie Ruth's hand.

Nellie Ruth held out her left hand where Molly could see it better. The tiny diamond on her ring finger wasn't large by any standards, but no one could tell that to Nellie Ruth. "John L. asked me last night...Bought the ring in Muskogee this morning!"

"I bet he didn't want you to change your mind."

"Isn't it lovely?"

"Yes, child, it is...Would you do me a favor young lady? Can you check on John L. and the horses?...I think your father wants to ask me something."

Nellie Ruth and Tobe looked at Molly with questions in their eyes, and then exchanged glances as Boot cocked his head. Tobe shrugged, but Nellie Ruth went to check on her fiancé's horse wrangling.

Tobe reached out and took Molly's proffered hand. She looked at him with a softness he had never seen. "I never knew how much you two meant to me until I thought I lost you. You asked me a dozen times and I foolishly said no. Can you find it in your heart to give an old bulldog another chance?"

Tobe stood mute, almost thunderstruck by what he had just heard. Slowly, he knelt beside her. Boot sat down beside him and rose up into a begging position. "Molly Allgood...I love you with all my heart and soul. Will you do me a great honor and marry me?"

She nodded as tears welled up in her golden brown eyes. "Yes...the answer is yes."

Tobe leaned in and kissed her tenderly as Sky smiled and waved to John L. and Nellie Ruth. The engineer blew a blast from his whistle that the whole town could hear.

FORT SMITH, ARKANSAS
JUDGE PARKER' COURT ROOM

A gaunt, red rimmed and hollow eyed Ben Larson stood in front of Judge Parker with his head bowed, hands and feet shackled.

THE NATIONS

In the courtroom were the parents of the young couple from the stage coach; the widow of the store-keep in Wewoka; Marshal Hank McGann's widow being supported by her brother-in-law, Jack McGann; the family of the banker in Bartlesville and other families from all over the Nations. All were there to see the last survivor of the notorious Larson gang sentenced. At that particular time in the history of the Nations, Judge Parker's verdicts were not subject to appeal. He had absolute power to administer justice as he saw fit in full accordance with the law.

Judge Parker glared down at Ben from his five foot high cherry bench and spoke with that booming voice that was feared by all—miscreants and his marshals as well.   "Benjamin Josiah Larson!"

Ben jumped at the mention of his name as it reverberated throughout the court room. He looked up for a brief moment at Parker then just as quickly, his eyes went back to the floor.

"The jury has found you guilty of complicity to commit murder...fourteen counts." The judge paused and seemed to be burning holes through Ben with his gaze, and then continued, "Vicarious accomplice to murder...eighteen counts. And murder in the first degree...six counts. The total absence of remorse typifies your sociopathic nature. It is painfully obvious to this court that you have no redeeming qualities and are a scourge to all decent people. In the Decalogue or as they are known, the Ten Commandments, the fifth commandment of the Augustinian division is, 'Thou shall not commit murder'. The Hebrew Torah contains numerous prohibitions against unlawful killing, but also allows for justified killing in the context of

281

warfare in 1 Kings 2:5–6; self-defense, Exodus 22:2–3; and capital punishment in Leviticus 20:9–16. The New Testament or Christian Bible is in agreement that murder is a grave moral evil, and maintains the Old Testament view of bloodguilt.

"You and that pack of wild dogs, curly wolves and highbinders you ran with killed for the pure joy of killing, without regard to gender or concern for moral turpitude. You, sir, are an abomination in the eyes of this court and, in fact, all mankind, and you and your type should be scourged from the face of this earth." He paused again. "The authority given to me here in the Western District of Arkansas by the United States Department of Justice will allow me to dispense the full weight of this court upon your worthless head. Even though my personal opinion is that the death penalty should be abolished, in your case, by God, I am happy and privileged to exercise the full and maxim punishment for your plethora of heinous crimes. I know the punishment I am about to pronounce will not restore the many lives you have taken or were complicitous in taking, but at least the survivors and family members will receive a modicum of satisfaction of seeing your life snuffed out at the end of Maledon's noose.

"The annual miracle of the year's awakening will soon come to pass, but you won't be here...The rivulet will run its purling course to the sea, the timid desert flowers will put forth their tender shoots, the glorious valleys of this imperial domain will blossom as the rose...still you won't be here. From every tree top, some wild wood songster will carol his mating song, butterflies will sport in the sunshine, the busy bee will hum happily as it pursues its accustomed vocation...the gentle breezes will tease the tassels of wild grasses and all nature...but you won't be here to enjoy it, for I command the Sheriff of Sebastian County to convey your worthless hide to George Maledon on the 18th day of June, the year of our Lord, 1885, whereupon he will hang you by the neck until you are dead, dead, dead...And may your abominable soul burn in hell for all eternity...Get him out of my sight," Judge Parker said as he slammed his gavel.

FORT SMITH, ARKANSAS
GALLOWS
JUNE 18, 1885

A crowd of over a thousand people from as far away as four hundred miles, and including three states plus the Oklahoma Territory and the Indian Nations, gathered in front of the twelve man gallows for the public hanging of one person—Ben Larson.

A line of Deputy US Marshals kept the throng that included men, women and even children, from crowding too close to Judge Parker's gibbet. There were four separate photographers between the marshals and the gallows, each hoping they had the best angle for the hanging. A temporary fence had been erected and tickets had been sold by the county at fifty cents per person to help hold down the expected crowd. The enclosure, however, was packed and yet twice the number milled about outside the gates and required additional marshals to maintain order.

The diminutive George Maledon in his traditional black suit and his usual dual revolvers strapped about his waist walked across the catwalk to the gallows where he had previously set in the center—Larson's noose. He turned and motioned to the marshal at the side gate. The man opened it—two marshals armed with Winchesters entered, side-by-side followed by two other marshal escorting Ben—shackled hand and foot—one on each arm. They were followed by two additional marshals also with repeating rifles.

As the procession made its way toward the gallows, Ben became increasingly agitated, especially when he passed Preacher Morse at bottom of the stairway reading in his Bible from the book of Psalms, "'Yea, though I walk through the valley of the shadow of death, I will fear no evil: For Thou art with me; Thy rod and thy staff, they comfort me...'"

The two marshals literally had to drag him up the thirteen steps—Ben screaming and crying at every step closer to his death. Once at the top, Ben was positioned over the center most trap door, his wild eyes jerking back and forth, while Maledon put the black hood over his head, only partially muting his blubbering screams. He then positioned the freshly oiled new rope noose around Ben's neck—the thirteen coils on the left side and Maledon's traditional slack loop draped over the top of his head. Ben's knees began to buckle from fear, but the marshals on either side held him upright.

Bass, Jack, Tecumseh, Tobe and John L. stood in front of the marshals that were holding the crowd back directly in the center of the gallows.

"Never thought I'd see the day I'd look forward to seein' a man die," said Tobe.

"I tol' the little worm he'd be asqueelin' like a pig under a gate," commented Jack.

"Think meby what the Judge said was right," said Bass.

"What was that?" asked John L.

"It is not the severity of the punishment that is the deterrent, but the certainty of it."

Abruptly, George Maledon pulled the lever and the crowd gasped almost in unison as Ben's shackled feet dropped through the trap door. They jerked twice and then once more—then were still. The last of the Larson gang was dead.

***

EPILOGUE

MUSKOGEE, OKLAHOMA
JANUARY 15, 1910

Hogy Carter walked from the cemetery back to his hotel. In his room, he sat down to finish the epilogue to his story about Bass Reeves and The Nations:

Bass Reeves was buried today, January 15th. He died on January 12, 1910 from complications of Bright's disease. I had the honor to be among the some two-thousand people who attended his funeral today, including the governor of Oklahoma, the honorable Charles N. Haskell. The Muskogee Phoenix wrote of the legendary lawman, "In the history of the early days of Eastern Oklahoma the name of Bass Reeves has a place in the front rank among those who cleansed out the old Indian Territory of outlaws and desperadoes. No story of the conflict of government's officers with those outlaws, which ended only a few years ago with the rapid filling up of the territory with people, can be complete without mention of the Negro who died three days ago."

I suppose one of the greatest tributes to his devotion to duty and his own personal honor, was when one of his sons killed his wife in a jealous rage. A warrant was issued for his arrest. Bass volunteered to serve the warrant saying, "He is my son; it is up to me to bring him in." Bass brought him in; Judge Parker tried him, found him guilty of manslaughter and sentenced him to twenty years in the prison at McAlister. Bass Reeves was one of the greatest peace officers in the history of the American western frontier and is said by many to be the best Deputy United States Marshal in the long storied history of the Marshal's service.

Hogy stopped writing for a moment, opened his leather portfolio that he kept his notes in and pulled out a yellowed scrap of paper that Bass had given him in their final interview. He had told him it was a note he had found wadded up in the bottom of the wagon after they had dropped off the prisoners at Maledon's jail. It had apparently been written by Ben Larson during the final leg of the trip into Fort Smith. *I guess it's like that poem Rufus Buck wrote to his mother they found on a scrap of paper in his cell after the Judge had him and his gang hung back in '96,* he thought. Hogy carefully unfolded it and read the poorly printed page again for the umpteenth time—it read like a poem or maybe even a song:

Farmer,Stienke

Shackled to the bed of this Tumbleweed Wagon,
  Ridin' to a place where outlaws die;
Fort Smith's dead ahead of this Tumbleweed Wagon,
  I can see the gallows yonder 'gainst the sky.

Too much time for thinkin' in this Tumbleweed Wagon,
  Only grief and trouble on my mind.
Wouldn't be a ridin' this Godforsaken wagon,
  If it wadn't for the gal I left behind.

Oh, Lord deliver me from this Tumbleweed Wagon,
  I promise I'll repent of all my sins,
Lord God! Please spare me the hangin' judge's vengeance,
  I swear I'll never do no wrong again.

I wonder. How do men end up in this Tumbleweed Wagon?
  With the prairie wind a-moanin' through their souls?
It's a one way trip to hell in this Tumbleweed Wagon,
  And the Devil don't give no pardons nor paroles.

Oh, Lord deliver me from this Tumbleweed Wagon,
  I promise I'll repent of all my sins,
Lord God! Please spare me the hangin' judge's vengeance,
  I swear I'll never do no wrong again.

Oh, Lord, deliver me from this Tumbleweed Wagon,
  I promise I'll repent of all my sins,

THE NATIONS

Lord God! Please spare me the hangin' judge's vengeance,
I swear I'll never do no wrong again.
I swear I'll never do no wrong again.

Hogy carefully folded the note back up, returned it to its place in his portfolio, picked up his pencil and continued the epilogue:

So it was, in the twenty-one years Judge Isaac C. Parker presided over the Indian Territory from his court in Fort Smith, Arkansas, 13,490 cases—344 of which were for capital offenses—appeared before him; seventy-nine men danced on his gallows, thirty white, twenty-six Indian and twenty-three black. Sixty-five of his marshals gave their lives in the field in the line of duty—one third of their number. Bass Reeves was one of those who survived. He was the first black Deputy United States Marshal to be commissioned west of the Mississippi. He served 32 years as a Deputy Marshal and is regarded by many as the best lawman in western history, regardless of color, with over three thousand felony arrests and, by his own account, fourteen men killed in the line of duty, twice as many as James Butler "Wild Bill" Hickok. Bass was never wounded in his long career, even though he had numerous close calls—he had his hat shot off; his gun belt shot off; a button shot from his vest; the heel from his boot; and his reins shot in two on various and sundry occasions.

The Oklahoma Territory and the Indian Nations were combined and admitted to the union, November, 1907 as the state of Oklahoma, the forty-sixth state of the United States of

America. Bass's long time partner and best friend, Jack McGann, married a widow, Angie O'Reilly in 1894. They never had any children. He settled down in 1896 to become city marshal of Tishomingo, Oklahoma, formerly the capital of the Chickasaw Nation. Jack was shot in the back by a drunk in 1908 at the age of seventy-three. Bass, Jed Neal, and John L. Patrick attended his funeral and were pallbearers.

Neeley McClaren kept his word and turned himself in as promised; Horatio T. Budlow kept preaching, in jail as often as not; Jed Neal became a highly respected Deputy US Marshal and died of pneumonia in 1909—he was buried in Fannin County, Texas.

Tobe died in 1899 of congestive heart failure; he was survived by his widow, Molly Bassett, his daughter Nellie Ruth Patrick and eight grand children. His daughter's husband, John L. Patrick, served as town marshal of Sand Springs, Oklahoma for ten years and then was elected to the Oklahoma state senate, where he is currently serving his fourth term. The Tumbleweed Wagon was retired in 1896 after Judge Parker passed away at the age of fifty-eight. The judge was black of hair and beard when he assumed the bench in 1875 at the age of thirty-seven, but the same was snow white, just twenty-one years later. Some say it was because of the stress of the job...or of those seventy-nine souls that departed this world from his gallows.

Bud Ledbetter, Heck Thomas, Bill Tilghman and Chris Madson, the Oklahoma Guardsmen, turned to movie making as actors and writers. Tilghman wrote and directed the silent film,

"The Passing of the Oklahoma Outlaws", because he felt Hollywood was over glamorizing the old west outlaw. The Guardsmen played themselves as did Arkansas Tom Jones (Roy Dougherty), the only survivor of the Doolin–Dalton Gang. If the fates had been more kind, there should have been a fifth Guardsman of Oklahoma—Bass Reeves.

****

PREVIEW OF THE NEXT

BLACK EAGLE FORCE NOVEL
by
BUCK STIENKE & KEN FARMER

Coming Soon

BLACK EAGLE FORCE: BLOOD IVORY

CHAPTER ONE

CAPE TOWN
SOUTH AFRICA

The first orange rays of the South African sun illuminated Table Mountain and her virtually sheer red cliffs to the north of Cape Town long before the sprawling city of one million stirred for the Monday morning grind. Six members of the Inkatha Freedom Party, or IFP, waited impatiently in a run down hotel room for three others. The sound of a noisy Nissan pickup truck, locally called a *bakkie*, with a leaky exhaust manifold could be heard as it pulled up in front of the building. Mandla Ndebele cursed aloud as he pulled the tattered curtains apart and watched Andile Mathebula and his two younger sisters disembark from the dirty white truck and slam the doors.

"Damn you, Andile, why can't you ever be on time?" he said to no one in particular. "And you don't have to wake up the entire neighborhood...stupid jackal."

"Calm down," directed the ostensible leader of the splinter faction, Londisizwe Sibanyoni, in a deep bass voice. The six foot, ten-inch tall Sibanyoni glared at Mandla, then crossed his long legs at the ankles. He looked over to his cousin, Nahila, and smiled. "How about another cup of coffee? It's been a short night."

She arose, walked to the tiny kitchenette and poured a cup of the brew in a cracked ceramic cup. Almost six feet tall, the twenty-four year old had fallen in with her firebrand relative after finding no work in her trained field of accounting.

Sibanyoni wanted so much for his Zulu kinsman and was tired of waiting for the mainstream politicians to make it happen. His plan to kidnap a senior executive of the De beers Corporation would pay handsomely and quickly—at least according to him. Now that the day of action had arrived, a certain air of calmness seemed to settle in on Sibanyoni.

Across the dirt street, a pair of dusty speckled red roosters took turns greeting the dawn. Dogs barked in response to the crowing, and lights began to flicker in windows below the third floor of the wood frame hotel where the six conspirators awaited their comrades. A series of knocks came from the door. Two knocks, followed by a single, then two in rapid succession were clearly heard. Sibanyoni tilted his head toward the door as he looked at Mandla. The lanky twenty-nine year old pulled a Yugoslavian M57 pistol in 7.62mmx25mm from his waistband and he approached the door. He checked the safety in the *off* position as he thumbed the hammer back to full cock and addressed the unseen persons outside. "Who is there?"

"Zulu breakfast service," came the coded reply.

Mandla lowered the pistol and hid it behind his thigh as he turned the corroded brass handle on the door, pulling the door open wide.

"Come in. You are late," he said and scowled.

"Not my fault. Couldn't get the truck started," Andile explained.

"I thought Londisizwe told you to check it out before today and fix whatever it needed."

Andile shot an angry look at Mandla as did his two sisters, who had entered the hotel room close behind him.

"Hey, I'm not made of mon..."

"Stop it!" Sibanyoni ordered. "And close the door, woman! Just because you were born in a mud hut, you don't have to act like it!"

The youngest woman, only nineteen, wore a traditional white cotton sari wrapped around her long lithe frame. Her battered rubber flip-flops had seen better days, but she moved with a certain air of grace belying her poverty as she turned to close the door.

Sibanyoni rose to his feet, Andile bowing to him slightly.

"My apologies, Commander. The battery cable was corroded. I thought..."

"You and your other assistants are here. That is all that matters now. You have the RPGs?"

"Yes sir. Three, like you requested, hidden in the bakkie bed. I procured pistols for the two lookouts as a backup."

"Can your women shoot?"

"I taught them myself."

"Fine. We'll review the plan one more time and then we need to leave to get into position. The target will depart for the mine in less than an hour."

The other eight assailants gathered round the small coffee table to review the satellite photos of the roadway and the corresponding street maps of northern Cape Town. He pointed at the helipad located three miles from the executive's home, then moved to a spot three-quarters of a mile back down the hill. "From here, there is only one way in or out to the helipad. We'll set up the station wagon here," he said pointing to the intersection where the lower lookout would be stationed. "Any questions so far? Now is the time to ask if you are not sure."

The others shook their heads and Sibanyoni continued.

Across town, inside the compound surrounding the estate of De Beers diamond company Executive Vice President Georg M. Bakken; a tall slender figure turned off the shower and dried his shoulder length premature silver hair with a thick white Egyptian cotton towel. He had been up since 5 AM with stretching, yoga exercises and a martial arts Kata to help keep his lean forty year old frame limber.

His Kata of choice was known as *Three Steps,* which involved a series of moves designed to defend against attacks with one move, followed by a counter attack involving two moves. There were designed moves for incoming assaults from bare handed attacks as well as knife, club or other weapon. The steps were even broken down into response to various directions of assault. Mark had trained for many years and was now an eighth degree black belt in Akido.

Slipping on a terry-cloth robe, he sat down to review security camera footage from the previous night. Nothing from the eight external wall sensors or cameras indicated a security concern, as was usual. The night security detail would have notified him had there been an incident, but his training led him to double check every day before he turned to the sixty-inch monitor on the wall and picked up the remote. *Skynews* broadcasted the world events that may have concern for his employer.

He checked the headlines, and then switched over to the local news. Living in South Africa for over a year had made the transition easier for Mark Ingram, as he had been able to pick up a considerable amount of the Zulu language from earlier posting in east Africa. Besides his native English, that he spoke with a distinct west Texas twang, Mark was conversationally fluent in French, German, Dutch, Portuguese, and Vietnamese—with a working knowledge of Chinese and Malay. Nothing out of the ordinary had come across the local news channel, so he slid open the closet door in the guest quarters, pulled out a tailored silk and wool blend gray pinstriped suit, a white long-sleeved oxford cloth shirt and a blue-gray tie that coordinated nicely with his blue eyes and laid them out on his bed.

Mark shaved, combed his silver hair straight back and dressed. He then reached onto the night stand and retrieved his Colt

Gold Cup .45 and slipped it into the shoulder holster under his left arm. The saddle colored leather nestled organically around the stainless slide—the eight round magazine stuffed with Glaser Safety Slugs. Each of the 145 grain projectiles contained hundreds of number 9 lead shot under a blue plastic ballistic ball that facilitated flawless feeding. Two spare magazines that hung inverted under his right arm carried an additional eight rounds each. Three special fifteen round extended mags rode in a custom designed carrier that laid down the center of his back. Any hit from the deadly rounds in the center mass of an aggressor would result in a one way trip to the morgue.

He slipped the gray suit jacket on and headed out the door to breakfast in the dining room. The guest quarters was situated only seventy-five yards from the main house. Mark made the crossing of the closely manicured lawn and listened to the first morning calls from native birds as dawn broke on the hillside villa. He entered the eight thousand square foot house through the French doors overlooking the gardens and made his way to the kitchen.

"Morning, Mr. Ingram," the towering executive chef Ibi Obongo said with a ready smile.

"Nice day, isn't it Ibi?"

"Nothing finer than a spring day," he replied. "Anything special for you today, sir?"

"Boerewars or sosatie with some of your famous pap would do nicely."

"Have some fresh off the braai, Mister."

Mark nodded as picked up a mug of fresh tea from the Turkish samovar atop the marble counter. *Working for a wealthy business executive had its perks*, he contemplated as he took his place at the otherwise empty table. Before Mark had half finished his first mug of tea, Ibi silently moved beside him and laid the white china plate filled with a tasty locally produced antelope sausage and a single marinated lamb shish kebob beside a serving of krummelpap, or crumb porridge, a local staple similar to polenta. Mark likened it to grits and preferred to eat it with salt, pepper and a pat of real butter. Chef Obongo could make Mark anything he requested for breakfast, but preferred a hot protein meal to start the day off.

"Looks great, Ibi. Thanks."

"My pleasure, Mister Ingram,"

Mark picked up his silverware and began to dig in to the antelope sausage. The balance of spices accentuated the natural flavors of the wild game. Cumin, paprika, salt, onion powder and garlic powder, with a mix of hot dried peppers Mark could not identify peaked his curiosity. *Gonna have to get this recipe from Ibi. Would be great with mule deer.*

Mark pressed the button on the center garage door where the armored Suburban was parked. As the metal door rolled up into position, he carried a heavy black ballistic nylon bag and approached the vehicle. He set the bag on the ground, pulled a small device from his outside coat pocket and tapped a couple commands on the key pad. Sophisticated electronic sensors scanned all the frequencies used for remotely detonated devices and he made a slow pass around the white SUV. When he had completed a full 360 degree scan, he tapped another code and a green clear icon appeared on the screen. He slipped the scanner back in his pocket then walked to a tall cabinet on the back wall of the huge forty-by-sixty foot garage. From there, he grabbed a long metal telescoping pole with a ten-inch lighted mirror on one end. He pushed a small black button on the butt end, illuminating a string of white LED lights surrounding the mirror. Mark checked the interior of each wheel well and the complete underside of the vehicle in just under seven minutes. Once he was assured no visible modifications had been made to the vehicle, he returned the device to its storage locker and secured it.

His procedure rarely changed. He was meticulous, thoughtful and completely professional about his work. He knew more than his employer's life was on the line when the two of them were out of the protection of the security details at corporate headquarters. Executive bodyguards were often the first to die in encounters with terrorist groups and kidnappers.

There was no place for complacency in his vocabulary or his life. His grandfather had taught him that on the ranch in the Big Bend area of west Texas. The US Marines had reinforced it in boot camp and in recon training. By the time he finished Marine sniper training, he was one of the most deadly men on the planet. His shock of shoulder length silver gray hair was somewhat of a throwback to his west Texas roots. When Mark was a kid, one of the ranch hands had been half Comanche Indian. He was older and had fought in Vietnam as a Marine.

He told tales of his wartime experiences in a casual, non-boastful manner that always impressed the young Mark. After the war he had returned to ranching and grown his hair long, securing it behind him with simple leather thong. Mark always thought it made him look invincible—so once he was not bound by the regulations of the Marine Corps—he let his hair grow long too. The week before he shipped out to Saudi Arabia in support of Operation Desert Storm, his Comanche friend presented him with his own Ka-Bar fighting knife.

"Running Wolf, I cannot accept your knife. I know how much it meant to you in 'Nam."

"Then my friend, you know just how much I want you to to have it. It has good medicine. Killed many Cong plus saved my life many times. Maybe it can do the same for you."

From that day forth, the Ka-Bar seldom left his side. It accounted for several Iraqi soldiers who overran the tiny little town in Kuwait when Saddam's forces attempted a counterattack. His M-14 may have fallen out of favor with the military brass and bean counters, but Mark never felt undergunned with the bigger 7.62mm round. But that morning, the need for smaller close-in firepower dictated the use of a Sig 556 with a short barrel and a folding stock. It fit into the black nylon gym bag along with eight 30 round mags filled with twenty-eight 55 grain hollowpoints and two tracers at the bottom of each mag. At the end of a magazine it was sometimes nice to have a reminder that the time to swap out for another had come. Besides, with numerous vehicles in urban fighting, the ability to set an opponent's punctured fuel tank afire could be just what the doctor ordered. Every little advantage helped, and Mark recognized them all.

He used the remote to unlock the Suburban and slid the black bag into the front passenger seat. Satisfied he had secured the vehicle, he walked back into the house to pick up his first three passengers of the day—the Bakken children—two boys and a girl, all of whom attended the International School in Cape Town, a highly respected as well as well protected school for the children of diplomats and businessmen alike.

As the three kids ran out of the house, Mark could not help but smile. He tried to keep a professional emotional distance from the children, but was not entirely successful. The three towheaded youths bubbled with enthusiasm and possessed a playfulness appropriate to their age. They always were fascinated by Uncle Mark's sliver hair. He had tried to explain the premature graying process to them, but to no avail, so he just took the familiarity in stride. If truth were told, he would have been honored to have the children as his own. But the realities of his lifestyle left him single and childless. He ushered them and their backpacks into the Suburban and securely belted them in for the ride. As they passed the main house, their mother waved out the bay window at the passing SUV. In the left rear seat, Sylvia, the youngest blew a kiss to their mother. Sibyl Bakken could not see inside the darkly tinted windows, but blew a kiss back. Mark waved as the electronic sensors picked up the vehicle's identification chip and opened the reinforced ornate metal gate, allowing the big vehicle to exit.

Driving from the right side of the car on the left side of the road had taken almost three months for him to feel natural and instinctive.

Sibanyoni sat in the passenger seat of the late model gray Ford Territory TX, driven by his younger cousin, Nahila. The SUV would not draw undue attention in the predominately white suburbs as the four Zulu activists lead the two other vehicles across town to their planned abduction site. Behind them, at a discreet distance, was a blue late model Volvo V70 station wagon—Mandla Ndebeleat was at the wheel—with Andile and his sisters bringing up the rear in his well-worn pickup truck. Magnetic signs proclaiming to be a legitimate lawn and landscaping service had been added to the doors of the truck shortly before the group departed their meeting place. A pair of worn out weed eaters and leaf blowers were tossed in as camouflage atop bags of lawn clippings that concealed the deadly Chinese-made RPG-7s in the bottom of the truck bed.

Sweat formed across Mandla's brow as he eagerly anticipated the confrontation. All the details had been reviewed, the weather was cooperating and, as far as the group was concerned, their operational security was air tight. He took one hand off the steering wheel and wiped his forehead against the sleeve of his light blue cotton shirt. His accomplice in the left seat was still cool and collected as the lead Ford SUV turned north on Hillcrest Drive and began the climb toward the ambush site. He noted Mandala's actions and smiled. "What's the matter? Case of nerves?"

"Screw you, Simi! I'll do my part, you do yours!"

Simi laughed heartily while he mentally reviewed the blocking and assault positions assigned to each person. The road narrowed as it approached the helipad summit with steep hillsides on both sides of the two lane road. No houses or driveways offered escape avenues, and Mandla had the job of blocking the downhill escape route by closing off the roadway from behind of the targeted Suburban. With overwhelming firepower, the team planned to disable the SUV, kill the single body guard, and disappear into the teaming city below with their precious De beers executive hidden inside the blackened windows of the Ford Territory TX.

Mark eased up to the intersection and pulled to a stop at the traffic sign. Dropping the three children off at school had gone as planned. In the absence of any political threat to the De beers Corporation, his job had a certain routine that could lead to complacency. A silver-gray Ford SUV passed though the intersection ahead of him, the occupants partially concealed by the darkened windows. He did catch a glimpse at the female driver and noted she was tall, had nice bone structure, but her eyes were hidden behind designer sunglasses. He watched the car pass through and continue up the hill, then started to pull out when a blue Volvo approached. He yielded right-of-way to it. The driver paid him little heed, but the passenger looked at him for a second before glancing away. After the Volvo cleared the intersection, Mark pulled though and continued westbound on Bougainvillea Terrace as a noisy white pickup truck passed behind him. He watched the truck in his rearview mirror and tried to note the magnetic sign. It took him a second to process the name, Green Thumb Landscaping, as it passed by at the speed limit of 40 km/h. *Have to check that one out. Haven't seen it before.*

Two minutes later he pulled into the drive at the Bakken Estate and checked his watch. *07:45 - right on time.* He exited the Suburban and entered the house. Georg and Sibyl had just finished coffee after breakfast and he was ready for his trip to the field office at the Namibian Skeleton Coast mine site. Mark picked up the suitcase from the master bedroom and moved it to the doorway and waited. Georg stood up and walked around the table to give Sibyl a parting kiss.

"Call me when you arrive," she insisted, as was her custom.

"Do I ever forget?"

She smiled and shook her head, "No, and I don't want you to start now...You know what I think about those helicopters!"

"I know, I know...I'd take a bullet train if we had one."

"Love you!" she called after him.

Mark lifted the suitcase with ease and held the door for his employer. The two walked without talking as Georg checked his iPhone for emails. Mark saw him securely seated in the left rear passenger seat, and then placed the suitcase in the far back and closed the rear door. In moments, the metal security gate to the complex swung wide and the two headed off to the helipad.

A cell phone jangled to life in Sibanyoni's shirt pocket. He retrieved it and glanced at the caller ID. "What's the word?"

"They are on the way now."

"Thanks, cousin," he replied as he terminated the call and selected a number on his speed dial.

Mandla answered on the first ring, "Yes?"

"One minute out."

"Got it," Mandla replied as he started the Volvo. He and Simi were parked a hundred yards up Capeview Lane, a side road that dead-ended into Hillcrest Drive. He placed the car in drive and began to slowly edge forward.

Andile had his truck pulled over to the side of Hillcrest just thirty yards past the turn off to Capeview. His hood was up to feign engine trouble—he was standing beside the bed with his hands on an AK-47 as was another man of the assault team. Others with weapons were spread out, hidden in the brush on the downhill side of the hillside roadway.

Londisizwe and his cousin Nahila waited uphill from the parked truck with the Ford's engine running. Mandla would block the retreat downhill and the Suburban would be disabled. Sibanyoni had given strict orders not to fire the RPGs at the passenger compartment. They wanted the executive alive. The bodyguard didn't count.

Mark rounded the curve and caught sight of the pickup with its hood up. He lifted ever so slightly off the accelerator as he scanned the surroundings. He knew the roadways around the Bakken residence like part of his own anatomy. He had driven every street when not actively involved in security operations and had walked every foot path through the neighboring parks.

306

Out of the corner of his eye, he detected movement to his left. A quick glance confirmed a blue Volvo station wagon with two occupants—both black males—moving towards the intersection. Hairs began to rise on the back of his neck when the landscapers both locked eyes on the Suburban simultaneously. His left hand slid unconsciously to the zipper enclosing the gym bag with his Sig strapped in the front passenger seat. As his Suburban passed into the intersection of Capeview and Hillcrest, a previously unseen gray Ford SUV pulled out from behind the raised hood of the parked and presumably disabled Nissan pickup truck. The Territory TX pulled fully into the left hand lane of Hillcrest and slid to a stop, effectively blocking the Suburban's path.

"Get down!" Mark yelled at Georg as he slammed the brakes hard.

***

TIMBER CREEK PRESS